# DAVID W. REES

*To: MIKE LODIK*

*YOU ARE A MENSCH'S*
*MENSCH. IT HAS BEEN A*
*RARE PRIVILEGE AND HONOR.*
*TO KNOW YOU. OH, ALSO,*
*SO ENJOYABLE.*

A STORY OF MURDER AND DECEIT

SET IN THE CITY OF PITTSBURGH

## *The*
# HEADLINE MURDERS

Printed in the United States of America
ISBN: 978-1-59571-858-7
Library of Congress Number: 2013901762

Design and Printing:
Word Association Publishers
205 Fifth Avenue
Tarentum, Pennsylvania 15084
www.wordassociation.com

DAVID W. REES

A STORY OF MURDER AND DECEIT

SET IN THE CITY OF PITTSBURGH

*The*
# HEADLINE MURDERS

# *C*HAPTER ONE

Marsha LeGrange. She was—and is—stunningly gorgeous, with a figure that would make a Miss America jealous. And in school, there she had been: absolutely gliding along, all the sought-after senior boys chasing her, on her way to becoming not only the best cheerleader, the best tennis player (male or female) in her high school and valedictorian of her senior class. The gliding stopped, though, when at age fifteen her father died. She'd been pushing a wheelbarrow full of responsibility up a rocky mountain trail ever since.

Not much time for those popular boys. Boys and tennis were exchanged for working part-time twenty-plus hours a week and studying even harder so she could get a college scholarship. Still, she was voted best cheerleader and she was named class valedictorian.

She was still pushing that wheelbarrow, now, however, as a litigator. Only days earlier, Marsha had been worrying about keeping her job at the law firm of Wilkins, Wilkins & Dunn. This Great Recession was costing many lawyers, paralegals, and legal assistants their jobs, not only here in Pittsburgh, but all over the country. But today she would become a star. Untouchable? Maybe. She could only hope.

Three weeks ago, a senior partner had handed Marsha the trial file. The case alleged severe injuries to a woman, caused, she claimed, by an accident she was involved in with a person insured by Interstate Insurance Company, one of WW&D's largest clients. "It's yours now, Marsha," the senior partner had told her. "Best guess is, you'll be picking a jury in seven to fourteen days."

Seventeen days later—only a few hours ago—she came back to the office with a victory for the defendant, her client. In that four-day trial Marsha had proved that the woman's severe injuries were caused by a fall down the basement steps in her own home a week after the motor vehicle accident she'd had with the man whom Interstate insured.

Jeff Guilfoyle was the first to stop by to congratulate her. Jeff—tall, in great shape, a beyond-handsome man. Marsha had been to his home several times and had met his lovely wife and their two young sons. Jeff was the youngest senior partner at the firm. Some were saying he was only a few years away from being elected managing partner. Everybody took to Jeff Guilfoyle. Jeff, like the other senior partners, could come and go as he pleased.

"Hi, office star," he said. "You are going with me to the Rusty Bucket to celebrate your triumph today." Telling, not asking.

The Rusty Bucket was where lawyers in Pittsburgh went to trumpet their victories or pour booze on their wounds. It was only a block from the Allegheny County Courthouse and on any given late afternoon or early evening you could find a table or two surrounded by lawyers from the firm.

"Sure," she said. "I'll go along with you to the Rusty Bucket, if you're buying."

At the Rusty Bucket, she counted three tables surrounded by lawyers from WW&D. Everyone got up and said hi to her when she and Jeff walked by, and all of them praised her for her victory. Martha Le-Grange—one day worried about her job, now the center of mostly male lawyer attention. She was used to plenty of male attention, but this was a different kind. This was for Marsha, the victorious trial lawyer, not Marsha, the lovely young single woman.

A tall glass of her favorite Chablis was placed in front of her as soon as she sat in a chair that a senior partner held out for her. How, she wondered, as she smiled and nodded her thanks, *did they know my favorite brand of Chablis?*

Late afternoon filtered through more praise into early evening. The celebration of her victory added to the high she walked in on. She was trying to go slow on the wine, but after the second glass she began to feel just a little more than a buzz. She shook her head. Unwilling to leave. But she had a late date and it was time to go. As she carefully made her way to the door, everybody had their eyes on her.

She turned at the door, smiled, and waved. "Gotta go," she said. "Late date." Marsha knew men stopped in their tracks to take her in. But she hadn't been with a man for way too long.

After she got to her condominium on Pittsburgh's South Side, she got ready for her date. She changed the white cotton sheets on her queen-sized bed for champagne-colored satin ones. Next, she lit candles, one on either side of her dresser mirror. Then she stripped, taking care in how she hung up her suit and silk blouse, but kicking her pantyhose, bra, and panties into a corner of her large, mostly pink and lavender bedroom.

From the small brass box on the nightstand, she took out the last half of a joint, lit it, took a long, slow drag, holding it . . . . Then into the bathroom, to the old-fashioned iron tub, where she turned the hot water on full blast. Soon there were halos around the mirror lights. When the water got to just the right level, she took more of the harsh smoke into her lungs. Very carefully, then, she placed the joint in the standing brass ashtray, which she kept right by the tub especially for evenings like this.

She touched a toe to the burning water and felt perspiration bead above her upper lip. In went a long leg, perfected during hours of exercise at the Fitness Arena. Finally, she was submerged except for her arms and head.

Should she take another toke? Why not! She reached over, got the joint, and took in more smoke, held it, barely touched it to the water, then pinched it with a wet finger and thumb. After dropping it into the ashtray, she sank deeper into the water and floated in steaming luxury.

Eyes closed, she withdrew into herself, seeing in her mind's eye her tall man, the one with the broad shoulders, narrow waist, and oh-so-gentle hands. The one she would be seeing tonight. She caressed herself with Apenon soap, imagining that it was him doing the caressing. Drifting. Higher now than she'd been when she got home.

Sometime later, she got out of the tub pink, drowsy, and floating. She wiped the fog off the bathroom mirror to take a look at herself. "Perfect tits"—that's what a man once told her. Slowly, she wrapped herself in a huge yellow towel. After drying, she let it slip to the floor and walked naked to the bedroom where she dabbed on some Marietta, her favorite fragrance.

From her lingerie drawer she selected a black lace thong and matching bra. Her nipples tingled as she hooked herself into the bra. The thong slid right on, tickling her thighs until it was in place.

Flushed, she lifted her eyes to the dresser mirror and caught her reflection in candlelight, feeling the marijuana pull her deeper into herself.

Then, in the mirror, she saw him.

Turning, bracing herself on the dresser as she moved, she waited for her man. Right on time, just as she'd planned it—and he was whispering her name. "Take off the bra, Marsha." He stood behind her. His breath was warm on her neck.

She did, unsnapping it, then with a shrug of her shoulders, she let it drop to the floor. His hands cupped her breasts as his fingers moved on her nipples; then they were sliding down her sides and after that ripping at the thong. She was swaying.

His hands steadied her as she moved away from the dresser, standing, still swaying, between it and the bed now, and she felt warmth spread in waves from her center. He guided her to the bed, his erection against her, then turned her and ever so gently helped her down onto those satin sheets as her legs parted for him. . . . And with just enough sense left to know there was no date, no man again tonight, she fumbled in the nightstand drawer for the vibrator. Found it. Then put it to use.

Her shuddering increased as her lover hummed.

"More. More!" Seconds before she lost all control, she reached for the pillow and covered her mouth. And then she was mindless, unaware of her own screaming.

Marsha never saw John Lee "Jackie" Simpson, who was even better looking than her fantasy man, but he saw her. Jackie had been in her condo since before she got home.

Months ago he'd found her spare key where she'd hidden it in a fake rock outside her back door and had it duplicated. Though he had been staying out of sight in the next room, her home office, he had smelled the marijuana and heard Marsha's moans. And he knew exactly what was going on.

This wasn't his first evening alone with Marsha LeGrange.

After he was sure consciousness had deserted her, Jackie moved into Marsha's bedroom and stood tall and erect over her, staring, imagining all that he would do to her when the time was right. Marsha Le-Grange was driving him mad; his muscles and tendons were clenched to near snapping. She'd been doing this to him even before Boston.

What if she woke up? Part of him wished that she would. No problem; then he'd have to rape and kill her—sooner, unfortunately, rather than when he'd planned. Waiting to do it had been torment. What had kept him from her was one important event: He sorely needed one more part of his plan to fall into place.

When Marsha awakened the sheets were damp under her. She smiled knowingly. Another special evening. She rose, went to the bathroom, came back and set the alarm before letting sweet sleep come again. How nice everything was.

# $\mathcal{C}$HAPTER TWO

On Monday, April 15, Dr. Judith T. Jenkins was first raped, then brutally murdered. It happened sometime in the early evening. That night the eleven o'clock news on every channel showed Newton S. Sylvester, prominent Pittsburgh financier, civic leader, and political power broker flanked by two homicide detectives as they led him off to the Allegheny County jail, charged with that rape and murder.

Clifford Reavis hadn't watched the news on the fifteenth of April—he heard about Sylvester being on it later—because he thought they'd be doing their usual last-day-to-pay-taxes story, the one showing people crowding into the post office to get their tax returns date-stamped. Otherwise there would be reports of fires, the latest shootings and accidents; then there would be the weather. The current weather condition he was adept at determining. He looked out the window or stepped outside to get that information. The future weather? He could pick it up off the Internet or next day's newspaper.

But before he went to bed that night, he did get that feeling again, the same one he'd had when he walked with his pregnant wife Beth on the day of her murder. Beth had been Beth Reavis, Clifford's wife of only five years.

One evening Beth and Reavis had been walking on an East Carson Street sidewalk in Pittsburgh's South Side when Paul Petro, drenched with nearly three times the legal limit of alcohol, ran his Jaguar XKE up onto the sidewalk and crushed Beth against the front wall of a restaurant. Reavis still believed that he could have saved her if he hadn't waited too long to dive at her and try to push her out of the way. Beth and their unborn child were killed instantly.

On Tuesday, April 16, at 9:33 a.m., Reavis's bedside phone lit with a call, but did not ring. He had it on "DO NOT DISTURB." At ten-thirty he swung his long, bony legs over the side of the bed and struggled to a sitting position. He saw the red light flashing on the phone beside his bed. After a while he stretched, very slowly, hearing only a few joints click. He had a stiff left hip that made pulling his socks on tough, and his left knee gave him some trouble, but no high blood pressure, heart problems, diabetes, things like that. Standing now, he stuffed both feet into a pair of beat-up slippers and trudged down the hall to his second floor bathroom, fighting the curiosity that would draw him to his phone that perched on the multi-phone base unit on the third floor of his house. He splashed cold water on his face, which only made him shiver and didn't wake him up. Though he did floss and brush his teeth, he decided to pass on shaving for the time being. He put on his glasses and stuffed in his hearing aids.

He wasn't waking up fast enough. He paused to let his curiosity war with his desire to climb back into bed. Curiosity won again. It always did.

He walked down the short hall to the elevator and took it to the third floor of his five-story home, where he had his office, not doing the one flight of stairs due to the left hip, which had been sore and stiff for months now. So much for the golden years.

Once in the office he bent over the base unit to his phone setup. He pressed the play button and heard: "Clifford, this is Tim. I know you're not up yet, but call my office as soon as you get this. I need you."

That was it. "Tim" was Tim Garrity, a lawyer, friend, client and the man who once had rescued him from jail and then kept him out of prison. He sounded worried.

Reavis had met Garrity in night law school at Pittsburgh's Duquesne University. Each had chosen night law school because they had full-time jobs during the day. Night school was where they became great friends.

Tim wasn't in when Reavis called back. Tim's secretary, Marge, whom Reavis had dated, was the one to tell him. "Oh, yes, Clifford," she said. "Tim wanted to know if you could see him during his trial lunch break. He's trying the Trindle murder case, so he can only see you when the judge breaks for lunch."

"What time's that going to be? Why's he want to see me?"

"Oh, I'm *sorry*." She sounded excited. "Usually, the judge stops the trial for lunch at noon, on the nose. The case? It's about Newton Sylvester. It was on TV last night."

"I didn't catch the news last night. What is it, a new murder case?" Tim Garrity mostly represented people charged with murder.

"The police think Mr. Sylvester raped and murdered a Carnegie Mellon professor. Newton Sylvester, Clifford, the one who's always in the paper for political, charity, and society things."

*That* Mr. Sylvester. "Tell Tim I'll be there at twelve fifteen."

He heard Marge let out a breath. "Oh, good, Clifford. Tim was worried you wouldn't be able to make it on such short notice."

After hanging up, Reavis limped down the stairs the one flight to his bedroom. Using his foot, he pushed around the shirts and underwear on the floor until he found a flannel shirt he could wear. He put it on over the T-shirt he'd worn to bed last night and stuck it and his long legs into the pair of Levis he found draped over the chair by his bed. He went to the window, opened it, and looked out. There were puddles in the alley below; a few raindrops got him. Raining. Clifford Reavis, the weatherman. He located a Pittsburgh Penguins hoodie, put it on and headed downstairs for the front door.

Outside, sockless feet sloshing inside his loafers, hoodie over his head, Reavis slogged across the street to the Giant Eagle and bought a

*Pittsburgh Post-Gazette* with headlines that read: "PROMINENT FINANCIER ACCUSED IN RAPE–MURDER."

The story was sketchy. Dr. Judith Jenkins had been a full professor at Carnegie Mellon University's School of Drama. The police had found her last night in her townhouse, naked, bloody, and dead. Newton Sylvester had been arrested and charged with the crime. The story went on to say that, according to a an anonymous source with the police, the arrest and charges were based on "a substantial amount of physical evidence that linked the financier to the crime."

The rest of the story was filler, detailing Sylvester's many civic activities. What the story didn't mention, but what Reavis knew from talk around town, was that if you sought high elective office in Allegheny County, where Pittsburgh was located, or even in Pennsylvania generally, you'd better have Newton S. Sylvester's support. Sylvester had that kind of money and power.

The story did say that Sylvester and the victim had known each other, and there was a hint in one paragraph that their relationship might have been intimate: "Friends of Mr. Sylvester refused to confirm or deny whether Dr. Jenkins and Sylvester were more than mere acquaintances."

The paper ran a half-page photo of Newton Sylvester, flanked by homicide detective Donnie Cimoni, whom Reavis knew and respected, and another homicide detective Reavis had seen but didn't know. There was a bandage on Sylvester's left cheek.

Reavis, when he thought about the crimes Sylvester allegedly had committed, had to remind himself that Tim Garrity had been his good friend ever since law school, and that he owed him. It had been Garrity who had gotten Reavis—a sure bet to be convicted of aggravated assault and attempted murder of the man who killed his wife and unborn child—off scot-free.

At the time, Reavis hadn't cared whether he got convicted. After he lost Beth and their baby, nothing mattered.

# *C*HAPTER THREE

April 16. Noon. Reavis was on time for his appointment with Tim
Garrity. He wore a corduroy suit. He liked corduroy because it didn't
need to be pressed much.

"Tim's not back from court yet, but you can wait in his office, Clifford.
That will give you a chance to nose around in there." Tim's secretary
Marge loved to dance and had a great rear end. Reavis had taken her
dancing at Sand Castle's Jukebox Sunday Nights. Outdoor dancing
right beside the Monongahela River.

*What did she mean by that "nosing around" comment?*

Garrity's office, which occupied a high corner of the Grant Building,
was huge. Reavis walked to the window and looked out, seeing all the
way down the Mon, almost to the Point, where it met the Allegheny
River to form the Ohio. He turned from the window. Tim's office was
done in reds and dark browns, colors Reavis had in his living room,
colors he liked for men's offices. Dominating the room, in the center on a raised platform, was Tim's mahogany desk, and attached to
the two walls that weren't windows were certificates proclaiming the
courts in which he was permitted to appear. Including the United

States Supreme Court, which shared the wall with photos of Tim and his lovely wife and three sons.

Reavis was trying to read a letter upside down on Tim's desk when Tim shot through the door. Not seeming surprised or irritated that Reavis was reading his mail, Tim waved for him to sit down. "Glad you could make it, Clifford. Knowing how late you sleep, I wasn't sure you could."

Tim Garrity, nearly ten years younger than Reavis, had the kind of curly gray hair that women liked. He had the body of an athlete, but was shorter than average, and making up for that, he must have thought, by wearing shoes with built-up heels.

Garrity had been one of the best criminal lawyers in Pittsburgh for years. He was tense today. The muscles on either side of his neck stood out; he kept moving his head around, cracking his neck. Trying murder cases had a way of making lawyers uptight. The Trindle case, the one Tim was in the middle of trying now, was getting pretty good play in the news because it was a murder case. TV cameramen would be catching Tim and Robert Trindle going in and out of the courtroom in the courthouse. Usually, there was an interview with one of the victim's family members, calling for justice. What the public did not know was that more often than not, the brothers and cousins of the victim had been charged with or done time for armed robbery, aggravated assault, and burglary.

Reavis watched now as Tim fought to switch mentally from murder trial to murder case.

"Marge tell you what this case was all about?" Tim said.

"Newton S. Sylvester."

Garrity nodded distractedly. "I got him out of jail first thing today, before the Trindle trial started. The only way I could do that so fast on a first-degree murder case—or even get him out at all—was by telling the judge the DA's office didn't oppose high bail. Not only the DA, but nearly every judge in Pittsburgh owes Newton Sylvester for his past support. If he was ever found innocent they would someday, again, need that same support." Tim's face showed a wry grin. "Since judges have to be retained by the voters every ten years, they'd sooner err on the side of letting him out on high bail than by keeping him in jail."

He was drumming a pencil on his mahogany desk, looking at Reavis. "All I know was that he swore to me that he wasn't guilty. But we only had five minutes alone. I know virtually nothing else about the man. He wasn't a client before the mess he got himself into last night. He was a referral from another firm, one that sends me a lot of business."

Reavis said, "I hear he's got a lot of bucks."

Garrity leaned back, sighed. "He's loaded. Not to mention having tons of quiet political influence. Clifford, I've spent only those few minutes with Sylvester, so I don't know much. He does have a bandage on his face. The police are supposed to have found blood on some of his clothing. I only know that from reading today's paper."

Tim put his hands palms down on the desk and looked evenly at Reavis—looking silently for a favor from the investigator who had been his friend for years.

"Sure. I'll look into it for you, Tim," Reavis said in answer to the look. What he didn't say was that if it turned out the way he thought it would, he'd be off the case. No way was he going to be looking for some technicality that would get a rapist and murderer off.

"Obliged, Clifford." Then Tim bent over the Trindle trial notes in front of him and seemed to forget all about Reavis. The Sylvester case could wait. Trindle was now.

Reavis let himself out of Tim's office. As he got to Marge he began somehow feeling guilty for not asking her out anymore. He'd been feeling that guilt ever since they'd last dated. Good—he saw something he could ask her about, a picture on her desk.

"Who's that?"

"My fiancé."

Reavis tried to hide his surprise, mumbling, "Lucky guy."

After leaving Garrity's office, Reavis called Pat Tazer, another longtime friend. "Can you get me anything on the Sylvester case, Taze?"

"Got copies of the first reports and crime scene photos as soon as I heard Tim Garrity was representing him. I've been expecting your call."

So Reavis's next stop was the investigation branch of the Pittsburgh Police Bureau, on the North Side. He got his car and drove over to it.

Pat Tazer and Reavis had met one night when Reavis happened to sit on the bar stool next to the big cop—six-five, a hard two-forty, and thirty-some years younger —at the 18th Street Café on the South Side. Tazer half-turned on his stool and said:

"I don't want no skinny, four-eyed bastard I don't know sitting next to me, pal." Tazer made a sweeping motion with his arm. "Out!"

Reavis, half-shot himself, had wound up and aimed a roundhouse at the big man. Tazer caught Reavis's arm in mid-air and, next thing Reavis knew, Tazer was carrying him over his shoulder down to the end of the bar. Where he dumped him on a stool.

Reavis charged back to Tazer's end. "Try that again," he said, "and I won't miss next time."

Tazer threw up his hands in surrender and called to the bartender, "Hey, Will, get my buddy here a shot and a beer." They'd been friends ever since.

When Reavis opened the door to the squad room, he saw that Tazer wasn't the only one in the twenty-by-thirty-foot room. Three detectives were playing a poker machine in the corner. Tazer had made a deal for it with Vice—they'd picked up the machine on a raid.

The way Tazer raised his head would have put a slow motion replay to shame. "Oh," the big cop said, "it's that skinny, four-eyed bastard." But he didn't weigh two-forty anymore. Pat Tazer pushed his three hundred-plus pounds back from the desk and leaned back. Reavis thought briefly about grabbing Pat's chair before it tipped. "I heard Tim picked up the Sylvester case, so I knew you would be calling."

Tazer looked over to see if the three poker-machine players were watching. They weren't, so he dug a file about half an inch thick out of his middle desk drawer and pushed it across the desk to Reavis.

Inside were copies of reports and crime-scene photos. Reavis sucked in some air as he looked through the dozen or so copies of the eight-by-ten, black-and-white photographs of the former Judith Jenkins.

"Write down what you want, but don't take any of the copies," Pat said.

Reavis read that two uniformed officers had been first on the scene after a call came in on the nine-one-one line. The male caller, who refused to give his name, said he'd heard a woman screaming in the victim's townhouse, located in the Mexican War Streets section of Pittsburgh, on the North Side. Heinz Field, home of the Steelers, and

PNC Park, where the Pirates played, and the Rivers Casino were on the North Side now, too. Money was moving there. The money people had been trying to get people to call the North Side where it met the Allegheny River the "North Shore." Upscale. A few blocks away, angry young men would be shooting one another, at least once a week. Over drugs, territory, disrespect, by mistake, or often because of a woman.

The caller went on to report that he'd seen a tall man, who at first he didn't recognize, running out of the Jenkins home. Then Sylvester looked right at him, or so the caller said, and that was when he recognized him from seeing him on television—one of those WQED public-television fund-raisers. The man who reported seeing Sylvester said there was blood all over Tim Garrity's client.

The police found Judith Jenkins in a second-floor bedroom of her home, lying in a pool of her own blood. Her face was half caved in and her neck was sliced. The murder weapon, an ivory-handled steak knife with the brass initials *N. S. S.* inlaid in the ivory, was lying a few feet from the corpse.

Donnie Cimoni wrote the homicide report, retracing the steps the police took to secure the physical evidence. With a search warrant, the homicide detectives proceeded to Fox Chapel, "the home of the alleged perpetrator." Sylvester answered their knock at 9:22 p.m., dressed in a pair of flannel slacks, white shirt, and slippers. There were three gashes on his left cheek, each about two inches long.

The report recited how the search warrant was served: Sylvester, fully apprised of his rights, let them in, saying they didn't need a warrant, that he had nothing to hide. He also signed the standard Miranda Rights police form that said that he had been read his right to remain silent and to retain counsel, and that he waived them.

According to Cimoni's report, a plastic trash bag was found in the corner of a closet in one of Sylvester's bedrooms. In it were a pair of Dockers, a white shirt, and a pair of New Balance running shoes, all blood-soaked. A steak knife set, the pieces a perfect match with the murder weapon, was found in Sylvester's kitchen. One knife was missing from the set.

Sylvester had shown the detectives the knives, but couldn't explain the missing one, the bloody clothing, or the scratches on his cheeks. He told his inquisitors that he'd taken a few sips of a martini about six thirty, which was right after he arrived home from his office, and that he must have conked out on the couch. The next thing he remembered was being awakened by their knock on his front door.

The report also stated that there were no signs of forcible entry at the Jenkins townhouse. Sylvester, who admitted knowing the victim, said he didn't have a key to Dr. Jenkins's home. The bloody Dockers the detectives found, however, had a key in the right front pocket. And it opened the front door of Judith Jenkins's townhouse. Sylvester couldn't explain that either.

There were no lab reports yet. DNA would take even longer.

At the bottom of the report was a note that read, "See Offense Report 898-12."

"Taze," Reavis said, "can you get me eight ninety-eight twelve?"

Tazer leaned across the desk and pushed a much smaller file toward Reavis. Offense Report 898-12 detailed Jenkins's complaint about receiving an obscene phone call two weeks before her murder. She told the police that she hung up on a phone freak who said he'd been in her bedroom. Not until she received her own underwear in the mail did she call the police.

That time, none of Dr. Jenkins's neighbors could recall seeing anyone strange coming in or out of her townhouse. As for the neighborhood, an amalgam of those who were months behind on their utilities bills and the ballet and symphony crowd, who could say what someone strange looked like? The police had to drop the investigation of Jenkins's harassment complaint. No leads.

Before Reavis left Pat Tazer's office he asked him to call the nine-one-one people and clear his listening to the recording of the call from the guy who'd reported the Judith Jenkins murder. Tazer was on the phone doing that as Reavis left.

When Reavis did listen to the call-in recording, he couldn't tell much, only that the caller was indeed male and didn't have an accent. Twice the nine-one-one operator had asked the man for his name, and both times was rebuffed, the man saying he didn't want to get involved.

Starved by the time he got home, Reavis decided to make himself a couple of steak hoagies. Made anywhere else in the country they would be called steak subs. The key to making superb hoagies, he'd found, was in the roll. Better put—Mancini's rolls. Fill one with sandwich steaks (any kind seemed to be okay) and then add mozzarella cheese, fried green peppers, mushrooms, Heinz Ketchup, and onions, and you had yourself all the meal you needed. He set to work on a couple.

Reavis took the steak hoagies and the elevator to the fifth floor of his home, a twenty-five-by-twenty-five-foot room, sitting above what had been a flat roof that was now the open-air fourth floor. The side of his fifth-floor room that faced north was comprised almost completely of thick glass. This room was where he liked to do his heavy thinking. He got an Iron City beer out of the fridge and walked over to the windows and slid them open.

He looked out at the Monongahela River and a cool breeze slipped into the room. When he sat in the recliner in one corner of the room, he could still look out towards the Monongahela and hear the river-boats. Usually, after some time up here, he ended up with answers. Today, though, he had plenty of those. What he didn't have were any more questions. So far it looked like Newton S. Sylvester all the way.

And what if it was Sylvester? *Don't tell me, he thought, about a sick mind, about a killer who needed understanding and help.* Bullshit. If Sylvester did do it, he should be locked up. Or worse.

The sun was going down and it was getting cooler. He went to the large closet and took out a thick Steelers hoodie, which he pulled on over his head. He cursed when he felt the hearing aid being torn from his left ear as he was pulling the hoodie on. He was in luck; the hearing aid had dropped into his lap. He put it back in and gave the loosened one in his right ear a push back into place and then sat back. Reavis drained the last of his Iron. No, he wouldn't help to clear a rapist. Not even for Tim Garrity he wouldn't. Tomorrow he would meet with Sylvester, as he'd promised Tim. And if things still looked the same after that meeting, he would tell Newton S. Sylvester exactly what he thought of him. Then tell the man he could get himself another investigator.

# *C*HAPTER FOUR

One day Jackie came across a journal Marsha LeGrange kept under her bed. She had dated the journal, and the first date began with her thoughts about her initial interview with Lester Wilkins, managing partner at WW&D. She had labeled the second page "LESTER WILKINS, Esq." She used two columns. The column on the left she labeled "Pluses," the one on the right "Minuses." On the plus side she had started off with the words "commanding presence" and wrote about his looks, calling him intelligent, engaging, that he was a widower, and then: "early partnership?" She had drawn little hearts all around the pluses.

She only had one minus: "Age?"

Once Wilkins had asked her to dance at the law firm's Christmas party, and she spent two pages of her journal talking about their two dances, what a wonderful dancer he was and how good he felt to hold.

To say her words enraged Jackie would be like saying lions preferred meat. Yet, at the same time, Wilkins was exactly what he needed for her.

Marsha LeGrange had it all, Jackie believed. Somewhere around five-six, a perfect body, which she didn't spend a lot of time showing off; her dark hair shone like Jackie's mother's, and she had no problem getting men to notice her. He had to admit, too, that she worked her tail off and had a great legal mind.

To say that he was jealous of Wilkins, frustrated because he couldn't match what Wilkins had to offer a woman, and now hated Marsha and Wilkins both would be an understatement. After reading Marsha's journal, he couldn't sleep without pills, which he saw as a weakness in himself. Jackie hated to depend on anything or anyone but himself for his peace of mind. He had promised himself that as soon as he was done with Marsha LeGrange he would quit the pills. Just like he'd done with alcohol.

Long ago, he'd learned that the only woman he could depend on, the only one who could give him peace of mind, was his grandmother, Sarah Lee Simpson, whom Jackie knew loved him. She always told him the truth—unlike his momma, who would tell him she loved him, but whom he would catch sometimes looking at him as though she hated him.

He believed Nadine Harris might love him too, and was certain that he could depend on her. He refused to admit it, but after he read Marsha's journal he needed to be with Nadine more than ever. Badly. He left Marsha's condo immediately after he'd read her journal the first time and was on his way to Cleveland.

After he got to Nadine's, a six-bedroom, five-bath beautiful nineteen fifties stone home with a sculpted yard in the suburbs outside of Cleveland, Jackie had only raised his hand toward Nadine Harris's doorbell when the door opened and Nadine dragged him inside. In three breaths, their clothing lay strewn in her hall and on the living room rug, the clothing marking the trail right up to where they locked bodies on the couch in her living room. Finished for the first time, they gathered and then took their clothes with them to her bedroom and started again. When they were done and panting, yes—some of the strain Jackie had been feeling after reading what Marsha LeGrange had written about Lester Wilkins had vanished. Some, but not nearly enough.

Jackie and Nadine had met in law school where they were in a study group with four other first-year law students. Jackie, Nadine, and the four others didn't measure up to most of the students because none of the members of the group came from the right kind of background.

Jackie was able to attend law school because of a rich man's money. Stuart Randolph, the man who Jackie believed was his father, paid his way. Which shamed him. Nadine worked her way through school as a nurse, seven p.m. until three a.m., five days a week.

Jackie tried to keep his distance from her, but it wasn't always easy.

He'd always had an easy time talking to women. He knew women liked him—and were happy to fuck him. Plenty of females from high school, college, and law school let him know that he was more than welcome in their beds. All they cared about, though, in high school and college was his looks and how many touchdowns he scored in the last game. In law school they cared about how he could help them get better grades.

Nadine had let him know she thought he was attractive, but didn't push it. She could match him in legal aptitude and looks. What she did push was a strong friendship. Jackie didn't trust any woman to be a friend, but he let go a lot of that mistrust with Nadine. Over their three years together at law school, Jackie had let himself get loose enough to be as close a friend to her as he could.

On the day they graduated from law school, Nadine made him get in her car, telling him she had a surprise for him. She then drove to a motel, signed them in, and took him to the room she had rented. They stayed in that room for nearly two days, until he got scared about how he was feeling about her and ran off in the middle of the second night while she slept.

Three years later, Nadine located him again and called, told him she had married and that she really needed to talk with him, that she needed help. Jackie's question was: Did he want to be that kind of friend—a friend in need?

He gave it a chance, and they met at a restaurant in a suburb outside of Cleveland. Nadine had sunglasses on when they met and when he went to put his arms around her for a hug she shrunk away. He drew back and looked at her. "What's wrong?"

She said, "My husband beats me. He's not a successful businessman like he let on to me. He's a vicious criminal. I found out that he was and told him I knew." She took the sunglasses off and Jackie saw that both of her eyes were blackened. She pushed her blouse over to where he could see her left bra strap, and all Jackie could see was black, blue, and yellow.

She said, "He threatened to kill me and the kids if I left him. The only person I could think of to call was you. I don't know what to do."

Jackie knew. The man had to die.

Jackie convinced Nadine that her husband's death was her only escape. But they had to have a plan that would keep Nadine and her kids together and safe from her husband, his criminal associates, and the law.

They decided that Nadine would act the terrified, submissive wife—which wouldn't take much acting. They made their plans, mostly by telephone, and always pay phones back then. Nadine's job was to find out about her husband's finances, his schedule—every secret he had. Eventually, using a small video camera, she got the password for her husband's computer. They trained it on Harris's computer and before long the keys his fingers touched gave them the password.

After that it was easy to learn everything they needed about where his money was, and the codes they needed to transfer it were not hard to discover. "Chucky" Harris kept lists of both in what he thought was a computer that couldn't be breached.

Jackie quit his law job and followed the man night and day, learning all he could about him. One of the first things he learned was that Chucky Harris had a mistress and that the mistress's husband had done time for voluntary manslaughter. The irony was that this man, Elvis Mason, worked as a bodyguard for Nadine's husband.

When they were ready, Jackie made sure that Nadine and her two little boys were away, visiting her sister in Michigan. He did the rest. He got into the house with a key Nadine had given him, waited for the husband and his mistress to get out of their clothes and get into bed, and then strolled into the bedroom and shot Chucky Harris in the back of the head and the woman in the forehead while he held a shirt belonging to bodyguard Elvis, the woman's husband, in front of himself to catch the blood splatter from both shots.

The next part was a little tricky, but would seal the deal. Jackie called Mason on Chucky Harris's bedroom landline and did his best imitation of Harris's voice, telling the bodyguard to get over there right away, that he was in trouble. Then he hung up. He left the front door open and waited for Mason. The bodyguard pulled in about twenty minutes later and ran to the front door and knocked. When the door opened from just the knocking, he went inside.

All Jackie had to do then was wrap the blood-spattered shirt around the gun he'd used, get into the bodyguard's unlocked car, and tuck them under the front seat. Sure enough, Mason must have put two and two together in Chucky's bedroom and realized he would be the prime suspect in the two murders, because he was soon out of the Chucky Harris residence, in his car, and speeding away.

Jackie called nine-one-one and reported hearing gunshots at the Harris residence, described Mason and his vehicle, and said the car took off real fast out of the Harris driveway soon after he heard the gunshots. He refused to give his name to the nine-one-one operator.

The morning before the murder Jackie had transferred Chucky Harris's offshore money to an offshore account of his own. Problem solved: Harris was dead. The police found the blood-spattered shirt and murder weapon in Elvis Mason's vehicle. They also had casino surveillance video showing Elvis leaving the casino in a hurry in the right time frame. Harris's bodyguard—Chucky's mistress's husband—went to prison for life and Nadine inherited. Nadine and her kids were safe and she and Jackie were two rich young lawyers.

They split three million, three hundred thousand, eight hundred and ninety-two dollars, which they had sucked out of all Chucky Harris's accounts. Nadine got the house.  Nadine opened her own law firm. Jackie had plans of his own.

Now they were as close as Jackie was able to let them be. Nadine, gorgeous, sweet, wracked with guilt about the murder and filled with love for her two safe, pre-teen boys, and filled with love and need for Jackie. Thankful for whatever time and attention he would give her.

Jackie had heavy needs and probably some type of love for her, too.

But felt no guilt about Chucky Harris.

# CHAPTER FIVE

Like a diver out of oxygen, Reavis thrashed his way to the surface. Fighting for air. He tore at the sweat-soaked sheet that was cutting off his oxygen and fought free of the dream that wouldn't let him breathe.

In the dream he'd been running naked up East Carson Street with a butcher knife, closing in on Paul Petro, Beth's murderer. The man who had killed his wife cut down a dead-end alley and disappeared in the murk. Reavis heard a noise behind a caved-in garbage can and folded the can even more when he kicked it aside. He saw a man-shape lurch from behind the can and slashed at that shape with the foot-long knife, ripped flesh, heard a moan, saw Petro trying to stand, then slump, fall face-first to the concrete alley and claim a spot among orange peels, chicken bones, and coffee grounds. But when he put a foot on Petro and shoved him onto his back, the dead eyes that returned his stare were Newton S. Sylvester's.

At 11:06 a.m., wired with the three cups of coffee it took to break away from the dream, already having bad thoughts about the man he was on his way to see for being in his dream, Reavis guided his new silver Monte Carlo onto the ramp from Route 28 to Fox Chapel, a suburb of Pittsburgh where Newton Sylvester and a lot of other rich people lived.

The iron gates anchored to fieldstone pillars that formed the entrance to Sylvester's driveway were open. Reavis drove his silver car into the gray-brick driveway rimmed with trees about to blossom in a long arc up to and then on by the main house.

The main house, weathered red brick with a steep slate roof, was at least two-thirds of a football field long. Detached from it was a six-car garage with a vintage white Rolls Royce displayed in front of it. Reavis believed a person could go a lifetime without seeing a car like that around Pittsburgh.

A man in his mid-fifties and wearing a black undertaker's suit admitted him, but when Reavis started to follow him down the dark hall, the man turned and put a hand lightly on his arm. "Please wait here, sir. I'll announce you."

The man excused himself, moved down the hall and disappeared. Looking around then, like a kid does before he sneaks a cookie, Reavis started down the hall.

To the right was an auditorium. Antique furniture was clustered in five groups to disguise that auditorium as a formal living room. Twin black-marble fireplaces took up most of its far wall and portraits of long-dead people wearing black-plumed hats and outfitted in crimson and purple looked down their noses at Reavis from the other walls. Persian rugs let some of the mirror-like hardwood floor show. He edged closer to the room for a better look.

A long-fingered hand touched his shoulder. Reavis flinched. "This way, Mr. Reavis," the man dressed like an undertaker said. "Mr. Sylvester will see you now."

Reavis followed him to a dark, paneled room. The dark curtains were drawn. A white-haired man rose slowly from a high-backed chair in the darkest corner. Tall—today at least—the man was stoop-shouldered, his skin drawn tightly over a fading winter tan. According to the police records Reavis had seen, Newton Sylvester was younger than he was, but he looked over seventy today.

"Mr. Reavis," Sylvester said as he offered a surprisingly strong hand, "I am Newton Sylvester." Sylvester did his best to smile. But his right eye wouldn't stop twitching. "Please." He gestured to a chair with a pincushion seat. "Won't you sit?"

After they were seated, Sylvester said, "You're Margaret Mueller's friend, aren't you?"

Peggy Mueller was the woman Reavis was dating. Well, maybe a lot more than dating.

"Yes." Reavis wanted to ask what was it to him about him and Peggy Mueller, but didn't. Instead, he said, "How well did you know Dr. Jenkins?" Sylvester blinked, looked away, reached down and pulled at the sock on the leg he had crossed. "I first met her a year ago. I was—am—a member of the Mayor's Committee to Promote Pittsburgh. So was Judy."

Newton Sylvester's eyes began to fill.

"And one of our projects," Sylvester said, "was to encourage producers to make more movies in Pittsburgh. Judy was a professor in Carnegie Mellon's School of Drama. She had a national reputation and many contacts in the movie business."

He sighed and straightened in his chair before going on. "I quickly developed more than a business interest in her." Sylvester took a monogrammed handkerchief out of his suede morning coat, which hung on him like skin on a prune, and dabbed at his eyes. "I've been divorced for over ten years now. I discovered that Judy enjoyed racquetball, so I joined the health club where she played." He paused, folding his handkerchief three times before he got it right. After he tucked the handkerchief back into his jacket pocket, Sylvester fixed Reavis with a look and said, "That's where I met Margaret Mueller. She called me this morning. Told me she was seeing you. What a good man you were."

Reavis took his glasses off and started to clean them with his favorite knit tie, maroon with black horizontal stripes. He wasn't about to talk to this man about Peggy Mueller. He thought he might be falling in love with her, which was in conflict with the deep feelings he still had about Beth. Sylvester had pressed Reavis's strong guilt sore.

Sylvester went on. "Then I arranged to run into Judy at her club, the Fitness Arena, and we played racquetball. She was a real competitor." Sylvester uncrossed his legs, made a point of looking Reavis in the eye.

"She finally agreed to have dinner with me. We had a good time. She said she would like to do it again. And we did, five or six times."

Sylvester had to look away now.

Reavis had noticed the lines at the corner of Sylvester's eyes, the vertical grooves between his brows. He still had the twitch under his right eye. "Does the man who showed me in live on the grounds?"

"Faircloth? In an apartment over the garage. With his wife, Monica. They've been with me for years."

Reavis asked where Faircloth was on the night of the murder.

"I don't know. I haven't asked him. This kind of thing isn't what I like to discuss with people like the Faircloths. He and his wife have Mondays to do with as they please. They were out somewhere, I know that, but I didn't ask them where."

Reavis would. "What about the blood on your clothing, *your* steak knife with *your* fingerprints on it, the murder weapon? How do you explain all that, Mr. Sylvester?"

Sylvester looked helplessly at Reavis. "I have no explanation for any of it." He fingered the bandage on his left cheek. "I don't know how I got this cut on my cheek, either. I remember coming home about six, six-thirty that night. That's the time I come home every night. I always have a martini as soon as I get my suit off and get into my slippers.

Drinking the martini was the last thing I remember doing until I answered the door for the police."

Sylvester held out his hands, palms up, leaned towards Reavis, and shrugged. "Mr. Reavis, if I had done something like what they say I did to Judy, if I had done something like that, I wouldn't have answered the door for the police," Sylvester touched the bandage on his face again and regarded Reavis closely. "Would I? Wouldn't I have called a lawyer?"

Reavis had been in the same situation, police at his door, years ago, after he'd slammed a knife between Paul Petro's ribs, just missing his heart. That's how he'd ended up in a jail cell. No, his instinct had been to run and hide that night. He wouldn't have answered the door for the police. Crazy with rage as he had been, he'd had the good sense to toss the knife he'd used on Petro into the river. He'd refused to answer any police questions and called Tim Garrity as soon as he could after he was arrested.

"Are you," Reavis said, "in the habit of taking a nap as soon as you get home? Is that something you do a lot?"

Sylvester shook his head. "I can't say that I never take one. Maybe every month or so I'll fall asleep for fifteen, twenty minutes." The multimillionaire financier looked puzzled. "That's what gets me. I must have been sleeping for hours before the police awakened me."

"Did you feel drugged, funny, strange in any way when you awakened?" Reavis said.

Sylvester wrinkled his forehead. "Not actually."

"How about before you got home. Did you feel strange before you got home, before you made yourself that martini?"

"I was in rush hour traffic . . . East Ohio Street." Sylvester looked at Reavis. "You know how that is. You have to stay pretty sharp on Route 28. No. I'd say I was wide awake the whole way home. I had to be, in *that* traffic. I felt perfectly fine. As a matter of fact, I was more keyed up than anything else."

Sylvester looked away, brushed at his eyes. "Judy and I had a pretty good time last Saturday night. She invited me into her home. I was thinking about calling her after I got home the day she was killed." Shaking his head now, off somewhere in his thoughts. "But I never did."

Could Sylvester be innocent? With all that evidence that said he wasn't? It didn't seem possible. Unless someone had planted the evidence.

Reavis leaned forward in the pin-cushion-seated chair that was making his ass stiff. "What I'm trying to get at," he said, "is the possibility that someone might have drugged you." *All the physical evidence that Homicide found*, Reavis thought to himself, *could have been planted.* He said, "The glass you had your martini in, has it been cleaned?"

"Dirty glasses don't last long around Mrs. Faircloth."

"What about the gin and vermouth that you made your drink with the night of the murder? Do you still have those bottles?"

"Mr. Reavis, I had far more than one martini last night. And I still had difficulty getting to sleep. I doubt that there was anything in my drink that put me to sleep." He turned away, glanced at the door and, barely raising his voice, summoned Faircloth.

The butler appeared in seconds. "Yes, sir?"

"Get Mr. Reavis the Beefeater's and vermouth bottles, will you?"

Reavis waited for the butler to get the bottles and leave again before going on. Then he directed his questions to what the homicide detectives had said and done, seeing if they had violated any of Sylvester's rights—not yet realizing that he was now looking for ways to help Newton Sylvester. Sylvester's answers didn't identify anything wrong with what the homicide investigators had done.

Reavis switched tactics. "What do you know about Judith Jenkins's personal life, Mr. Sylvester?"

"Really very little," Sylvester said. "She talked mostly about her work, what we were doing on the committee, things like that. I do know she has a daughter somewhere back east. I think she said the young lady was a sophomore or junior in college. Judy never talked about her ex-husband."

Sylvester looked down at his large hands and Reavis took the opportunity to give him a closer look. The loose suede jacket was deceptive; Sylvester had a pretty good pair of shoulders on him. And he would look much younger—Sylvester's actual age—without the white hair.

Sylvester continued. "Judy Jenkins"—and then a tear slipped out of his eye—"was simply a nice lady to be with, an altogether attractive and intelligent woman." And then he broke down, bent over, hands over his eyes, and shaking.

Reavis didn't know what to do. Should he go over and comfort Sylvester? Leave him alone? He figured the best thing to do was sit quietly while the man poured out his grief. Had she refused to go to bed with Sylvester two nights ago? Insulted him, maybe? Had they argued that night? Perhaps he had pushed himself on her?

After Sylvester got himself together, Reavis said, "Did you two ever fight?"

A sobbing chuckle. "Mr. Reavis, we did not know one another well enough to argue."

"Have you noticed anything odd lately, any strange people, calls, anything like that?"

"No . . . there's been nothing out of the—" Sylvester straightened. "Wait. There is one thing. Terry, my dog, was poisoned. I was quite upset about it."

"Poisoned?"

"I had him tested by the vet," Sylvester said. "He would get loose. Terry could be quite an embarrassment sometimes. As soon as someone came up the driveway he'd be flying at the door. Making a real commotion. Faircloth loathed him, though he tried not to let on."

A noisy dog. Poisoned. That was something he'd have to look into. Still, Reavis didn't want to give up on the idea that Judy Jenkins had done something to set Sylvester off, made him kill. He thought he knew a way that could get the man to come out with something.

"Mr. Sylvester, I nearly killed someone once. The man who murdered my wife. I was enraged." Reavis studied the man across from him, watching for any change in expression. But Reavis didn't have to look for anything subtle—Sylvester was looking at Reavis as if he had just confessed to assassinating the president. Reavis pushed it. "That's right." He glared right back at Tim Garrity's client. "He was drunk in the middle of the day. Jumped the curb in his sports car on East Carson Street and slammed her into the front of a restaurant." Daring Sylvester to say something.

Somewhere else in his thoughts now, no longer looking at Sylvester, Reavis was remembering what had once landed him in jail. "That bastard never even said he was sorry. Tried to say his brakes let go. Son of a bitch was so drunk he couldn't even open the door to get out of his car. Blew a point thirty-four on the breathalyzer. I had my hands around his throat when the police arrived." He made his hands into claws. "The DA charged him with homicide by vehicle, but he got out on bail. "I took to following him." Reavis stood. "Twice I went after him with a butcher knife." He turned, started pacing, his back now to Sylvester. "The first time, I got him. Everyone thought he would die."

Petro hadn't died though; somehow he'd lived. Had shown up for Reavis's preliminary hearing, in fact. Like it was yesterday, Reavis could picture how Petro had looked at the hearing, pointing at Reavis with one hand, while trying to keep his balance with the other. Petro, drunk—even at the preliminary hearing. Back in those days assistant DAs didn't have court reporters at preliminary hearings, so there was no record of his testimony. Making it impossible for his testimony at the preliminary hearing to be introduced as evidence against Reavis at trial. And no one who was at the preliminary hearing could testify about what they heard Petro state—it was considered hearsay. Petro had to reproduce his testimony at trial. That would turn out to be very important.

Remembering that someone else was in the room with him, Reavis turned back to face Newton Sylvester. "The point is, I tried to kill Paul Petro. And I don't think I'm a violent man. Yet the fact remains . . ."

"Mr. Reavis, how could you have done that?" Newton Sylvester's eyebrows were raised, his mouth open in wonder. "Other than self-defense, there is no proper excuse for killing another human being. None. The Sixth Commandment."

Now Clifford Reavis was staring at Sylvester, and what he saw pissed him off. Sylvester was looking at him like something you didn't touch.

He almost asked Sylvester, who was he to judge? But he didn't. Because now he had his answer—Newton S. Sylvester couldn't abide with what Reavis had tried and failed to do to Paul Petro. For any reason. It wasn't just what Sylvester said; Reavis could see it in the man's eyes. No, it wasn't Sylvester who'd raped and murdered Judith Jenkins, unless he was some kind of split personality. He couldn't have and still looked at Reavis as he was doing.

Reavis went on with his questioning, playing with the idea that something had made Tim Garrity's client come undone, lose his head, do something in a rage that he was blocking from his memory. "Have you ever been treated for mental or emotional problems, sir?" Still pissed, emphasizing the sir.

Sylvester flinched, Reavis's tone of voice obviously getting to him. "I'm sorry," he said, "would you repeat that?" Some of the way he had been looking at Reavis was leaving his face.

Reavis said it again.

"Never," Sylvester said emphatically. "I have never had any mental problems."

"How about drinking? You said you always have a martini after work. Is that the extent of it?"

"I drank a little more while I was going through the divorce. I won't deny that. But nothing I would consider abnormal under the circumstances. Certainly nothing I ever needed help for." He shrugged. "I've been pretty free of problems. Until now." Sylvester looked like he was thinking. Then he said, "Money has a way of insulating a person, I guess."

"Nothing, then," Reavis said. "No amnesia, blackouts, anything like that?"

Sylvester shook his head.

"How about drugs? A steroid for some ailment, an antihistamine, even over-the-counter drugs can change your personality, produce rage?" he asked.

Sylvester started to shake his head again but Reavis waved him off. "Think a moment before you answer, please, Mr. Sylvester."

Sylvester sat back. For a long while. In the end, however, his answer remained the same. "I know what you're looking for. I know how things look for me, that if I had some kind of mental problem, or a bad drug reaction, it might help my case, at least get me a lighter sentence. But that kind of thing, a history of taking drugs of any kind, prescription or non-prescription, bad drug reactions, emotional instability—it just isn't there."

They sat locked in silence until Sylvester brought up what had become the obvious. "There's only one possible answer, Mr. Reavis . . ."

Reavis finished the thought. "Someone else did it, made it look like you did."

"Yes, and you have to find out who."

Sylvester was no longer judging Reavis. All he wanted now was help. Even if it was from a guy who tried to take the law into his own hands more than once.

"Do you have any enemies?" he said. "Because, let's face it, if you didn't do it, someone went to a lot of trouble to make it look like you did." Reavis turned back and moved closer to Sylvester, now looking down at the man. "Who hated you that much?"

"I've been thinking of nothing else for two days now. I am sure there are some people who don't break into a smile when they think of me. I'll give you some names if you like. But rape? Murder? No one."

"I would like you to tell me their names," Reavis said.

Sylvester did, and Reavis wrote them down.

Reavis rose to leave, out of questions, temporarily at least. At the door the very rich man caught Reavis by the shoulder, squeezing harder than he must have intended. The look in his eyes contained no disdain now. Sylvester was fighting back tears. "Please help me."

For the third time, Reavis had to bring his new Monte Carlo to a screeching halt. This time barely a foot behind an Audi 5000 stopped at a red light. He would have to put Newton Sylvester out of his mind. He'd only had this car a couple of months.

*But if not Sylvester,* he wondered, *then who?* That's what made him keep nearly rear-ending cars at red lights—asking that question.

# CHAPTER SIX

"What do you think of him?" was the first thing Tim Garrity asked about Sylvester when he returned Reavis's call.

"For somebody who probably grew up a couple acres away from his next door neighbor, got driven to a private school every day by a chauffeur, he's not a bad guy. A little stuffy, but he seems to be okay."

"Fill me in."

Reavis did and, it took a while after he'd finished before Garrity said, "From what you say, I can't see where any of Sylvester's rights were violated. Not in the way the police got a warrant and executed it; not even because they questioned him without a lawyer. They read him his rights, gave him a chance to call one." The lawyer paused. "So, I'm not going to be able to get any of the evidence suppressed."

Reavis got the feeling he always got when he hadn't been able to come up with something. Somehow it was his fault the facts weren't turning out right. It especially bothered him now that he was convinced of Sylvester's innocence. *Or was he innocent?* "What about a polygraph, Tim?"

"What good would a polygraph do? "They're inadmissible. You know that."

He hadn't yet told Tim what was bothering him. "Tim, I believe the man. Maybe I only feel sorry for him, I want to. But I do want to know if I'm being bullshitted. Tim, if the test shows he's lying, then I won't have to waste my time tracking down leads that won't end anywhere we want to go." Finally, he got around to it. "Tim, I won't do anything to help get some rapist off. I have to be convinced Sylvester's innocent."

"That's where you're lucky, Clifford. I had to take his case. The firm that sent me Newton S. Sylvester sends my firm a lot of business."

Reavis knew that it's very tough for attorneys to turn down business referred by other attorneys. He'd graduated Duquesne University Law School and he kept up his license to practice law. But he could choose what he wanted to do. What he really liked to do was investigate. And, being a lawyer, or working for one, he could investigate criminal cases without needing a private detective's license.

"Look, Tim," Reavis said, "if the polygraph says he's lying, you can confront him. He might break down and tell us the truth. Maybe you could convince him to plead guilty. It's not first degree, anyway. If anything, it's a crime of passion. Maybe plea him to voluntary manslaughter. Take a chance on a lighter sentence because of his age and that he's never committed a crime before."

Garrity said, "You're getting rusty, Clifford. No. If it's him, it's murder one. The knife with his initials, Clifford. At her place? Right now, let's face it, the DA's Office has a lock on a murder one conviction. If the polygraph shows he's lying, maybe I can pressure the guy into a plea. If he'll go for that, I'll try to talk the assistant DA into dropping the rape charge, letting Sylvester plea to second or third degree murder. Maybe," Garrity said, "I can even get the assistant DA to go along and recommend a lighter sentence to the judge, at least make no recommendation."

"I think he's innocent," Reavis said. "I think he was framed."

Reavis heard the lawyer sigh. "We need a hook on this case, Clifford. Maybe you've just given me one. I'll call Sylvester tomorrow and set up a polygraph. We've got nothing to lose."

"How's Trindle going?" Reavis said.

"I can't get a read on the jury, Clifford. It's a mixture. I'm getting some who won't look at me. That kind always scares me. Every once in a while I'll get a smile out of one of them, though. Then I feel a little better. I'll get a better idea when Trindle takes the stand. The jurors will be less guarded when they're watching him testify. I'll promise you one thing, though: I'm getting out of town when this one's over. My nerves can't take it like they used to."

Reavis didn't want to remind him that, yes, he might be able to get out of town when the Robert Trindle case was over, but that his mind would then be working full-time on the Sylvester case, wherever he goes to hide.

Reavis had done some work on the Trindle case for Garrity. He liked Trindle, who looked like a fortyish truck driver and seemed mild-mannered. Reavis put him at about six even, maybe a pretty hard hundred ninety pounds. What he remembered most was going to a bar with Trindle, looking for a witness.

That bar gave meaning to bars people called "buckets of blood." Some of the drinkers had prison tats, almost everyone there had the look. When Trindle and Reavis opened the door to the bar there was the usual bar noise. The tattoo guys started flexing, looked to see who just came in. When they saw Trindle, however, they turned their heads away and the bar got very quiet. It stayed that way, no one looking over at Reavis's and Trindle's table the whole time they were drinking their beers. The witness wasn't in the bar.

Reavis, thinking that if anyone would have something bad to say about Sylvester it would be his ex-wife, made her his first stop.

*White* was a better word than *pale* to describe Grace Sylvester's coloring. She had soaked her full lips in inviting red lipstick that matched the polish on her nails. And she had dark, thick hair.

She turned, beckoning him to follow her down her narrow front hall, then looked back and caught him staring at the slit in the long satin thing she was wearing. His face got warm. She smiled, loving it that Reavis was sneaking a peak. She stopped at the end of the entrance hall and gestured gracefully, the ballet dancer. "Please, sit anywhere you like."

Grace Sylvester wouldn't move, so he had to brush against her to get by. She felt firm, but not too firm beneath her satin thing, and he caught a whiff of her good perfume.

It was 8:28 p.m., and dark. The drapes, open, gave Reavis a matchless view of Pittsburgh—the Point, downtown, Heinz Stadium, PNC Park, the Rivers Casino—a Mt. Washington, Grandview Avenue view. From here on Grandview Avenue the lights of the city below looked like jewels. On Grandview property overlooking the city went by the linear foot.

He sat on, and felt buried in, a white overstuffed piece of sectional furniture. The rug was snow white, the wallpaper a winter scene on foil. But the room made Reavis feel warm. No doubt because of the rug's thick pile and the overstuffed furniture. And because of the splashes of red Grace Sylvester had added to her room—a vase here, silk flowers there, two paintings on a wall with a lot of red in them.

"This shouldn't take too long, Ms. Sylvester."

She was sitting opposite him, legs tucked beneath her. "Grace . . . please. Take your time, Clifford." Her voice was cigarette throaty. "May I call you Clifford?"

He nodded and was again conscious of his face feeling warm.

"When I read about Newton," she said, "I just couldn't believe it." She paused, looking him over. "You're much taller than I imagined you'd be."

"I've always been tall," was all he could think of to say. Then felt like it was a stupid thing to say.

She shifted on the sectional; he tried not to stare, but, once again, she caught him doing exactly that. "You're really quite an attractive man. In your own way."

"Thank you." Usually, he didn't have any trouble talking to women, but the way this one looked at him made him nervous. "My own way?" he said.

"It's hard to explain." More thigh through the slit. She played with what had to be real pearls and seemed to be giving his question some thought. Finally she shrugged—proving that she wasn't wearing a bra. "I really can't say what makes you so attractive."

None of them ever could. He folded his arms and sunk deeper into the sofa. Reavis had a sudden fear of being trapped, not able to get away from Grace Sylvester.

That got him. Being worried about getting away from a woman who looked and smelled as good as Grace Sylvester. Why did that worry him?

"You're interested in someone," she said, "aren't you, Clifford?" Sounding disappointed.

"What makes you say that?"

"Aren't you?"

Reluctantly, he nodded. "I have been seeing someone."

"Yes. I'll bet you have." She did something with her legs and skirt, ending the fine-thigh show. "So what would you like to know about Newton?" All business now. Still friendly, though.

"Just general things." Reavis relaxing, feeling more at ease. "Things like, did he drink, have a temper?"

"Temper." She laughed. "I tried everything to get that man to show some emotion." Grace Sylvester regarded him frankly from eyes as dark as her hair. "He wasn't a cold man, Clifford. He was more like a steady seventy-two degrees. Room temperature. Never hot; never cold. He was not repressed, either. He wasn't bad in bed. But, otherwise, he was bland; that's what he was, a nice, bland man. When I told him I wanted a divorce . . ." Grace Sylvester smiled.

He motioned for her to go on.

"Nothing. He didn't say a thing. Just got up—we were sitting at the dinner table—actually excused himself, went down to the basement, and played with his model trains the rest of the night. He never did ask me why I was leaving him." She looked away, said, "Model trains. They were his passion."

Grace Sylvester didn't say anything for a while. Then she looked sharply at Reavis. "I'll bet you're not."

"Not what?" he said.

"Bland." Checking him out some more. "You've got too much devil in your eyes. I can read it in those eyes of yours, even through your glasses." She narrowed her eyes and shook her head. "No, you'd never be bland. I can tell. Something about you simply sends a woman that message. That's one thing that makes you attractive."

Newton and Grace Sylvester, she went on to say, were still friends. "I just know Newton didn't do it," Grace Sylvester told him as he left. "He's absolutely harmless. Oh, except for politics. Money is a big stick to politicians. And while Newton may be bland, he still knows how to use that big stick."

Reavis didn't think he did it either. He was more sure of it after he got the results of Sylvester's polygraph test, which showed that the man who was charged with rape and murder was telling the truth when he claimed that he didn't rape and murder Judith Jenkins. The gin and vermouth bottles Reavis had picked up at Sylvester's—what did the lab have to say about them? Nothing in them but Beefeater's and vermouth. No drug residue.

For the next week and a half Reavis pecked away at the Sylvester case. He went through courthouse records, civil and criminal, pulling the Sylvesters' divorce file. There was nothing in the criminal indexes. Reavis was looking for maybe a DUI to show a drinking problem Sylvester would not acknowledge. He even googled Sylvester and Judith Jenkins. Nothing.

He interviewed Judith Jenkins's daughter, Margie, and he interviewed Edward Jenkins, the victim's ex-husband, before they left town after the funeral. He interviewed the computer expert's friends, professional associates, and neighbors. Dr. Jenkins had neither enemy nor best friend. Simply put, she was devoted to her work. And that was about it.

He also interviewed Sylvester's friends, neighbors, business associates, political allies, and political enemies. And he interviewed the hired help, Charles and Monica Faircloth. No one could believe Sylvester did it, but no one could name anyone who hated Sylvester so much they'd frame him for rape and murder, either.

Marge called and said Tim wanted to meet him. They did on Friday, April 25, at the Common Plea, a restaurant near the courthouse and city-county building, which both had courtrooms.

Tim was there when Reavis got there; he could see him in the back. And went over and sat.

"Marge told me you got a not-guilty on Trindle, Tim. Way to go."

"They were out two days. That's always a good sign. I'm glad I decided to put him on the stand because he came across real good. I told him to make sure when he answered questions to look at the jury when he answered. And never to look at me for an answer. He did a good job of it. We kept it simple. The guy had an honest look. Clifford, it's how you look and how you say it that does the job with juries."

Reavis knew that.

Tim went on. "It didn't hurt that the jury saw what scumbags most of Arloski's family were. You and I talked about it. The assistant DA didn't have the greatest case. Trindle and Arloski arguing at Lotta's Bar, then Arloski leaving. Witnesses in Lotta's didn't have great memories about how soon after Arloski left, Bob Trindle went out the same door. Bob had a simple story. He left after Arloski, before Arloski could come back to Lotta's with family help. He said he never heard a shot and never saw Arloski after he left the bar. Went straight home. That's a tough story for a prosecutor to break.

Tim leaned back in his leather chair again. "So, what's the story on Mr. Sylvester?"

Reavis told Tim he was certain that Newton Sylvester had been framed. There was no question about him staying on the case. He went over what he'd been doing, looked at Tim, wondering whether he might have missed something.

Tim said, "You even googled them. Checked to see if they were on Facebook, YouTube, whether they were on Twitter and all that other new high-tech stuff. Man, you're current. Which one was it, Peggy or Bobby who got you going on that?"

Reavis admitted that both Peggy Mueller, the woman he was seeing, and Bobby, who had a masters in computer science and who hung with Reavis a lot, had helped him with the Internet things.

Tim gave his head a slow shake. "I can't think of anything you missed, Clifford. I'm seeing Sylvester Monday. Maybe something will come up then."

Reavis was with Peggy Mueller the evening after he had lunch with Tim Garrity.

Reavis had met Peggy in his big church over on the North Side. He just happened to sit next to her one Sunday. She gave him one of her great smiles that day. When they got up to sing, he could tell she wasn't too short for him. He could smell a slight touch of her scent, and he liked it. He put a little more into his hymn singing that day. After the service, the pastor asked everyone to give someone a hug before they left. Reavis and Peggy both turned toward one another, nothing planned, and he got a good hug. Reavis had worried that he'd made it last too long, but she hadn't pulled away.

Reavis waited that day for everyone in the pews in front of him to pass by before he stepped out, backing up some so she could get out ahead of him in the aisle. They walked out to the front doors together and talked awhile. Reavis didn't get that much information out of her that time.

The next Sunday, he made sure to find a way to sit next to her again, and everything went from there. He soon learned that she was a long-time widow and that she had three grown daughters and a bunch of grandkids that she adored. One day he asked her what kind of music she liked. "Doo-wop,"she said.

He asked her if she would like go with him to Jimmy Beaumont and the Skyliners' fiftieth anniversary concert at the Benedum Center in two weeks, and she told him "Sure."

They loved the concert. Porky Chedwick, the Pittsburgh DJ of Reavis's teen years, was there; they brought him out from backstage and introduced him. Ninety, Porky was then, the "Daddyo of the Radio," Pork called himself. "Your Platter-Pushing Papa." Porky would say on the radio, "I'm so cool that I make the Statue of Liberty drool.".

Peggy broke into his thoughts. "What was it you said the first time you took me out, Clifford?" He looked down at her. Peggy stayed in shape, and she had a great shape, too. She was close to his age, no more than ten years younger, but Reavis believed she looked much younger than that. They were taking one of their walks and had stopped in the middle of the Tenth Street Bridge to look down at the Monongahela River, dirt-brown and angry now, swollen by spring rain.

He didn't know what she was getting at. "What? I said a lot of things that night. You mean when I said all I worked were cases that interested me?"

Peggy squeezed his arm, looked up at him. "You sure got one, didn't you?"

He looked at her, frowning. "I sure did." He shook his head, trying to figure out what he'd missed during the investigation of the case. "I thought there'd be something. There always is. The police messing with his rights . . . something." He tossed a piece of broken concrete into the river, listening for but not hearing a splash.

Peggy said, "I don't believe for a minute that he did rape and murder Judith Jenkins, but if he did, you wouldn't want him to get away with it, would you?"

His foot got stuck in the iron bridge railing spokes and it took him a full two minutes of yanking hard to get it out. After he got it out, he said, "No, I wouldn't stay on the case if I thought he was guilty." He was sure of that.

"Then why are you looking for a police error, technicalities?" she said. "Shouldn't you be out looking for the man who did it?"

"I have been looking, Peg," he said. "Even people who didn't like Sylvester. Everybody seemed to like Judy Jenkins, none of them seemed capable . . . I'd swear . . ."

"What makes you so sure he didn't do it, then?" She now sounded like she needed to be as convinced of Sylvester's innocence as Reavis was.

"I just am, that's all," he said. "Don't forget, Sylvester passed the polygraph." She started to say something, but he held up his hand. "I know, the polygraph can be beat; he could have blacked out killing her . . . the polygraph couldn't pick that up."

But the polygraph wasn't why Reavis was sure Sylvester was innocent. He couldn't tell Peggy the real reason he knew Sylvester was innocent: the look of revulsion on the millionaire's face when Reavis told him about nearly killing Paul Petro.

And Peg? Tell her about trying to kill Paul Petro? He hadn't known her long enough. Maybe someday he could talk to her about Beth's and his unborn child's murder, how he should have been able to save her. Maybe not.

She put her hand in his. If felt small, but warm and strong, too. Peggy Mueller, he'd come to know, was strong. She'd had to be—working full time and raising three kids all by herself. "Couldn't there have been somebody you missed, Clifford? Someone who knew them both?"

"That's what gets me, Peg. It had to be that way. It couldn't have been someone who, say, Judy Jenkins came in on in the middle of a burglary, or someone who followed her home. Whoever it was also framed Newton Sylvester, and had to know he was going to do that before he even killed her." A jealous lover was the best bet but Judith Jenkins did very little dating; she simply didn't have a jealous lover in her past or present. Including her ex-husband.

He got a flash thought of how the Carnegie Mellon School of Drama professor looked in the police photographs, lying naked in her own blood. Whoever killed her had to be crazy. That's what got him: How could someone as out of control, as the photos of Judith Jenkins proved her killer had to be, have the presence of mind to turn around and do such a perfect job of framing Newton Sylvester? There had been blood and tissue under her nails, too. Reavis was sure when the DNA results came back, the match would be made with Sylvester.

When Reavis and Peggy reached Second Avenue, they made a left, intending to head down Second to the Point.

"A nut," Peggy said.

Reavis looked around to see who she meant, but he couldn't see any nut. "Where? I don't see . . ."

"No, Clifford, I mean the murderer could be unbalanced, insane. Maybe he didn't even know Dr. Jenkins or Newton Sylvester. Maybe he picked them out: one to rape and murder, one to frame."

"Are you talking about a serial rapist—a killer and also a guy who frames someone for his crimes?"

"I don't know about serial," she said. "But at least this one case."

It was a clear night. He'd dropped Peggy off at her home in the suburbs. Reavis, on the roof below the fifth floor of his narrow home, lying in a hammock out in the night air, headphones on, listening to the Dubs singing "Could This Be Magic," "Don't Ask Me To Be Lonely," and some Skyliners' songs.

The night, the music and the beer began to loosen the hold the Sylvester case had on him. He thought about what Peggy had said about a nut who raped, killed, and framed. How would he ever prove that? Eventually something got to nagging at Reavis. An answer? He hoped. But whatever it was, it wouldn't float to the top. Maybe whatever it was would break through by morning. A lot of times answers did that with him.

# CHAPTER SEVEN

*A crazy.* Reavis was sitting up in bed rubbing sleep-clogged eyes. Was that it? Was that really the answer? Or was he really off base? That was what bothered him all weekend. By Sunday, though, he thought he might have found a way to test his psychopathic-stalker theory, as well as get some clues to the man's identity. He called Bobby Sunday night to tell him he was going to be over early Monday, that he needed him to look up some things on the Internet.

Monday morning Reavis was up before the alarm clock went off. Bobby, who slept as late as Reavis, would be getting up early, too. Bobby with his masters in computer science. Internet information was exactly what Reavis needed. Bobby had grown a foot since Reavis first met him, but still wore those red tennis shoes like he had on when they first met. He also had a full beard now. Some people thought he looked like a mountain man. Some people called him "Shoes," because of the tennis shoes.

Here's how Reavis and Bobby got so close: Years after Reavis had moved to the South Side, about noon one day a young kid was sitting on the front steps of one of Reavis's rental properties where Reavis was working. When he saw Reavis coming, he got to his feet real fast and brushed at his shirt and pants. "I was wondering if you could use some help," he said.

Reavis took one look at him that day: maybe fourteen, fifteen, five-six and skinny. Looking Reavis right in the eye, the boy said again, "I hear you might have work for somebody like me. I'm stronger than I look and I'm very smart. I pick up new things fast." The boy had some bad pain—not physical pain—on his face, in his eyes, that first day and his hands were locked together in front of him. All he would tell Reavis was that his name was Bobby. No last name. Not where he was from. Nothing. But Reavis couldn't turn the little guy away.

"Where are you staying, Bobby?"

Bobby said he just got to town. Hadn't found a place yet.

He put Bobby to work then and there. Bobby worked his ass off the rest of that day and into the evening. About nine o'clock Reavis dug his wallet out of his Levis, took out three twenties and handed them to Bobby. "Where do you want me to drop you?"

Bobby took the money, said thank you, and lowered his head for a while, then looking up at Reavis, said, "I guess the bus station, maybe I can sleep there."

"You want to do some work for me tomorrow?"

"Sure, Mr. Reavis. I'll work for you as long as you want. I need the money."

Reavis said, "You can stay at my place tonight if you want to and don't mind sleeping on the couch. I've got an extra bedroom upstairs, but it's full of junk. No bed."

Bobby took a step or two back and looked like he was trying to read Reavis. Like maybe he thought Reavis was trying to get up to something with him. Then he nodded, with a what-do-I have-to-lose look.

"Done," Reavis said. "But I don't wake up to any alarm clocks. I'm usually not up and around until an hour or two before noon. I sleep late and I work late. If you get up before me, just go out to the kitchen and find something to eat."

Now Bobby was grinning. "That's what the man down the street told me. He wasn't sure if you would be here yet. He told me you were a late sleeper. I like sleeping in too."

Bobby slept on that couch for months, Reavis feeding him and getting him signed up for a savings account. All Reavis ever had to do was show the boy how to do something once, and he picked it up. It had been that way ever since. Now Bobby was usually the teacher. Reavis hadn't known it that first day, but they were going to be together all these years. Bobby could do all Clifford gave him to do. That was Reavis's nickname for Bobby—*Do-all.* Reavis smiled while thinking his next thought. He would yell, "Hey, Do-all," and the kid would come running.

Bobby did everything: lifting concrete block, finishing cement, sanding, painting, whatever. After all this time, Reavis still didn't know Bobby's original last name. The kid still wouldn't tell him that, where he was from, or what he'd been doing before Reavis found him waiting on the doorstep that first day.

Reavis could have found out everything. That's what he did—find things out, but something told him not to. Give Bobby the privacy.

Then one day about three years after they met, Bobby, talking softer than usual, said, "You know a lot of attorneys, Clifford. Can you get me one? It's about my last name."

*Finally!* Reavis, managing his breathing. Trying to look normal.

"I want to change my last name—legally." Bobby had a look on his face, trying to look calm, almost making it.

"Oh," Reavis said. Bobby still not giving up his real last name. "You know I'm an attorney, Bobby, but I don't practice much law, even though I'm licensed. I'll call Tim Garrity and see if he can fix you up with someone. But, Bobby, you have to give your attorney your real last name. The attorney will need it when he does the name change; it will be in the court filing, which will be a public record." He looked at

Bobby until Bobby locked eyes with him. "I've never looked into your background and I promise I won't now. You've always been Bobby or Do-all to me." Reavis gave Bobby a big smile then and said, "Do I at least get to hear what your new last name is going to be?"

Bobby giving Clifford Reavis that grin of his. "How's 'Doall' sound?"

Reavis had grinned, too, thinking his next thought. Like a father, he had given Bobby his last name—"Doall." Now it was going to be legal.

Reavis caught himself smiling at his memories, and called Bobby, whom he'd already talked to about the case. After he got to Bobby's, he laid out the Sylvester case to him in more detail than he already had, telling him his new idea: that a total stranger might have raped and killed Judith Jenkins and framed Tim Garrity's client for the crime. Then asked him if he could find other cases like it on his computer.

"If they're there, I can. Okay, let's start looking, Clifford."

They took the stairs to the second floor of Bobby's three-story, a building that for the first three floors was laid out exactly the same way as Reavis's. Bobby's computer room was on the second floor, the back room, which was the width of the thirty-feet-wide home. There were no windows in the room, but there was nothing to look out at anyway, except for walls and roofs of homes a few feet away and down at the alleys between them. His computer, huge monitor, laptops, and a couple dozen disks sat on a series of three side-by-side tables—like you'd find at a bingo hall—put together to make one long table. Against the opposite wall he had just put in a new, long blackleather sofa and matching leather recliner with a small refrigerator in between, the refrigerator also serving as a table for sofa and recliner users. Wherever someone sat they could watch what they wanted to see either on the computer monitor or on the fifty-two-inch flat-screen TV he had mounted in the middle of the wall, three feet higher than the monitor.

Bobby had installed lighting in the ceiling, which saved him from needing any lamps. He could turn any of the three rows of lights on, down or off from the doorway, with a remote he kept on top of the refrigerator, or with the computer.

Reavis and Bobby agreed on the search words they would use, like *murder, rape, professional, powerful, wealthy,* and *educated.* Words that would describe the crime and the kind of people involved.

Bobby called up Google and typed in the words. Within seconds a March story popped up in the online versions of both the *Pittsburgh Post-Gazette* and *Pittsburgh Tribune Review*. Both headlines read:

### DOCTOR MURDERED

Another rape-murder. The man accused of the crimes and his victim were both physicians. The victim was Stacy Bonato. According to the story, and as with Sylvester, a tip had led to the discovery of physical evidence, all incriminating Dr. Robert A. Taylor. The story in the *Post-Gazette,* sparse in detail, probably because the murder was discovered and Dr. Taylor arrested for it just before the morning paper went to press, went on to say that Bonato and Taylor had known each other socially. Follow-ups in both papers led to more information.

Reavis called Pat Tazer and told him what he and Bobby had turned up on the Stacy Bonato murder.

"Did you find any others like it?" Tazer asked. Reavis said, no, that was the only other one, and asked if Tazer could get the file for him.

Then Reavis had another thought. "You know, Taze, how 'bout you get me copies of the call-in recordings on the case, too, and get me a copy of the one on the Sylvester case again. I'm thinking we might hear the same guy on both recordings."

"Yeah, I can get it all for you," Tazer told him.

"I'll be right over."

"Whoa. I'm not that fast. Give me a day, Clifford. I'll need the extra time to get the call-in copies."

Reavis put the phone down, looked at Bobby, and asked him if he had the makings to put some steak hoagies together. He did. Reavis made them each two and they spent some time talking about how close Bobby was to his earning his PhD in computer science and about a professor of his, Dr. Sharon LeVon, who was mentoring him. Bobby seemed to have more than an educational interest in her.

After comparing the way the Pittsburgh Penguins played hockey to how the Philadelphia Flyers played the game, Reavis slowly got up, making sure his ass was in gear. It wasn't, so he had this stretch he had to do. That done, ass in low gear now, he thanked and high-fived Bobby Doall, and took off.

# *C*HAPTER EIGHT

The next afternoon Reavis's big cop buddy, Tazer, tugged a folder from under the other ones on his desk and showed it to Reavis. Then held up a small box and said, "The call-in copies."

"Way to go, Taze. Thanks. Can I see that file now?"

The Pittsburgh police sergeant handed it to Reavis. "Take it to that empty desk over in the corner."

Reavis grabbed the murder file, went over and sat down, rapping his right knee on the desk. Halfway through the file he had forgotten all about any knee pain. Dr. Judith Jenkins and Newton S. Sylvester, Dr. Stacy Bonato and Dr. Robert Taylor—the cases were carbon copies. Taylor's fingerprints had been found in every room of the victim's apartment. Not surprising. Stacy Bonato, a resident physician, Taylor, chief of cardiology at Mackey Hospital in Oakland, had been lovers. The lab people had matched the blood and tissue found under Bonato's nails with Taylor's. Also, it was Stacy Bonato's blood the police found on a bloody shirt stuck under the spare tire in Taylor's SUV. The young doctor had been raped. No semen. Again, there were scratches, this time on the back of the physician accused of killing Stacy Bonato.

Once more a man had called nine-one-one. He identified Robert Taylor as the man in blood-soaked clothing whom he saw running from Stacy Bonato's apartment. He also was able to give the nine-one-one operator the first three letters of the license on the back of Taylor's SUV. The caller, however, would not say how he knew Dr. Taylor. As in the Sylvester case, the caller had refused to identify himself.

Like Newton Sylvester, Robert Taylor claimed he fell asleep soon after he got home the night of the murder. His wife was out at the time, and, as it turned out, seeing a man whom she'd been having an affair with for over two years. Interesting: the one night Mrs. Taylor couldn't supply an alibi for her husband. Her regular night out with *her* lover.

Finished reading, Reavis called across the room to Tazer, "Can I listen to the call-in recordings now?"

Tazer reached for the small box and brought it over to Reavis.

First Reavis listened to the Sylvester call-in recording again, then the Stacy Bonato call-in recording. To be sure, he listened to both once more. He stood up, pumping his right arm, and then had to double over in pain. He had smacked his knee again.

Reavis motioned Tazer over. "Listen to these Taze. It's the same guy!"

"I already listened to them, Bones. I do believe you're on to something." Pat Tazer wasn't moving out of his chair.

It was the same guy all right, and the son of a bitch sounded excited. Reavis believed he detected a little smugness in the tone of the call-in on Stacy Bonato.

"Time for us to take another look, Clifford?" Tazer wasn't telling Clifford Reavis, only asking him.

"And do what, Pat? Your homicide guys didn't sit down on Taylor and stop. They talked to everyone they could. Donnie Cimoni, your best homicide detective, and his partner worked the Sylvester case. Who do you have that's any better than Donnie in Homicide? Let me talk to Tim Garrity, see about getting voiceprint identification on the two call-in recordings to be sure. Then you and I can take another look about what to do. All we're going to do now is scare the guy, maybe have him run for cover. We have no idea who he could be. He thinks he's in the clear, so let him keep on thinking that way."

That's the way Reavis and Pat Tazer left it.

Now, two weeks later, Reavis was sitting at his kitchen table, both of his big hands working at the Steeler beer stein that celebrated their sixth Super Bowl win. What other team had won six Super Bowls? Pittsburgh, city of champions.

Reavis used the beer stein for his coffee. He couldn't quit thinking about what he'd turned up on the Bonato–Taylor case. He had worked it like it was his own case, interviewing thirty-three people and reviewing every police report before he had to give up.

He was thinking about one of those interviews now, his meeting with Dr. Margaret Russell, Stacy Bonato's best friend and roommate, who was also a resident at Mackey Hospital.

It had taken him a while to find Margaret Russell. She had moved. He understood: How could anyone live where their best friend was raped and murdered?

From the way she sounded when he called to arrange that interview, he thought maybe he had awakened her. "Well," she said, when he told her why he wanted to see her, "my schedule is pretty tight. Maybe we could do this by telephone." She didn't say anything for a few moments. Then: "I thought the police were satisfied that Dr. Taylor did it."

"They are, but I'm not," Reavis said. "I'd rather meet with you, if you don't mind." Reavis knew from experience the phone was a poor substitute for talking with someone in person. More often than not, he'd found, it was the look on a witness's face, maybe something dropped in conversation—not an answer to a specific question, just something dropped—that turned out to be important. Every investigator would tell you the same thing. It's facial expressions, body language, what people let drop, what just pops out of their mouths. So he pressed Margaret Russell. "I think a psychopath killed Stacy and framed Dr. Taylor. You might know something that could help identify him. You might even help prevent another murder."

"If you think . . . I was going to work out this afternoon. Stace and I used to work out together when we could, but I guess I could see you."

Margaret Russell had come to the door in spandex shorts, bright blue with black stripes down the sides, and a white oversize sweatshirt. She was attractive, he guessed most people would say, but was a little too tall and tense looking for him. Too young, too.

The pine coffee table in her living room was piled high with medical journals and notebooks. Two half-empty coffee mugs, one with a broken handle, and two big glass ashtrays full of Newport cigarette butts also fought for space on it. There was an Exercycle in the corner. Reavis took all this in as he gulped the coffee Margaret Russell got for him. It was good. He would try for another cup before he left.

"I have a friend named Margaret," he said. "Are you a 'Margaret,' a 'Maggie,' or a 'Peggy'?'"

"Maggie, most of the time." She looked beat. Her pretty smile couldn't quite make it to her eyes. "You're a 'Clifford,' aren't you?"

"I seem to be. I don't get 'Cliff' from anybody I know."

Russell sat back, her arms folded over her stomach, looking at him and waiting for Reavis to get to his questions about her dead friend.

"Everybody at the hospital says you and Stacy were best friends, had been for years." He finished the coffee and held up the empty cup. "Good coffee."

"Thank you." She took the obvious hint, rose, took his cup, and went to get him more. When she returned, she said, "Most of us survive on this stuff and—I hate to admit it—some of us use cigarettes, too." Russell brushed back a strand of blond hair with one hand and shook a cigarette from the aqua-colored pack on the coffee table with the other. She lit it quickly and went on. "About Stace, yes, she and I had roomed together since the beginning of med school. She was my best friend. Neither of us had much free time, but what we did have we usually spent together. Unless she and Bob were getting together."

She inhaled deeply, then let the smoke trail out. "You know, it's almost a relief, you telling me it might not have been Bob . . . Dr. Taylor." She took a quick drag of the Newport this time, leaned forward, and looked into Reavis's eyes, shaking her head. "He didn't have any reason to kill Stace."

Reavis couldn't see any either. His investigation had revealed that Taylor and his wife went their separate ways, that she knew about Stacy Bonato and her husband and could have cared less. She had a boyfriend of her own. Stacy Bonato was no threat to their marriage. The Taylor marriage was wide open. "Did anyone ever break in where you and Stacy had lived before she was murdered?" He was remembering that someone had sent Judy Jenkins a pair of her own panties and matching bra.

A look crossed Maggie Russell's face, like she didn't know whether she should tell him something. She took another drag from her cigarette.

"She . . . there was something. Someone took one of her panties and bra sets." Russell blushed. "The kind that are more to look at than wear for very long." Looking at Reavis, seeing if he was too old to get where she was going.

Reavis was partial to red. He had to stop himself from asking her what color, but he managed to simply nod to her that he got it.

She went on. "The weird thing is that one day she received a package at the hospital and the panties and bra were in it. Stace opened the package in the residents' lounge. Took a lot of kidding about her taste in underwear. We talked about it later and she told me that someone had called her and, using some kind of phony accent . . . what did she say it sounded like?" She stopped, then shook her head as if she couldn't remember. "Anyway, he told her that he'd gotten into her bedroom and taken her underwear."

She put out her cigarette and shook another one out of the pack. She looked at Reavis before lighting it. "Stace and I thought it was one of the male residents. Maybe he got them at one of our rare parties here." She looked like she wasn't so sure now.

Reavis, remembering that conversation with Margaret Russell, thought that not only was taking Stacy's underwear the kind of trick some male resident might pull, it's what the same guy had also done to Judith Jenkins.

Who was he? Where did he lurk? How did he choose his victims? Randomly?

*Randomly.*

That brought him to his feet here in his kitchen as he thought about the rapist and murderer's two victims. The idea that someone out there might be choosing victims at random. How different, he wondered, was that from how Paul Petro had chosen his Beth to kill? That's how Reavis saw Beth's death, as murder. Certainly not premeditated like the two he'd investigated, but Reavis's heart couldn't make that distinction.

He could feel the locks let go. Rage crawl out. Physical—rage was for him. A jolt. His stomach bunched. On TV news, he'd seen people saying they could forgive this one or that one, someone who took a loved one's life. His pastor preached the same thing. Reavis wasn't there yet. He was what his pastor called a "saint in progress." It didn't seem that his mind, deep down where it counted, could distinguish among the deaths of his wife Beth, Judith Jenkins, and Stacy Bonato. His pastor preached forgiveness and Reavis believed in it. So far, though, he couldn't get there with Paul Petro. Still there. Reavis shook his head slowly. After all these years.

What would he do if he found this killer? Try to kill him like he had with Petro? No, he tried to convince himself, last time it was personal: his wife was murdered, Petro the murderer. He didn't know Stacy

Bonato and Judith Jenkins. Killing wasn't right. Back then he had nothing to lose. Now there was a lot to lose, a life he mostly liked. And, yes, now there was Peggy Mueller.

He hunched his shoulders, dug his hands into his pockets, went back and sat at the table. Why should he be worrying about what he would do if he found this killer? He was nowhere close to finding him.

Because once again he was out of questions and people to put them to.

# *C*HAPTER NINE

Marsha LeGrange got money back from the IRS this year. She'd put two thousand away, thinking she would owe, and had found out she didn't. She received her refund yesterday, another $541.23.

That's why she felt so good when she woke up this morning. And feeling good was why she chose her favorite suit to wear, a black wool-crepe suit that had set her back. To wear with it, she chose a silk blouse. For her favorite suit, her favorite blouse. Right? It had tiny white flowers sprinkled on a black background and a short raised ruffled collar.

Silk was Marsha's weakness. She liked the way it looked, but even more she liked the way it felt against her skin.

Marsha usually walked to work, three miles from where she lived in a condominium on the South Side. There was a cold steady rain this morning, however, so today was one of those days she took the bus. Because of all the walking she usually did, and the three nights a week she worked out at the Fitness Arena now, she was headed from real-goodshape to reallygreatshape. Occasionally, she would catch herself flexing in front of the mirror on the back of her bedroom door, then looking around guiltily, as though she was afraid someone else was in the room with her. She liked feeling and looking at firm muscles again. She reached down and ran her hand down the outside of her thigh, firm and heading to the firmer it once had been. It had been years since her legs had been steel-hard—that brief time in high school when she spent every free minute playing tennis.

Combining natural athletic ability with unlimited practice, she'd become the number one seed in all the local tournaments back in Missouri and was easily the best tennis player in her school. *Boys included,* she remembered with pride. She gave a quick shake of her head, regretting that she'd had to cut back on the hours she practiced tennis. At age fifteen, sudden as death, tennis no longer came first for Marsha. She'd no longer had much time for fun.

The bus dropped her off right in front of the building where WW&D had its offices. Her suit safe under a trench coat and umbrella, head turned to the side against a slanting rain, she scampered for the building.

When she got inside, she shook the umbrella off and walked over to the newsstand, where she glanced at the *Post-Gazette*. Newton Sylvester. She could see another article on the paper's front page. The man she saw a lot at the Fitness Arena, even before he'd been arrested for murder? Just the other day she'd been talking to Sylvester there. He was a nice guy. Marsha couldn't picture him as a rapist and murderer. She bought the paper.

She got through some of the story riding up on the elevator. Marsha had taken up racquetball since joining the health club. Was Judith Jenkins the woman she'd seen Sylvester playing racquetball with at the Fitness Arena? She particularly remembered seeing Sylvester and an attractive woman because of his loud laugh when he'd missed a shot. Loud laughing was out of character for Newton Sylvester. When the elevator stopped at her floor, she tucked the paper under her arm, promising herself that she would finish the story later.

Marsha's work day started out normally enough, but her secretary Carol's midmorning announcement that Lester Wilkins was on the phone changed that.

"Lester Wilkins?" Marsha said, wondering if she'd heard her secretary right.

"The very same," Carol said.

Marsha grabbed the phone. "Are you free for lunch today?" Mr. Wilkins said.

*If I wasn't,* she thought, *I'd make sure I got free.* "Yes. Sure. Certainly, I'm free, Mr. Wilkins." Then she looked at her appointments to see if she would have to do any shifting.

"Good. How about lunch at The Bucket then? Little after eleven?" He paused. She had her mirror out. "That way we can get a good table, have plenty of time to spend chatting. I'll stop by for you."

*Plenty of time to spend chatting.* She fussed with her hair and got ready to apply new makeup, congratulating herself that she'd worn the best suit she had. "Fine, I'll be ready," she said.

"Carol," she called out to her secretary after she hung up, "can you give me a hand with this mess? Lester Wilkins will be stopping by. He's taking me to lunch."

Looking at him across the table, Marsha decided that it was men like Lester Wilkins for whom the pinstripe suit had been invented. In his late forties, she guessed, he was on the low side of tall, and was just-perfect lean. The suit he wore today, dark blue, very light wool, fit him perfectly. All he ever wore were dark blues and charcoal grays. But always, she had noticed, he slipped in a dash of color in his ties. Today's was mostly red with tiny blue ducks on it. His best feature was his silver-gray hair, which he wore longish but always well-trimmed. His dark brown eyes seemed to shine as he sat listening to her.

The waiter came. She ordered a Reuben with some chips; he a salad. After the waiter left, she clasped her hands in her lap and looked at him, wanting him to get to why he'd asked her to lunch. Wilkins was a widower. She wondered if this was business or personal and wasn't sure which she wanted.

"Marsha," he began, showing the smile that had charmed so many juries, "I make it a point to find out as much as I can about the people in our firm. But in your case that's been easy. A lot of people are talking about you."

She sat up straighter, looked harder at him, cocked her head an inch or two to the right and put on a hesitant smile.

"One of those people talking about you is Hank Watson. I believe you know Hank?"

Hank was the Interstate Insurance Company regional claims manager. Interstate was an important client of Wilkins, Wilkins & Dunn.

"Yes," she said. "Hank and I are friends." Marsha had run into Hank soon after she'd started working out at the Fitness Arena. What she'd recently shared with Hank was the Giacamo case. He'd been the one she'd advised not to settle the case, to withdraw Interstate's two hundred fifty thousand dollar offer to the Giacamos' attorney, Murray Levin, and let the case go to verdict. He was glad he'd listened because the Giacamos lost. Marsha and Hank had gotten to the place in their friendship where both tried to get to the Arena at the same time so they could work out together. She liked to play racquetball with him too.

"Hank says," Lester Wilkins continued, "that everyone at Interstate is still talking about that verdict of yours on the Giacamo case. They haven't forgotten that you saved them two hundred fifty thousand dollars." The money they offered to settle the case before trial. He emphasized each word. "To give you an idea how important that verdict was to us, our billings to them are only slightly over the same amount every year. That on one case alone you nearly justified our firm's fees from Interstate for a year. That's how Interstate sees it."

Lester Wilkins lowered his voice. "Interstate recently completed a review of its defense costs, most of which are legal fees. And you know what?"

She leaned forward more, shook her head.

He put his hand on hers. It felt warm and dry. Then he seemed to catch himself and took it off a little quickly. "Interstate is increasing our share of their business. Hank Watson said one of the big reasons was your verdict. And you."

Lester Wilkins continued on in the same vein for a while, Marsha not saying a word. Then he seemed to begin winding down. "Some of the partners and I had an informal meeting the other day." He stopped, sat back, was taking her in. "The meeting was about you."

She couldn't keep from tapping her right foot. *Come on!*

Wilkins said, "We've decided to showcase you, Marsha. Greatly increase your responsibility. That means you'll be handling big cases now. Of course," he put his hand back on hers and let it linger there this time, "we'll always be there to help you if you need it."

She started to worry that she might not be able to handle it.

Seeming to read her mind, he held up his hand. "When you get the results we know you will, more and more clients will ask for you. We want that. It will help the partners with their case loads. And it will also move you that much closer to making partner." He paused again. She could tell he wanted her to be sure that she understood the full import of what he was talking about—the part about being considered for partner.

He needn't have worried; she could repeat what he had said word for word.

"Oh, Marsha, one more thing." He removed his hand from hers and turned up that great smile. "This morning we had a formal meeting, one with all the partners." He was grinning now. "Effective immediately you'll be making a hundred twenty-five thousand dollars a year."

*A thirty-five-thousand-dollar a year raise.* A hundred twenty-five thousand dollars a year in Pittsburgh. This wasn't New York City; money stretched a lot farther here. She had to say something now. But what? Little more than a month ago she'd been thinking Lester Wilkins didn't even remember who she was. "Mr. Wilkins, thank you so much. You don't know how good you've made me feel." *But he must,* she thought. The pride, delight—it had to be written all over her face. "I can't wait to get started, and," she broke into a grin herself now, "I have had my eyes on a blouse."

Wilkins, smiling knowingly, said, "With me it's ties." Their eyes met and his gaze held hers. "Not many like you come along, Marsha."

She didn't see Larry Haski until they were ready to leave and then, for once, she didn't let the sight of him get to her. Haski was by himself, as usual, in a corner booth, his back to her, where he could have seen her and Wilkins in the mirror behind the bar. Larry Haski did not seem happy. She never stopped to think that he might have followed them here from the office.

Larry Haski had it in for her—of that she was certain. But she didn't know why.

Back at the office, she wanted to tell someone. But that wouldn't be professional. *Being professional,* she decided ruefully, *could leave a lot to be desired sometimes.* Now, more than ever, she missed her dad. She could always brag to him.

She was too full of what went on at lunch to come down and concentrate. And, was she imagining it? Weren't there a lot of people looking in on her this afternoon? Yes, there had been a lot more of that than usual. She had a pretty good idea of why, too. Carol must have blabbed about her having lunch with Wilkins.

Unable to sit still, she got up and walked to the window. Maybe some of the guys would be having coffee downstairs now. Yes, she did feel like a cup of coffee. She usually didn't take breaks, but today, she told herself, she deserved one.

When she got to the Starbucks on the first floor, she saw Larry Haski and Jeff Guilfoyle sitting together. She pretended to be looking for something in her purse until Jeff noticed her.

"Marsha."

She acted surprised, like she'd only seen them for the first time. Jeff waved her over. He knew all right. *Look at that grin on his face.* Sure. Jeff would know. A full partner, he would have been at this morning's meeting where all the partners voted on her raise. A quick glance at Haski told her that, somehow, he knew too.

"Where do you buy your clothes, Marsha?" Haski said as she was sitting. Then, looking pointedly at Jeff, he let loose. "Because it looks like I'm going to have to buy a dress at your favorite shop, and wear it, to get noticed by Lester Wilkins." He turned his glare on her. "Isn't that right, Marsha?"

This was not what she'd come to hear.

Doing her best to keep herself under control, she looked briefly at the bastard. "Be nice, Larry," she said. Then, as she turned away from him, wanting no argument, she remembered the Sylvester article in that morning's paper. Composing herself, she managed to look at Jeff Guilfoyle, act like Haski had never said a word, and say, "That Dr. Judith Jenkins from Carnegie Mellon. Newton Sylvester. Unbelievable. Jeff, isn't Mr. Sylvester one of Tom Dunn's clients?" Acting like she didn't know, just to get Haski's focus off her, talk about something else.

"Yeah," Jeff said, looking relieved that she and Haski weren't going to get into it. "We were talking about that before you came down. Brought back some unpleasant memories of my own, you know."

She gave him a puzzled look.

"Yeah," he said, "someone I know was raped and murdered a couple months ago." Jeff looked across the table at Larry Haski and asked him in an unfriendly tone, "You remember her, don't you, Larry? Stacey Bonato, you couldn't stop staring at her whenever you saw her at the Fitness Arena. Or talking about her body with the guys."

Marsha took a chance and turned her gaze on Haski, who had a look of pure rage on his face as he glared at Jeff. His only answer was a grunt before he jumped up, knocked over what remained of his coffee, turned his back on them, and left.

Jeff said, "There goes just the kind of guy who would do something like that. Talk about a short fuse. Haski's got *no* fuse."

Rape. Larry Haski. Rage. Marsha could feel the small hairs on the back of her neck rising. She fell silent, thinking about the looks Haski was always sending her way. Jeff Guilfoyle was right. Though she wouldn't necessarily agree that Haski was capable of rape, she could picture him being violent with a woman.

Not pleasant, these kind of thoughts. So she let them die, got Jeff talking about their clients. Jeff's undergraduate degree was in computer science. One of the friends he'd kept in touch with after graduating from college started an information technology company and got back in touch with Jeff after he started practicing law. Jeff brought the friend and his IT company and three other tech clients with him when he joined WW&D. All four of the clients Jeff brought with him had their own internet companies. Now, the first friend to become Jeff's client, and he alone, accounted for fees the size of Interstate's.

Then Jeff's first four clients referred more companies like theirs to Jeff, and those companies contributed more fees to WW&D. Word was that Jeff's clients alone accounted for over two million in billing a year to the firm. Jeff made full partner so fast because he was a rainmaker. Finding new clients who would make it rain down fees on Wilkins, Wilkins & Dunn. Not to mention on himself.

Larry Haski invaded her thoughts, making her lose track of what she was thinking about Jeff. She began to brood about Haski.

"Marsha?"

Startled, her arm jerked.

"Hey, you there," Jeff said. "Don't let Haski get to you. He's a head case."

She slowly shook her head, unable to understand people like Larry Haski. What had she ever done to him? "I can't figure him out, Jeff." She looked at her coffee, untouched and cooling, then at Jeff. "What is his problem?"

"Come on, Marsha," he said. "You know damn well what Haski's problem is."

"No, Jeff. I don't. I really do not."

Jeff was studying her, seeing if she meant it. Finally, he said, "You really don't know, do you?" He ran his right hand through his thick, dark hair, then rubbed his eyes. "It's an obsession with him. He couldn't take it if a woman made partner before he did."

When Marsha didn't say anything, he went on. "He usually doesn't say much about what's going on inside that head of his, but one night I ran into him at the Bucket—he was loaded, sitting by himself in the corner—and he gave me a lecture about how women were ruining the legal profession, said that a woman's place was home raising their children."

Jeff looked across the table at Marsha. "When I confronted him with his statements the next day he said he didn't even remember seeing me the night before, let alone saying what he did. But"—Jeff put his hand on Marsha's arm—"he didn't take them back."

"Funny," she said, "I might have gone out with him at one time. He's smart and looks good in gym shorts. And if he wants to, he can be charming. I've seen him with some of his clients."

She saw the look in Jeff's eyes, like he couldn't believe what he was hearing. "Jeff," she said, "he is a good-looking man. You can't take that away from him."

"He's got a name for you," Jeff said.

"Name? For me?"

"'The Virgin Marsha.'"

She wrinkled her forehead. "'The Virgin Marsha?'"

Jeff said, "Don't ask me why he calls you that. Maybe it's because you don't do much dating. Or it could be that he thinks you can do no wrong as far as the partners are concerned? Who knows?" Then Jeff offered to say something to the other senior partners to help get Haski off her back.

"No. Thanks, Jeff." She didn't want that. "I'll handle it," she said, hoping the grateful look on her face told him how much she appreciated the offer.

"All right, I won't say anything," he said. "But watch out for him. He's got a temper. A real temper." Then he changed the subject. "Naomi wants to have you over for dinner again some night. We'll send the boys to grandma's." Naomi was Jeff's wife.

"Great," she said. "Your wife is a real sweetheart. Not to mention gorgeous. I can tell that she's just right for you. You've got two great sons, too. They don't have to go to grandma's for me."

Jeff blushed. "Come on," he said, reaching for her hand. "Let's go play lawyer."

# *C*HAPTER TEN

That evening she did some serious thinking while lying in bed. The "Virgin Marsha," was it? Marsha was anything but a virgin. She had had little time to date in college, but she had dated then and, in fact, a little late for many young women of her generation, had lost her virginity. Not with a football star or a big man on campus but with a guy she met on the tennis court one day when she was playing against her best friend. Carrie Stockhausen was and still is her best friend.

But the real irony of being called the Virgin Marsha was that her part-time law school job, on Saturday nights, was as an escort—she sold her body. Not in Pittsburgh. In the Cleveland suburbs. She was recruited here, after she had been thoroughly vetted. Her best friend, Carrie, had been recruited first. She had recommended Marsha to the woman who ran the escort service, Marilyn Moore, who also taught Marsha the tricks of the trade.

Marilyn had sources who were looking for beautiful women who'd done extremely well in college and who wanted to gain advanced degrees but were already in debt for college and had no way to pay for those advanced degrees. Let alone their college loans. How those sources found Carrie, who recommended Marsha, too—each of whom wanted to be attorneys and were carrying high college loan debt—neither Carrie nor Marsha ever found out. By seeking women beautiful of face and body and mind like Carrie and Marsha , at the same time she also avoided the need to hire drug addicts, or worse. Marilyn achieved a monopoly of the prostitutes who could add to and keep up with conversations at the finest society events. Yet give their clientele what they needed physically before and after those events.

Marilyn had called on Carrie first, then later, at Carrie's urging, Marsha. She explained to each of them exactly why she was contacting them and how much they could make. Carrie told Marsha she'd denied Marilyn the first time she was approached. Marilyn had told Carrie if she changed her mind to call her and she could arrange to have her come to her home, where she carried on her business of providing beautiful young women to rich men. Carrie was appalled by the idea at first, but after reviewing her college loans she realized there was no other way to pay them. Not to mention pay for law school and get the grades she needed to be selected for the school's law review, which would enable her to name the legal job she wanted.

Carrie went back and forth on the idea for a month and a half, still working her part-time jobs. Finally, she caved under the weight of her debt.

Without even mentioning it to Marsha, Carrie arranged to meet with Marilyn Moore at Marilyn's home. Marilyn showed her where she would be working and had her interview the prostitutes who worked for her. Each had a college degree and high college loans. Each wanted to get higher degrees. They were frank with Carrie, telling her that they often cried themselves to sleep, that their souls were raw with shame, but the work they were doing was the only way they had to pay for their loans and to even think of earning advanced degrees. Each did tell Carrie that their working conditions were more than they could have hoped for.

Carrie made her decision after talking to Marilyn's prostitutes. She told Marilyn that she would go to work for her, but said that she would only do it if Marsha made the same choice, telling her that she couldn't do the work without being able to talk with Marsha about it, have help talking about her guilt and shame. Selling their bodies knifed into them as they drove back to Pittsburgh each weekend. Marsha and Carrie worked only Saturday nights and each of them made at least five thousand dollars every weekend.

Marilyn paid taxes on the business income, which she called "professional recruitment," to the state and federal governments. Marilyn deducted all the necessary taxes from Marsha's and Carrie's paychecks and sent them a W-2 form every year. Both paid income taxes on what was described as a "recruitment liaison."

Marsha quit that lucrative job, with all of her school loans, her legal education and expense paid for. She also earned law review every semester. So did Carrie. Each also ended up with plenty of after-tax money in the bank.

Marsha quit selling her body to become Judge Ronald Kaufmann's law clerk. After that she became an associate attorney at Wilkins, Wilkins & Dunn.

Carrie started her own law firm.

Getting to know men nowadays, however, took more time than the companionship and sex they offered seemed to be worth. It wasn't only a male-female relationship, though. It was any kind of relationship other than the one she'd had for years with Carrie. And she and Carrie had a lot less time to talk on the phone and see each other than they'd have liked.

Marsha pushed herself up in bed and relaxed against the headboard, realizing that this was the first time that her long-unconscious decision about other relationships had found its way into words.

It was just that she had so little time. She looked absently at one of the pink cherubs on the wallpaper. Was that it? No time for them. Was that why she had no real friends other than Carrie, or was there something wrong with her? She fussed with the pillows to make herself comfortable.

Other than Carrie Stockhausen, Jeff Guilfoyle was as good a friend as she had. And what was Jeff's and her relationship about, anyway? A couple dinners with Naomi, his wife, and him. His cute kids home once, too. Talk at the office, maybe a few drinks together at the Bucket? Some workouts together at the Arena? What did she really know about him? And why couldn't she let Jeff do something about Larry Haski?

Larry Haski made Marsha nervous.

There was something besides Larry Haski that would not only have made Marsha nervous but would have terrified her. What she did not know was that Jackie Simpson was going to be in her home again tonight. He would wait there until she went to sleep.

As always, then, he would come into her room. Marsha didn't always sleep naked, but she did sometimes. Jackie liked to find out. Maybe, deep down, he wanted to wake her, have her see him standing over her. That would be her problem. His relief. He would be forced to rape and kill her.

He had wanted to take a souvenir tonight, one he could send her in the mail as he had with Stacy Bonato and Judith Jenkins. But she got home a little early tonight, so he didn't get a chance to pick one out.

He had to make himself take nights off from his visits to Marsha Le-Grange. He knew that. He was feeling more and more wired because of her. And, right now, he couldn't break his schedule to go see Nadine. He would, though, up the ante on Marsha as soon as he could. That would ease his Marsha-induced stress some. He was already working out all the time. That helped out some too.

But nothing except Marsha LeGrange lying beneath him, begging for her life, was going to get him where he now so desperately needed to be. That and a man to frame for her murder. Finding the right man to frame for her rape and murder was all that was holding him back.

Marsha LeGrange was already there for the taking. Where he needed to be was on top of her, doing what he'd done for his first time to Marie Martieri.

# CHAPTER ELEVEN

Nor could Clifford Reavis get to where he needed to be. Answers wouldn't come, so late one morning he left his home and drove to his newest renovation project, a narrow, six-room, single-family house with Inselbrick siding and a high peaked roof. He needed time to let things settle, for answers to break out of their hiding places. Renovating rundown houses was both balm and stimulant to Reavis. As he drove to his new project he remembered his first renovation, where he still lived. One day, Beth not a year dead yet, Reavis was on the way from the house where he had lived with Beth in Bethel to the South Side, where he drank. He saw a FOR SALE sign on a beat-up old house a few blocks from his favorite bar.

Clifford had become rich the hard way. Beth's company had a huge policy on her life, with Reavis the beneficiary. Also, Beth and Reavis had taken out million dollar life policies on themselves when they'd learned she was pregnant. Petro's liability carrier paid the high limits of his liability policy to Reavis and he collected on the stacked underinsured motorist coverage on his and Beth's two cars. All tax free. Money had never again been Clifford Reavis's problem. His problem was the hole that the loss of Beth left in his heart.

Reavis couldn't make himself return to his insurance-claims job after his wife's death. That's what his job had been: managing men and women who paid people like him when the negligence of one of the people they insured killed or injured someone.

He had been drinking away at the blood money but wasn't making any kind of dent in it. Still half shot from the night before and with typical boozy reasoning, one day Reavis decided that if he was going to spend all his time drinking on the South Side he might as well find somewhere to flop there. More important, the South Side was far enough away from their home in Bethel, a place with too many memories and too many neighbors and friends trying to do the right thing.

He stopped at the house for sale that long-ago day and looked around. Water stained the ceiling where its roof leaked, the plumbing was bad, and the plaster was cracked or missing. "That couch go with the place?" he asked the owner. When the guy said it did if he wanted it, Reavis said he'd take the place. He could plop on that couch every night. That's why he bought the place: a couch to plop on in a place near where he drank. Away from Bethel, now called Bethel Park. No grand plan. No plan at all.

He couldn't let himself get rid of Beth's and his Bethel home, though, so he kept it, staying there when the need to be with the little that Beth had left behind became too overwhelming. He would just open the garage door with his radio control and drive into the garage. All of

Beth's things were in their home, including her scent, though it had faded more and more as each month passed. Beth. Their good times. How much he missed her. Clifford Reavis, crying in the dark with nothing but the diminishing fragrance remaining of the woman he missed so much.

One night as he and a younger Pat Tazer sat drinking boilermakers at a bar off East Carson Street in the South Side, Tazer decided that they should renovate the beat-up house where Reavis flopped. Tazer coerced two other guys into helping them the next day, but after that only Taze and Reavis worked on the row house. Then it was only Reavis, Tazer always saying that he'd gotten things started for Reavis; it was up to Reavis to finish the job.

One day, chipping off some plaster, Reavis found a fireplace. It took three days to get the plaster off the red-brick fireplace. After a visit from a plumber and the guy who sold gas fire logs he had himself a beautiful working fireplace. And for the six days it had taken him to get it that way, he had forgotten to drink. He made the place his home then, and it still was his home. Then, just the living room, with the red-brick fireplace, and an eat-in kitchen and bathroom on the first floor. On the second floor a big bedroom and a smaller bedroom. Between the two bedrooms was a bathroom. The third floor became his office a few years later. Hot tubs, the elevator, and fifth floor over the roof, which he'd had carpeted and where he had a fence around the rim installed, were far more recent additions.

It took years for Clifford Reavis to begin dating. After he did, he loved catching the looks on the faces of the women he brought home from time to time, first flicking a switch that played slow doo-wop music from his stereo and then (in late fall and winter) flicking the switch beside it that lit the gas logs in the fireplace. What he did with the light switch depended upon the woman.

After he finished renovating that first place, Reavis bought another, just to work on, have something to do, then rented it out after it was finished. He had become a real estate investor almost by accident. Now he had over three dozen properties, all of them paid off, almost all with paying tenants.

Bobby had let Reavis know he would be working at the six-room Inselbrick Clifford Reavis was heading to. The Inselbrick was going to go. Reavis hated Inselbrick. When he got there a neighbor kid helped him drag the belt sander off the end of his black pickup.

Bobby came down from the second floor when Reavis got there and Reavis told him he was going to work on the front room.

"What, you're out of leads on the Sylvester case? You think by working on this renovation, letting yourself get into the work, your mind will let go and give you a lead?"

"That's the way it usually goes," Reavis said.

"I think I can save you another sore back and leg cramps," Bobby said.

"How's that?"

"We only checked similar cases in our area," Bobby said. "What if the guy's been doing it all over the country?"

"I never considered that he's been anything but local."

"Me either. It just came to me now. Popped into my mind out of nowhere. Who could believe something like that? The raping and killing only? Yes. Sure. That's nothing new. But then framing a man for those crimes, too? No way. I never heard of such a thing. You didn't either. Not in all the years you've been investigating these things. Let me get my tools together and we'll head over to my place. Find out."

# CHAPTER TWELVE

Reavis followed Bobby in his pickup to Bobby's place. When they got there the two of them headed for Bobby's computer room. Reavis had to brush aside hoagie bags and pizza boxes to be able to see the big burgundy laptop on the smaller table. He nodded toward Bobby's beer-refrigerator-table and Bobby got him an Iron City Beer. Then sat in his computer chair, swiveled around so he could be facing Reavis.

"So," Bobby said, "I'll search out-of-town papers to find out whether there were murders like our two in Pittsburgh."

"Yeah. That's what I should have done in the first place."

"You should have? Get over it. Don't forget, Clifford, the first time we were just working on a long-shot hunch we had no idea would pay off. Then you thought you could turn up something on the Bonato case here that would help yours. Now we know there is a Pittsburgh killer who has killed two women and framed two men. Your big clues—the call-in recordings, the rapes, murders, and frames—are near duplicates. How were we even going to consider that someone was raping and murdering women and framing other men for his crimes not only in Pittsburgh but all over the country? Let's find out. I've bookmarked a website that has online newspapers from not only this country, but from all over the world."

Bobby swiveled away to face his computer. "Let me get the site."

Bobby opened his browser and brought up the Web site. "Same search words as before?"

Reavis nodded.

Bobby typed in the search words they'd used to locate the Stacy Bonato case, then said, "Get behind me and see what came up." Bobby, who mostly seemed to keep his cool, sounded exited.

Reavis, still having stiffness trouble with the left side of his ass, got up slowly and limped over to get behind Bobby.

He didn't have his computer-reading glasses with him, either, but what he could see on the out-of-town newspaper archives looked like headlines about different rapes and murders. He read that you could get a free abstract that told you a little about the rape and murder articles and had to pay if you wanted the entire articles. "Just what I'm looking for, Bobby. Think I can afford the entire articles?"

They used the rest of the day to search out-of-town papers. Last year's February 10 Internet edition of the *Houston Chronicle* was that first paper Bobby found to let him know he was on the right track. In

Houston, he'd found three murders, all within the last two years. Each victim was a professional woman; the accused—all later convicted—were, like Newton Sylvester, rich and influential. Each murder made the headlines. In two of the articles, mention was made that an anonymous call led the police to the man they arrested. Follow-up articles pointed out that an overwhelming amount of physical evidence led to convictions in each case. In all of the cases the accused took the witness stand and swore he was not the killer.

Bobby found some recent back editions of the *Boston Globe* that yielded three more, the Boston murders having taken place in a three month period, the latest in January of this year. Again, the victims were career women, the accused important men. These cases were recent enough that they hadn't gotten to trial.

Now, much later, Bobby and Reavis were just sitting back in Bobby's computer room. Bobby got Reavis two soft pillows and put them where he could sit on them on the black leather sofa, then got Reavis yet another Iron to drink.

Bobby, sitting with a cold Iron City beer at his computer, turned around to look at Reavis, who was moving his neck around to help get the kinks out.

"Clifford, the long shot came in. Some guy is killing women and framing rich guys all over the country."

Reavis raised the cold Iron City sixteen-ounce to his dry lips. Bobby followed suit.

What more could they say?

Once home, he called Peggy and told her what he'd learned. "Peg, it hits you in waves. You get so focused on one thing that you miss the big picture. First," he said, "I was all excited. I'd proven, at least to myself and Bobby, that Sylvester hadn't killed Judith Jenkins. So I felt good. You know, that it wasn't Sylvester."

He paused to take a breath.

"It's like I lent you the Monte Carlo and you had an accident. I'd be worried you got hurt. When I find out you're not, I feel good. Then it would hit me about my wrecked car. That's how it was when I realized that one man was going around the country raping and killing women. At least twenty-three of them. Peggy," it still hadn't completely registered with Reavis, "all those women."

"And there will be . . ."

"Right." Reavis finished Peggy's thought. "That's what's really getting to me. There'll be more. That was the last blast. Realizing that." Reavis had to take a deep breath. "He's never going to stop."

"Clifford, you've got to call the police."

He'd already given that a lot of thought but had rejected the idea. "No. I can't. What I have wouldn't be enough for them. Besides, where would they start looking? I don't even know for sure if he's still in Pittsburgh. More important, if they get close enough to the killer, he'll just take off and start up somewhere else."

But Reavis believed he was still in Pittsburgh. In each city three women had died. Never more. Not ever less. Sometimes a year apart. Sometimes only weeks. Three. Even the murders were always the same, the same kind of evidence, the same kind of victim, the same kind of men framed. Always the women raped. No one ever questioned who committed the crimes, so the idea of a serial murderer had never surfaced.

The killer never broke his pattern, but that pattern had been constructed to such perfection that the idea of scripted murder had never surfaced. Undoubtedly there were complete investigations on each case, including talking to potential witnesses, but the important evidence, according to what Reavis and Bobby had read, was the bloody clothing, DNA matches, fingerprints, and other physical evidence, which always pointed to men like Newton S. Sylvester.

Reavis said, "What's the name of the guy you work with who has to dust his desk and line up his paper clips and pens before he can get any work done?"

"Tosco. Bob Tosco," she said. "People like Bob are called obsessive-compulsive."

"And what does Tosco do when one of the clowns at your office moves his paper clips when he's away from his desk?"

"He goes to pieces," she said. "Clifford, before he sits at his desk, he lines up exactly twelve paper clips on it. A pen on both sides. He leaves his desk to go to the men's room or something and some joker messes it up. When he gets back he can't do any work until he gets his desk back exactly the way it was. Twelve paper clips, each an inch apart, all in a row. A pen on either side."

Reavis said, "I think our guy's the same way, only with him it's not paper clips and pens, its rape, murder, and framing someone else. I think he has to have everything just right, do things the same way all the time, too, just like Bob Tosco. Only he has to line up his murders. I don't think he can break the pattern. That's why I believe he's still in Pittsburgh. He only got two women here, Judith Jenkins and Stacy Bonato, and he always gets three."

"He has some kind of quota?"

"Yeah, if I'm right about him," Reavis said. "And he's got one to go."

She was quiet a long time before she spoke. Then: "Clifford, promise me . . . if you find out who he is . . . you'll let the police handle it."

*Sure, Peg,* he was going to say. Or would he? Why not let the police handle it? Could it be because he had to see if he had the guts to get this guy himself? Or was it the hate for Paul Petro he could feel—acid eating away at the handcuff's he'd tried to keep on that hate? Was that what he was going to try, take that hate out on this killer? It had been so many years since Beth's murder. Why wouldn't it all stay down?

He had been looking at his clenched hands. Now he looked in the mirror beside the phone. What he saw was that his face was red and his jaws were clenched.

When he didn't respond, she said, "Clifford, promise me."

"No, Peg," he said. "No promises." One of his reasons, a real good one, he could give her. "Peg, the police even begin to ask questions, he finds out about it, he's gone. Gone but not done. He hits a new city. Gets new ID and a new look and he's at it all over again. Then he comes back here for number three. He would be sure to hear about the Sylvester investigation being reopened. No. If I don't do it my way, it's certain death for I don't know how many women, and prison for even more men. I couldn't take knowing that I was responsible for that."

Reavis couldn't completely admit the other reason even to himself: a chance to convince himself that he hadn't been a coward that night with Beth and Paul Petro. That he hadn't jumped late to save Beth because of fear.

"What will you do next, then, Clifford?" Her voice was soft, had a different tone.

"Get some help here and then hit the road."

As soon as he got off the phone, Reavis called Pat Tazer. "Can you get me some off-duty detectives to give me a hand on my case. I'll pay each of them sixty dollars an hour. Have them bring their cell phones. I've found twenty-one cases in other cities where I think it's the same guy . . . . Two shifts of three or four detectives, they can be recently retired. Send me three or four at noon, another three or four at six. All you have to do is tell them I'm doing some work on a foundation grant that's paying me to look into brutal murders. Please, for both of our sakes, don't mention that what they find out could impact two Pittsburgh murder cases. I can handle all the Pittsburgh area calling. I'll give your guys the out of town stuff."

They'll be there tomorrow. Have your checkbook out? Better yet, cash."

"Will do. Thanks, Taze."

As soon as Reavis got off the phone he started scribbling questions, about accused and victims alike, for Tazer's detective buddies to ask the people they would call in Houston, Boston, Phoenix, and all the other cities. Such as: where the victims, men as well as women, worked, which clubs and organizations they belonged to, what their hobbies were, what they liked and what they didn't like. He wanted to know the names of people they were now or had ever been married to, had ever dated, or were dating when they were raped and murdered.

Same with people they worked with, did business with, played with, and they were related to.

When all the information was gathered, Bobby Doall would feed it into his computer, let the computer tell them what the link was, the one link for all twenty-three murders. He had to find that link. Now it wasn't only Sylvester's liberty that depended on finding it. Woman number twenty-four's life depended on it, too. As did some rich man's freedom.

Two days later Reavis was at Bobby Doall's, sitting in his computer room, Bobby having cleared an area among all the empty pizza boxes, hoagie bags, and other takeout trash in the room. Reavis, who didn't feel stiff today, sat on the black sofa. He imagined that he could still hear the voices of the men who had saved him weeks of digging on his own. "Yes, ma'am," he could almost hear Jerry Distan saying, "could you give me the names of her three best friends? Thank you. Do you have their phone numbers? Sure, I can understand."

Bobby Doall was keeping his mouth shut while Reavis let his mind go back.

Reavis pictured Detective Sergeant Todd Martin, rubbing smoke out of his eyes, saying to a relative of one of the Houston victims, "Hi, I'm calling from Pittsburgh, Pennsylvania. I understand you were Pat Jaczewski's cousin. Yes, it was a terrible thing. Yes, I know you already talked to the police. I'm with the Pittsburgh Police Department. As a matter of fact, I have the report about your interview in front of me. Some new things have come up that I need to talk to you about. Got a minute. Good. Did your cousin work out?"

Questions and more questions. Reavis shifted his position and took a gulp from the can of Iron City beer Bobby must have handed him.

"Clifford." Bobby dragged Reavis out of his thoughts.

"How do you want me to give you what everyone gathered?" Reavis said.

"Just give me all you have on each case. Little Bobby, who first got his GED, then hit the 99th percentile on his SATs and was now working on his doctorate.

Reavis read his notes to Bobby and Bobby typed into his computer. Every now and then Bobby would ask a question, get Clifford Reavis's answer, and type more. Four or five minutes after Reavis had given Bobby all of his notes and Bobby had asked all of his questions, Bobby swiveled around on his computer chair and looked down at Reavis.

"The word systems that come up the most are *workout, gym,* and *health club.* According to Gary." "Gary" was what Bobby called his computer, and that was another question Bobby Doall would never answer: Why did he call his computer Gary? Gary the computer told Reavis and Bobby that out of the forty-six people, victims and accused alike, all forty-six had belonged to an exclusive health club. Reavis's calls to Dr. Maggie Russell and Newton Sylvester had yielded four of them: Stacy Bonato, Robert A. Taylor, Judith Jenkins, and Sylvester. Reavis had never thought to ask about health clubs when he first investigated either case. Both Sylvester and Russell, he remembered, had even mentioned working out.

In Pittsburgh it was the Fitness Arena. Peggy went there all the time before night classes. It was a place he'd never set foot in . . . and given his distaste for exercise, he probably never would have. But now he would, because Judith Jenkins, Newton Sylvester, Stacy Bonato, and Robert Taylor had all belonged to the Fitness Arena.

"Bobby, you work out at the Fitness Arena all the time. Didn't you know about two female members being killed, two male members accused of their murders?"

"Nope. I know almost everyone who works out at the Arena at night, but only by sight. I might have worked out right beside Newton Sylvester or Dr. Taylor, talked to them, but never knew their names. I'd have maybe known the two women, but again, only by sight, probably by how great they looked. I'm sure I must have seen something on TV about the murders. But, Clifford, all the murders they have on TV or in the papers. Most of the time I don't pay names much mind. The workout managers came and went at the Arena there for a while. They might have put it together. But no one ever said anything to me."

"You mean every time I talked to you about Stacy Bonato and Judith Jenkins being killed, you didn't recognize their names?"

"Right. I might have known them, but not by name. At the Arena we talk about working out, maybe the weather, local sports. If I saw their photos in the papers or on TV I would only have glanced at them. I don't pay much attention to that stuff. Usually, they'll just have someone outside the Allegheny County jail after eleven at night saying there's someone inside who's been charged with one crime or the other. Enough of that is enough," Bobby said. "Also, eighty percent of the people who join the Arena work out for a month or two and then slowly or suddenly stop coming."

"What do you think, Bobby, you think he's still here?"

"Three in a row in Phoenix and Boston, his last two stops before Pittsburgh, only two here. He's got one to go. But I don't have to tell you that do I, Clifford?"

"No, I'm pretty sure he's still here and getting closer to his next victims by the minute."

"And he's doing it at the Fitness Arena where I work out," Bobby said.

"You got it."

Reavis thought so, too. Reavis backed up his and Bobby's conclusions with this evidence: In the other cities, each had three victims, but they were spaced out over two years in most cities. But in Boston and in Phoenix, right before Boston, there had been three in a row, each about a month apart.

Here in Pittsburgh, as in Boston and Phoenix, the city had had two spaced roughly a month apart. Reavis was sure the killer was still one rape, murder, and frame short in Pittsburgh. But he didn't have a clue about what the killer looked like, let alone his name. Equally important, he didn't have any idea who his next two victims would be.

He would have to hit the road to find that out. It was already a month since Judith Jenkins and Newton Sylvester. Time was not on Clifford Reavis's side.

Bobby interrupted his thinking with: "You going to call Boston— George Matson?"

"He's the first stop."

"Make sure you have your flash drive with the audio output with the Pittsburgh call-in recordings on it that I set up for you," Bobby said. "I didn't recognize the guy's voice, but maybe someone in Boston will."

# CHAPTER THIRTEEN

Marsha looked up from the hard copy of the brief she'd been working on and there he was. Lester Wilkins.

"How's it going, Marsha?"

She leaned back, pushed a lock of hair from in front of her right eye, and slid her shoes on as quietly as she could.

"Good, Mr. Wilkins."

"Can you take a break for lunch one of these days? Lunch will be on me."

*Was this business or pleasure? Pleasure would be fine,* she thought.

"Sure. When did you have in mind?"

"Today, tomorrow. You name it. The only thing is, it has to be somewhere in the suburbs."

He must have recognized the puzzled look on her face. "This won't be about business. I'm asking you for a lunch date, Marsha. And you don't have to go. It won't hurt your career here if you don't. Meanwhile, if you accept, no one around here needs to know."

Her smile told him all he had to know.

"Tomorrow work for you?" he said.

"Great," she said.

"And, Ms. LeGrange. Out of the office, it's Les. Deal?" He put out his hand to shake.

She took it. His hand dwarfed hers. She couldn't keep the look of glee off her face. "Les is better." She didn't want to let go of his big, warm hand.

Later that day, she cornered Jeff Guilfoyle. "Jeff, Lester Wilkins asked me out to lunch. Pleasure, he said." She searched Jeff's eyes. "Is that ethical, a male partner and a female associate lawyer? Is it discriminatory behavior, a boss taking an employee out?"

"I'm not sure," he said. "What do you want it to be?"

"Ethical. Non-discriminatory. He's everything I admire in a man. Smart, nice, not to mention debonair. In a way, I've been hoping for something like this from him." She put her hand up, as if to stop any wrong thoughts Jeff might have about her. "But I haven't been doing anything other than hope. No flirting. Nothing like that."

"Go for it, Marsha. You know what they say about all work and no play."

At one o'clock the next day, Lester Wilkins picked Marsha up in front of the Grant Building in his navy-blue Mercedes sedan. She smelled new leather as she let herself in on the passenger side. That and just a hint of some nice cologne on her date.

"Have you been to Scoglio's out at Foster Plaza?" he said.

"No, but I've heard about it. Is that where we're going?"

"If you like."

"I would like."

She believed she would like any of his ideas. They both seemed to relax as they headed across the Fort Pitt Bridge on the Parkway West towards Greentree and Scoglio's. He was telling her that their house salad was the best around Pittsburgh and their menu was terrific. "If you don't see something you like, they will probably make it for you, anyway." Then he switched subjects. "And there shouldn't be a lot of attorneys there, since it's just a little bit outside of town. Give us time to talk about more than business."

Lester Wilkins, less sure of himself than usual. *A good sign,* she thought. *That means he must be worried about impressing me with more than his legal ability.*

Neither saw Jackie standing at the corner of Second Avenue and Grant Street, watching them as Marsha lifted a long right leg into the Wilkins Mercedes and close the door. Marsha had written about her date with Wilkins in her journal last night. Now he would start looking harder into the daily routine of Lester Wilkins. What was his schedule? What were his investments? Did he have any money he was hiding from his partners or the tax people? And how could Jackie get his hands on any of the money he could find?

Jackie could feel the tension he'd been feeling about Marsha LeGrange ease slightly. She had her man. Now she simply had to reel him in. Jackie didn't know what he would do if she couldn't. This was the situation he had been waiting on for way too long.

# CHAPTER FOURTEEN

Reavis spied Matson before Matson saw him. George Matson, built like a standing-steel safe, wore his gray hair like a yarmulke. But the thing people noticed first about him was his thick black eyebrows, the right one turned up at the end like a ram's horn. Matson looked like Ed Asner, who played the boss who rarely smiled on the *Mary Tyler Moore Show.*

Reavis, knowing what was coming, tensed up after Matson finally saw him and hurried over. "Good to see you, Clifford," he said, before clobbering Reavis on the back with a heavy hand.

Reavis's knees buckled. He coughed. "You, too, Mat," he was barely able to say.

"C'mon, Clifford, I've got a car out front."

Reavis didn't have any luggage, so they headed for Matson's car and were soon on their way to the city. "Say what you want about New York City taxi drivers," Reavis said after Matson, changing lanes, nearly tore the left rear fender off a cab, "but give me a dozen Boston drivers like you, and we'll stand off a fleet of New York City cab drivers any day."

"Hey, man. It's everyone for themselves here," Matson said.

Matson had a new office, one that Reavis had never seen. But he expected no surprises. He would find, he was sure, the same twelve-cup coffee maker, sitting on its own small table, that Matson had had for years. With it would be the brown plastic tray Matson had swiped from a cafeteria and on it there would be Cremora, sugar cubes, Styrofoam cups, and white plastic spoons. There'd be one of those gray-green metal desks in Matson's office, too, but there wouldn't be any pictures of his wife and kids. Matson was a bachelor.

And that's exactly the way it looked when they got there. Matson, nodding at the coffee pot, said, "Coffee's over there." Then he yelled at someone Reavis couldn't see. "Wilson, get in here with those files and call-in recording copies."

Wilson, who came on the run, turned out to be the uniformed man, spit-shine-sharp, who'd looked at Matson like a dog that didn't want to get kicked when they'd passed him near the elevator on the way in. He had the files and call-in recordings.

"Give them to me." Matson grabbed the files. Then he glared at Wilson, which was apparently Wilson's signal to take off.

Matson looked down at the files he was holding, then over at Reavis. "I haven't had a chance to go over these yet." His eyes fixed on Reavis, who hadn't started pouring himself any coffee. Reavis hated Matson's coffee. "Go ahead, Clifford," he said with a wave at the pot on the table, "get yourself some." He grabbed the top file and began reading it.

"Hold up, Mat, let's listen to your call-in recordings before we start reading the files.

After they'd listened to each recording three times, Matson looked at Reavis. "Same guy as in Pittsburgh?" he said.

Reavis handed Matson his flash drive. "Plug this into your laptop and you tell me."

After listening to Reavis's recordings, Matson said it first: "Five rapes, murders and frames—all by the same guy?"

"Mat, let's not bring in the detectives on your three cases. I'd like to keep this quiet, so the killer doesn't find out and leave Pittsburgh. Let's leave this between you and me for the time being. But we know your three Boston defendants aren't guilty. Would our belief that there's a guy going around the country framing men like those three get the men in Boston jails out? Can you call the DA's office and have him get the three defendants you have here out of jail based on what you and I believe? As quietly as possible. Tell him all you want, but that you want to keep this low profile. Can you do that?"

"Yeah, I think so. I think I can get him to go along with me."

Then Reavis and Matson reviewed the three Boston case files. After they finished, Matson was rubbing at his throat, sighing, and looking out from under his thick brows at Reavis. "I'm sorry, Clifford." Shaking his head. "We really fucked up." He wagged a hand at the files and call-in recordings sitting on the corner of his desk. "There's no excuse for police work like this. This kind of thing should never happen. Someone wrapped us three packages and we bought them like a buy-two-get-one-free sale. What can I do to help you on your case?"

Reavis had needed George Matson to agree with his theory. One man doing all that? To all those young women. So hard to believe. He said, "Your call-in recordings, Mat. I'd like copies of them on my flash drive."

"Yeah. Sure," Matson said. "It's the same guy on all three of our recordings, Clifford. No doubt about it. He didn't even try to disguise his voice. Why wouldn't he do that?"

"Simple," Reavis answered. "Why draw attention to himself by trying to disguise his voice? Who's going to be looking for one guy to be calling in three murders? How many detectives would pay that much attention to call-in recordings, anyway, when there's that much evidence against the men the killer framed? Look at your three cases. You had a different lead detective on each one. Why would he listen to call-in recordings on two cases he wasn't investigating?"

"Mat, let's get voiceprint analyses of these call-in recordings. I'll get Tim Garrity to get them for us. That will keep it unofficial while the expert is checking the recordings. We do not want to alert this guy to the fact that we have even a suspicion about him. We'll get all the call-in recordings to whomever Tim finds. I know that different jurisdictions treat the admissibility of voiceprint experts' testimony differently, but more and more are admitting their testimony.

"Whether voiceprint analysis experts' opinions are admissible, and in what courts, is a problem for later. But if you ask me, if we can produce an expert who says the call-in guy is the same everywhere, then there's a good chance that there will be a lot of police departments and DAs who will reopen their cases, like you did."

"Yeah," Matson said, "I'll contact the other police departments around the country and get copies of their call-in recordings. But I won't give them the real reason I want them. We don't want them opening cases right now and by doing that alerting the son of a bitch who raped and murdered all those women and put so many innocent men behind bars."

"Making calls. That reminds me," said Reavis. "When you make your calls, get the other police departments to help me out in their cities. I'll make up some project I'm working on for you." He thought a minute; came up with an idea. "Hey, what about making me some kind of official liaison to the Boston Police Department. Unpaid, of course."

Matson nodded. "Okay." He stood up, hands on his desk, leaning toward Reavis. "You are now Special Liaison to the Boston Police Department. How's that, Clifford?"

"Do I get my own badge?"

"You get a letter from me saying you're working with us and telling anyone who reads it to do all that you ask. I'll send an e-mail, too, with the letter as an attachment, to the chief in each city."

"Listen," Reavis said, "the e-mails and attachments to them will be fine, but they're still going to haul ass faster for you than me." He thought a bit. "Get them to send me—no, both of us—copies of the files they have on each case. Copies of the call-in recordings, too," he said.

"Right." Matson got a look on his face then. Reavis could tell what was coming, because it kept hitting him like that also. "Those recordings," Matson said. "We've been listening to a maniac."

# CHAPTER FIFTEEN

Marsha was startled when she saw Les Wilkins standing in the doorway of her office. Today he was wearing one of his charcoal gray, pin-striped, suits. And a tie with yellow polka dots on a charcoal gray background that exactly matched his suit.

She started to get up, straighten her skirt, but he waved her back down. "Finish what you're doing." He'd caught her bent over a file on her desk, a frown on her face. "I can wait."

She glanced sharply at her nails. They needed polishing. She wished she'd taken the time to polish them after lunch. "I can use a break," she said as she leaned back in her chair and folded her hands in her lap. There was a new feeling between the two of them now. Like, what next? They'd spent two hours over their lunch the other day and Wilkins had told her then that he'd like to see her again, outside of work. She had given him the best smile she knew how to make and said, "Me, too."

"Business today, Marsha. Here's that first important case I promised you. It has the Hank Watson, regional claim manager, Interstate Insurance Company, seal of Marsha LeGrange approval. Hank asked me to assign it to you." He held a file out for her to see. "Dr. Avanas is the plaintiff's doctor. And, we believe that the number of times he said he saw the plaintiff is, as usual, inflated."

Dr. Thomas Avanas, she knew, was a well-known "plaintiff's" doctor. Even if no other doctor could find so much as a bruise on someone who had been in an accident, Avanas would testify that they were nearly dying.

Wilkins said, "We've been trying for years to get to that guy. But he's always been too slippery for us." Wilkins squeezed his hands into fists. "Hell, I'll get him on the stand, show him his bill, and get him to say, 'Yes, that's my billing statement.' I'll point out to him that he's billing for treatments on a Sunday, say, 'Doctor, you don't mean to tell me you're treating your patients on Sundays, do you?'"

Wilkins leaned forward, his eyes on hers. "Then he'll just shrug, turn and face the jury, giving them that innocent smile of his—you should see how they melt—and say something like: 'Thanks for bringing that to my attention. I have a new assistant, my scribbling's a little tough to read. No, of course I didn't see her on Sundays, but . . . how badly she was hurt' . . . Then he'll turn to the jury again, smile, and say, 'Maybe I *should* have seen her on Sundays, too.'"

"I'd heard that Avanas was tough," she said.

Lester Wilkins, smiling wryly, placed the file on her desk. "Marsha, we've all had *our* chances at him. Now you're going to get yours." His look softened; she could tell he was thinking. "I'm beginning to believe"—and now the managing partner was smiling—"maybe Avanas might be about to meet his match." Then he nodded as if to say, yes, maybe so.

She did her best to look confident, but had no idea how she could get to a medical witness as good on the witness stand as Dr. Thomas Avanas.

"I wonder," he said, "does anything worry you?" Before she could respond, he told her, "I have never met a young lawyer with your degree of poise."

Then he changed the subject. "When are we going to get together to play some racquetball? I hear you're tough to beat." He gave her a look that she couldn't quite decipher. "Let's have a game or two some night soon. I'll buy the drinks afterward?"

She kept on with her best smile. "Why not make it loser pays?"

He said, "Tomorrow? After work?"

"Great," she said.

After he left, Marsha was too hyped up to get back to the work on her desk right away. *Poised? Confident?* That was how she had always *tried* to appear. But she sure did have to suppress the urge to tell Les Wilkins how she'd felt all morning before he'd walked into her office.

Tom Dunn, this morning, had walked past her in the hall without saying a word. Nothing, not even a hello. That had gotten her worrying, wondering if WW&D hadn't regretted giving her a raise based on only one lucky case, if she'd ever get the extra responsibility Les Wilkins had just given her.

She'd even been wondering whether she'd bombed at lunch with Les Wilkins. That maybe she was a one-lunch-stand. She hadn't been able to do anything for almost a half hour after what she had interpreted as Dunn's snub, worrying that maybe Larry Haski or someone else had poisoned his mind against her. Finally, as she usually did when she felt anxious, she buried herself in a case. That was the Marsha LeGrange Les Wilkins had come upon when he looked in on her. Never worry? Her? Hardly.

Les Wilkins. He was a different kind of man. He managed to say something nice to her every time he saw her at the office, especially at lunch the other day. He had always seemed to go out of his way to be nice to her at the Fitness Arena, too.

She and Les Wilkins were going places personally. She could just feel it. She liked his racquetball idea. She couldn't wait to see how they worked out together. Maybe no more *Virgin Marsha*.

She was still thinking of Wilkins when her phone rang—and it *was* Les Wilkins. "Marsha, I'm going to have to postpone our game tomorrow night. My brother Winnie just called. He's leading the firm's defense team on that bad-faith case we're defending in Atlanta. He says they need me to join the battle. I've got to catch a six o'clock flight for Atlanta tonight to be ready for depositions there tomorrow. Marsha, will you give me a rain check on the racquetball game?"

She tried not to let her disappointment sneak into her voice. "Sure." Then tried to put a smile on her face and in her voice, to sound like it wasn't all that bad. "If that's the best excuse you can come up with to avoid a beating."

"You're on," he said. "The moment I get back."

But she thought, after he hung up, *How long will that be?*

To avoid what she could feel was a bout of feeling sorry for herself coming on, she made herself work on her new case. She would see Hank Watson, the Interstate Insurance regional claim manager at the Fitness Arena tonight. Maybe they would talk about her new case involving Dr. Avanas. For sure, they planned to work out together. About forty, Hank had light brown hair, smiling blue eyes, and was very comfortable and a lot of fun to be around.

# *C*HAPTER SIXTEEN

Marsha was late getting to the Arena. Reviewing the Skomski case, which was the new case, the one involving Dr. Avanas, had taken longer than she thought it would. Hank Watson, furiously pedaling a Lifecycle when she caught his eye, wagged a finger at her. Bad Marsha.

"Guilty," she called out with a sheepish grin. "I won't be long." She ducked into the women's locker room, quickly changed, and headed for the Nautilus room.

It was crowded tonight. The first thing she did when she got there was punch Hank Watson in the shoulder. "I've got something to thank you for, don't I, Mr. Watson?"

"Oh . . . ?" But he had a sly grin.

"Hank," she said, "I know you told Lester Wilkins to give me that case with Dr. Avanas on it!"

The Interstate Insurance Company regional claims manager puffed up a little. "I have been pushing Wilkins, Wilkins & Dunn to use you on more of our cases and I did ask them if you could handle that one for us. Yes. But not because we're friends. I think you're the one who can get to that crook Avanas." He looked evenly at her. "Know why?"

"Why?"

"Because you're a woman, he'll let his guard down with you. Maybe. At least I hope he will. A lot of doctors think they're gods. Especially with women. All day long they order nurses around. Most nurses are still women. And all the women they see as patients *have* to depend on them." Hank Watson was smiling slightly. "You have softness, an easy way about you. But you're steel underneath. Like a dusting of snow," he said, "that hides a layer of ice."

"Steel . . . ice?" she said, not knowing if she wanted to be thought of like that. "You think I'm too hard . . . too cold?"

They both moved. It was getting close to their turn on the first machine, the hip and back machine.

"No, not too hard." He looked at her, a serious expression on his face. "Plenty hard enough, though. Cold? No, I would never call you cold. But you are tough. Look what you did to the Giacamos' attorney, Murray Levin. He's no rookie, you know. He's one of Pittsburgh's best plaintiffs' attorneys."

Maybe I shouldn't be saying this, Hank, but what if I just got lucky on the Giacamo case?" She looked at him, trying to gauge his reaction.

"Maybe I won't be able to get to Dr. Avanas."

Hank shook his head. Uh-uh. "I sat through that trial watching you. Your are very, very good. You'll get to him. You're a natural."

She let out a breath that she didn't know she'd been holding. Hank's saying that had given her something she needed. Her confidence was returning. She felt good.

She looked across the room and saw Jeff Guilfoyle, got his attention, smiled, and waved. Jeff must have heard about the Avanas case, too, because he not only waved, but gave her a thumbs-up.

Halfway through her workout, she looked in the mirror and saw a man looking back at her. He waved like he knew her, but she couldn't place him. Attractive. Obviously in shape.

Later Marsha got a feeling, like someone was watching her from the end of the room. Quickly, she looked down toward the multi-triceps machine. Someone *was*. That same guy. The smile on his face said that, yes, he had been looking, and that, uh-huh, he liked what he saw. Before she had a chance to think, she smiled back.

He didn't look away until it was his turn to wedge himself into the multi-triceps machine.

She kept looking. He was tall and had a nice size to his body, just the right amount of muscle. She kept staring, watching as he pushed at the weight machine, a ridge forming on the upper arm she could see. *Yes, she thought, a very nice body.*

Marsha nudged Hank. "Who's that?" She had to know. "Who is that man over there, Hank?"

Hank looked down to where the man was. "Marsha, come on now . . . you know damn well that's Larry Haski. I know you can't stand him, but . . . "

Marsha had told Hank all about Haski. But she hadn't been pointing at Larry Haski. The man she'd asked Hank about was leaning over the multi-triceps machine, first spraying with the cleaner bottle and then wiping away the cleaner and his perspiration with the little hand towels the Fitness Arena laid out for its members.

Then Marsha did see Haski, looking impatient, standing behind the man with shoulders to go with that nice smile of his. Haski wanted on the multi-triceps machine—right now.

"No, Hank, I mean the man in front of him." She inspected herself in front of the wall mirror, then tucked a strand of hair under her Adidas headband and sucked in her belly.

"Short, dark hair? Tall? Decent looking?" Hank said.

"Shhh. Not so loud. Yes. Do you know him?"

"Yeah. I've talked to him a couple times. He's strong. Stronger than Haski, even. What the hell is his name?" Hank put his hand to his chin, looked thoughtful. Then: "Mel . . . that's his first name. But what's the last?" He paused, still thinking, then shook his head and looked at her. "You know, I don't think I ever did get his last name. Though I could say that for most of the people I see here. Even the guys I talk to in the locker room."

Hank turned away from Marsha, studied the man for a while, then snapped his fingers. "Real estate. That's it. He has something to do with real estate." Hank, smirking, foot up on the weights part of the hip and back machine, chin resting on his knee, was studying her. "He's been asking me about you, you know? Wanting to know whether you were dating anyone."

"And you never told me?" Marsha put both hands on her hips, moved closer to him. Their faces weren't six inches apart. "Asked you about me . . . you didn't tell me?"

"Just kidding." The claims manager got a little-boy grin on his face. "You never seemed interested in the men here. You know," the grin broader, "I thought it was all career with you."

"Not to the point of domination." She paused a moment, wondered about that and then nudged Watson again. "Next time he looks this way, make sure you smile and wave. And if you get the chance"—letting him know with a look how serious she was—"make real sure you introduce us. You will, won't you, Hank?"

"We'll see."

Now the man named Mel was concentrating on working his calves on the multi-exercise machine. She watched him. He had his eyes closed as he slowly did calf raises. Veins stood out under long calf muscles. She noticed Haski again, directly behind this Mel man. Haski was finished with the multi-triceps machine, not bothering to wipe his perspiration off. He stood, hands on hips, shifting his weight from foot to foot, trying to let Mel, who had something to do with real estate, see what a hurry he was in.

Mel paid Haski no mind.

She compared the two. Both were somewhere around forty, she'd guess. Tall, about the same height, which made Mel tall enough for heels. Both were built like athletes, Haski slightly beefier than Mel.

Each had dark hair, Haski's a little longer than Mel's. Marsha knew Haski had a little gray in his, but wasn't close enough to tell whether Mel's was turning. There was something about his looks that she liked better than Haski's. Was it the strong jaw? Maybe his smile? Of course, that was it. Haski rarely smiled, had frown lines. She would bet Mel had tiny laugh lines dancing out from his eyes.

While she was watching, Mel finished with his calf raises and started doing chin-ups on the machine. Then he finished with those and was bouncing on his toes, letting his arms hang loose, shaking his muscles out. Strong legs. The eyes, she wondered, what color were his eyes?

Jackie was grinning despite himself. He was spying on Marsha LeGrange here at the Fitness Arena, had been for a long time; in fact, if circumstances had been right, he would have killed her first, before Stacy Bonato. But circumstances hadn't been right. She hadn't latched on to one of the big wheels here at the Fitness Arena. Now it looked like it could be Lester Wilkins. At least that's what Marsha LeGrange was writing in her journal.

Maybe things with the two of them were changing. He'd seen Lester Wilkins staring at her, talking to her every chance he got. Especially here at the Arena. Lester Wilkins would be just right. He sighed. *Finally.*

Jackie watched every move she made until he had to get on the next machine. She was wearing a pair of those spandex things. A lot of the women here wore them to hide a flabby ass or lumpy thighs. Not her. There were no lumps on her thighs. And she had one sweet rear end. Who should know better than him? He'd been studying her legs, rear end, and all the rest up close for over two months.

Jackie strapped into the next Nautilus machine, cinching the belt tight. *Asking for it.* That's what she was doing. Look at her, the way she was always looking at herself in the mirrors. She knew how she looked . . . almost as pretty as his momma. A shiver went all the way through him, then another. He had to hurry up, sit on a bench. She could pass for his momma's twin sister. No wonder she got to him more than all the others.

He made his mind switch his thinking. He could do that. It finally looked like Marsha LeGrange and Wilkins would get it going. Like that Jenkins bitch had—like that heavyweight doctor Stacy Bonato had walked in with? He let out a laugh, thinking about what he'd done to those two. Lester Wilkins, yeah, he would be perfect. Marsha Le-Grange sucked up to him enough, that was for sure, and now she was putting man–woman moves on him. And he wasn't resisting.

For Jackie to do it right, Marsha LeGrange had to start something with Lester Wilkins. Jackie saw him at the Arena a lot and tried to talk to him whenever he got the chance. Big man—senior partner in a successful law firm. That made him the perfect match for Marsha Le-Grange. Jackie needed Marsha to lure him back to her condominium. For the fingerprints.

Lester Wilkins was just like Stuart Randolph. Watching someone just like Stuart Randolph go to jail for what he, Jackie, had done was almost as important to Jackie as getting Marsha LeGrange.

Stuart Randolph was always around when Jackie was a kid, hitting on his momma, Janice Simpson. Jackie couldn't count the times Stuart

Randolph had picked his momma up in that big car of his and took her to the airport. Jackie didn't see his momma for a long time after all those times Mr. Randolph was always taking her from him.

Jackie's momma and grandmother told him his daddy died in an accident. But that's what people always told bastard kids like him. Jackie's belief was that he was Randolph's bastard son. Randolph had arranged a scholarship for Jackie to go to college, paid his way through law school. Why else would he do a thing like that unless he was Jackie's daddy?

Yes, Martha LeGrange was a carbon copy of Janice Simpson, his momma. Janice Simpson was supposedly always away at school when Jackie was growing up, then at a job that kept her away. *She should have been home with me,* Jackie thought. That's what mommas were supposed to do. Raise their kids. But Janice Simpson could have cared less about Jackie. Either that or she hated him. Oh, she would tell him she loved him, but then why did she look at him with hate in her eyes when she must have thought he didn't see her. He ended up being raised by his grandmother, Sarah Lee Simpson. For Sarah Lee Simpson Jackie would do anything.

Jackie was beginning to get anxious, worrying he might not get to Marsha LeGrange before his momma caught up to him again in this city. That was another thing: How did his momma find him in each city? She'd found him in both Phoenix and Boston. He talked to his grandmother on the phone and sent her all the money she would accept. He wouldn't talk to her about his momma, though. Nevertheless, Miss Sarah would always try to get him to talk about the woman. She would say things about his momma to get him to talk, but she never mentioned his momma's telling her she saw him in each city she worked in.

His momma never did seem to stop in on Miss Sarah. What kind of daughter was she? No better a daughter than she was a mother.

# CHAPTER SEVENTEEN

Marsha asked Hank Watson to stop at the health bar upstairs if he saw the man named Mel there; made him promise to sit at the same table with him if he could.

Usually, exhausted after an hour of struggling with the Nautilus machines, she liked to linger in the shower. Tonight she just got clean, making sure not to get her hair wet. She got her hair into a ponytail and then took some time getting her makeup right. Finished with that now, she took a quick look in the full-length mirror and hurried out of the women's locker room and up the stairs to the health bar.

She slowed when she got to where she could be seen by anyone and took a deep breath and then a quick look. Hank had come through. He and Mel were at a table together, talking like old friends. Both looked up at the same time and waved.

At the counter she ordered a pineapple drink—"All the vitamin C you need for the whole day. The natural energy of fructose," the sign said. She glanced in the mirror behind the counter. He was studying her.

Hank and Mel rose as she walked to the table and she saw that he did have blue eyes, like her father's.

"Marsha," Hank turned so that only she could see his evil grin, "Meet Mel Sadecki. Mel's been telling me the right way to use that decline press machine downstairs."

*Mel Sadecki?* "Hi, Mel." She held out her hand and he took it in his, which made two of hers and felt good. Her hand wasn't dry, though, so she pulled it away, wondering if he could tell she was nervous. There was no way to tell by looking at his face, but he was smiling. A shy smile, like a little boy's.

Mel Sadecki pulled out a seat for her, saying, "I've been telling Hank here," nodding at Hank, "how well you do with those torture machines downstairs."

"They are like torture machines, aren't they?" she said. "The first two weeks I used them I could barely get out of bed in the morning. All that pushing, tugging, and twisting, they still wear me out. But at least," she shrugged, "I'm not sore anymore."

"Used to be," she said, "I'd play tennis all day. Every day. That was back in high school, though. Back when I never got sore." She looked quickly at him. What did he care about what she'd done in high school?

Mel said, "You're making yourself sound like an old lady. High school wasn't that long ago, was it?"

"I'm over thirty." Did he think she was too young? Why hadn't she simply said thirty-two?

"Wow." Mock amazement. Over thirty, huh?"

"Oh, and you're some old man, I guess?" It was hard to tell just how old he really was. She couldn't see any gray hair and, she'd been right, he did have tiny laugh lines around his eyes. Would he be as old as thirty-five?

"Forty on the nose." Mel Sadecki was still smiling, but now she could see he was watching her closely. Was he thinking he might be too old for her? She smiled at him; forty was fine with her.

Hank, no more than an observer now, got up, looking at his watch. "Hey," he told them, "I've got to get moving. Need a lift home tonight, Marsha?"

Hank Watson knew that she always walked home from the Arena. The way home for her was safe. A little long after a workout, though. Hank also knew that she wanted to get to know Mel Sadecki better. "No, thanks, I'll walk. *As usual!*" she said.

Nodding Hank's way as he left, Mel said, "Nice guy. Insurance? Claims, isn't it?"

"Hank's the regional claims manager at Interstate Insurance, the youngest one they've ever had," she said. "He also teaches in some kind of training program that takes him all over the country. Sometimes he's gone for months at a time."

"And you," he said, "are a lawyer?"

She wondered briefly if he was the kind to be put off by that. "Yes . . . I am." She fought the need to tell him that she got her first big case today. "And what do you do?"

"Real estate, mostly," he said. "Not too much on start-up, development kind of things, the shopping malls, office buildings, things like that; mostly I look at existing situations. I'm not into leveraging. Tax things." Mel Sadecki smiled. "Very safe stuff. The real estate recession missed me. It's a buyer's market now if you have the cash."

His elbows were on the table and his chin was in his hands. He looked uncomfortable talking about himself. "Now what's this about tennis you were saying?"

"Oh, Marsha said, "I played all the time, up until I was fifteen. That's when my father died." She saw his jaw drop, his eyes narrow, like he was worried he'd hit a subject he shouldn't have. She wanted him to think it was okay, that she didn't mind talking about her father. "I guess I quit because I felt guilty playing tennis when my mother needed help with money. I got a job so we didn't have to use all the insurance money, but still have enough for me to go to college and law school." She'd never told anyone things like *that* before.

Should that worry her? Maybe she was talking too much, boring him. No. He was nodding, looking like he understood, like she could tell him whatever she wanted, that it was all right with him. He seemed very interested in everything she had to say.

"I'll bet you felt lost when your father died—almost . . . deserted." He looked like he was searching for words. "What about your mother?"

"I became the mother," Marsha said. "She let me take care of her after Dad died." She thought she'd kept the bitterness out of her voice, but she was afraid that anything else she might say about Agnes LeGrange might not sound right. "There I am," she said, making it lighter, "running at the mouth."

Mel Sadecki leaned across the table some more. "If I wasn't interested," he said, the look on his face making sure she understood, "I wouldn't have asked."

"Are you originally from Pittsburgh, Mel?"

"No. Small town in the South. Pittsburgh's my base, though, but I'm all over the country."

She felt her forehead wrinkling, her eyes widen. "I don't hear a southern accent."

"I think it's the travel. I don't get back home much. I guess I've lost most of it."

"A lot of traveling. That's probably why I haven't seen you here before."

She couldn't read his eyes; he was in a position now where the lights were reflecting off them. "Yes, I've been on the go a lot the last two, three years, I guess. But I've seen you." Said shyly—and again he reminded her of a little boy, looking as if he'd like to hide his head in his mother's skirts.

She liked how he looked in his charcoal suit—though now no tie—and his shirt with French cuffs, sapphire cufflinks that were only slightly darker than his eyes.

He said, "Every time I see you here, you're concentrating so hard, jaw clenched, fierce look on your face. I guess you haven't seen me."

She would be looking for him the next time.

# *C*HAPTER EIGHTEEN

"We've got to get him before he can get the next one," Matson told Reavis.

They'd been quiet. Both thinking. Reavis struggled to get free of the weight of the words Matson just dumped on him. But that was as futile as escaping mosquitoes in a tropical swamp. Reavis didn't want to be too late. Three times before he'd either been too little or too late.

The first time he was a fraction of a second *too late*—he even had his hands on Beth before Petro's XKE tore the woman he loved from him and mauled her.

The second time it was too *little*. That time he had waited outside Petro's house with his long knife, watched him stumble, drunk, to his front door. Reavis jumped out in front of Petro that night, wanting Beth's killer to see who it was before he slammed the knife between his ribs. He got him real good—but not good enough.

Petro pulled through. Before he lost consciousness, he told the police it was Reavis who had stabbed him, and they tracked Reavis to a South Side bar, dragged him out of it, and dumped him in a cell, charged him with aggravated assault and attempted murder.

"You better hope he lives, or it'll be first-degree murder instead of aggravated assault," the arresting officer had said. Reavis shivered now, remembering. Aggravated assault? Attempted murder? Back then he would have welcomed first-degree murder charges; he wanted Petro dead. He hadn't cared what would happen to him. Nothing mattered. Not then. Beth and their baby were dead.

The third time Reavis was also too late. He put the man who killed his wife and unborn child in intensive care for a week, in the hospital for three. But two weeks after Petro got out of South Side Hospital, doing eighty (drunk again) on that straight stretch of Route 51 near Century Three, he lost control of his black sports car one more time. That night his Jaguar XKE crossed over the center line and hit a Corvair head on, killing everyone in it, two couples from West Virginia on their way to a Pirates game.

Petro had orphaned five little kids that time.

He had also killed himself.

Here is how Reavis was too late the third time: That night, when Petro killed those four people and himself, Reavis was waiting down the street from Petro's house, fingering a knife and promising himself that he would finish Petro the drunk this time. So he was there when the Pleasant Hills Police pulled into Petro's driveway. He saw the young police officer get out, go up, knock at the front door. Petro's wife answered. Reavis saw the police officer tell her something; saw her bury her face in her hands. It was a hot night; Reavis had his car window open. The woman was wailing; she screamed, "I tried to tell him not to drink and drive! I would even hide his keys, but he would beat me until I gave them to him!" She was shaking her head, pounding a fist into her other hand. "It wasn't his fault. He was a sick man."

*What did sick have to do with it?* Sure, Petro was sick, but that sick son of a bitch had killed Beth Reavis, their unborn baby, four other decent people, and orphaned five little kids.

After Petro killed himself, the Commonwealth had no one to testify against him (Commonwealth of Pennsylvania vs. Clifford T. Reavis, Allegheny County Criminal Case Number 75-000495), so the DA's office didn't oppose Tim Garrity's motion to dismiss the charges against him. Tim had told Reavis that he believed the assistant DA didn't push his argument too hard when the judge heard Tim's motion. The assistant DA, too, probably thought good riddance.

Every so often Reavis would have Tom over in Criminal Records at the Clerk of Courts Office pull the case for him to read. Why? To remind him that he *had* tried to kill Petro? That he *had* the courage to do that. Maybe it was to prove that what he'd had with Beth was more than a moment; not even a moment for their baby. Reavis didn't know. It just made him feel better.

Now, here he was again, decades later, someone else—sick, too? Born to kill? Like Paul Petro? He was out there killing. Reavis caught himself grinding his teeth. How was he going to get this bastard before he killed again?

Petro was a tumor, one that couldn't be operated on. Reavis had to squeeze him from his mind, for now, at least.

"Clifford. You're out somewhere. What have you been thinking about?"

"Thinking I want to get this bastard before he gets his next victims. It set me to thinking about Beth and Paul Petro."

Matson knew the story. After they'd become the friends they were now, Reavis had told it to him one night over several pitchers of beer.

"Can you get me the names of all the men who paid cash at the Executive Fitness Arena here in Boston between the Phoenix murders and ours?"

"Why there?"

"Because that's the only way we can find out who our man is. In each city, the women raped and murdered and the guy framed all belonged to an upscale workout place. In Boston it was the Executive Fitness Arena."

# *C*HAPTER NINETEEN

Reavis saw Matson look the number up and then call the Executive Fitness Arena. Soon he was growling at someone on the phone. Then he hung up.

"What was that all about?" Reavis said.

"When I called, the receptionist comes on." He paused to swallow the last of his sugar donut and lick his fingers. Matson on his third cup of coffee. "And she starts on how busy Mr. Paris, the manager, is; asks can she help me instead of him."

Matson grinned, leaned forward, elbows on his desk, hairy forearms crossed in front of him. "I said no and asked if this 'real busy' Mr. Paris had a first name. 'Certainly,' she says, 'Mr. Paris's first name happens to be Richard.'"

Matson continued. "Well I know a Rocco Parisi who sometimes goes by the name Richard Paris. A while back, I sent him up for dealing coke. Later I testified against him at his parole hearing. He's scum, Clifford." Matson raised his right forearm, then brought it down, pounding a fist on the desk, splashing coffee out of his cup. "When that receptionist said Paris, I remembered Parisi testifying at the parole hearing that he had a job waiting for him at a health club. That's what they do to get out on parole, say they got a job waiting for them. Half the time it's in some other crook's business."

Matson got up and went over to pour himself more coffee, then sat again. "So," he said, "when she said Paris, I figured Paris and Parisi were the same guy. I told the young lady that if she didn't get his ass on the phone I was going to call his parole officer and tell him to violate Parisi because he was obstructing a murder investigation."

Matson was grinning now. "Parisi was panting when he got on." Boston's superintendent of police leaned out dangerously from his swivel chair, snatched the plastic spoon off the tray and dug it into the cup of sugar. Then he dumped a little on the floor as he guided the spoon towards his mug. After getting most of the sugar in and splashing some of the thick liquid out again as he swished the mess around, he turned back to Reavis. "I could hear his receptionist whining in the background. She was saying something about only doing what she'd been told." Reavis watched as Matson seemed to be thinking. "Parisi must have smacked her."

"So what about the club's membership records?"

"What's his," Matson said, "is ours. No need for a subpoena, court order, nothing."

"Yeah." Reavis's right eye itched. He removed his thick bifocals and rubbed it. "I'm betting he paid cash. Think?" he said, squinting at Matson.

"Yeah," Matson said. "He'd leave less tracks that way." Matson looked at his watch and then back at Reavis. "Let's get the hell out of here. We're not going to get anything done sitting around drinking coffee."

*Coffee. You could float lead on the stuff.* Reavis got up and, taking his time, walked over to the open window. From which he tossed out the dregs of the cup Matson had forced him to drink. He turned back and looked at his host. "You call this shit coffee?" Shaking his head and looking at the empty mug in his hand.

Matson just scowled.

Parisi, who wore an obviously expensive rug and had on way to much cologne, got up from behind his chrome and glass desk, gestured at it and said to Matson, "Please . . . please sit down, superintendent."

Matson's lips actually curled. He tossed his head in the direction of the door. "Cut the shit," he said. "Out." Pointing to the door.

"Well, just let me know if . . ."

"Out." Louder. Arm fully extended.

Parisi got a look on his face like a thirteen-year-old kid who had taken all night to work up the nerve to ask the prettiest girl in the eighth grade for a dance . . . and been turned down in front of his friends. He cut and ran.

Reavis had to hand it to Parisi, though. Everything was waiting for him and Matson when they got to the club—not only members' files, but also a hot-to-the-touch silver pot full of freshly brewed coffee. Reavis gulped Parisi's coffee and, while he was at it, wolfed three cheese Danish too. He caught Matson's eye. "Great coffee, huh, Mat? And"—pointing it out—"look at this spread. I don't know. Seems to me like the man's got some class."

He got the Matson scowl again.

Of the twenty-four men who had joined Executive Fitness between the Phoenix and Boston murders, only five had paid cash. The only information in their files were names, addresses, and phone numbers. Two of the five cash members were quickly eliminated. Both answered their telephones when Matson called. The assumption Reavis and Matson were working on was that the killer they were looking for had departed Boston.

Nobody answered when Matson knocked at the door of Harmon Richards, the man whose name was first on their list, which was down to three now. But they did get an answer at the house next door. From a lady with tears running down her cheeks. At first she opened the door only as far as the chain, but after Matson showed her his ID she opened it the rest of the way and nodded for them to come in.

The woman, shriveled, probably ten years younger than she looked, had them follow her to a spotless kitchen. There she lifted her apron and wiped at the tears. "It's Frankie, isn't it?" she said. "He's in more . . . after this morning, I don't think I could . . ."

"Who's Frankie, ma'am?" Matson said.

"Why, my son. Isn't he the one you're here about?"

"No, ma'am," Matson said as they watched all the tension leave the woman. "We're gathering some routine information on an old case. The people we want to see live next door. The Harmon Richards family. Do you know Mr. Richards, ma'am?"

"Oh, yes, that one," she said, rolling her eyes. "He's lived next door for over four years. Comes in at all hours. Frankie and Harmon don't . . . why just last night . . . "

"Thank you." Matson broke in. "I don't think Mr. Richards can help us after all."

No, Harmon Richards couldn't help. They were looking for someone Reavis and Matson believed was now in Pittsburgh.

Their second stop was at an apartment building in a neighborhood that Matson said was filling up with professionals. They were looking for Thomas Whitfield. The address: 3216 Longfellow Avenue, apartment 112. No one answered the door at Whitfield's apartment, so they walked down the back stairs to the superintendent's basement apartment.

The super's name was Toby Constantine. He was home and he invited Reavis and Matson in, limped over to a vinyl recliner with white stuffing poking out of both arms, motioned for them to sit on a vinyl couch that was bright red with a big chip out of one leg, then sat himself. Two plaques on the wall declared that Tobias Andrew Constantine was a lifetime member of both the American Legion and Disabled American Veterans. A purple heart hung between the two plaques. That explained the limp. Korea, Reavis guessed.

Constantine told them that apartment 112 had been rented to a Whitman Dutrates, but that Dutrates's company had transferred him while he still had six months to go on his lease. Dutrates paid Constantine a commission to sublet the apartment for him. It was Constantine who sublet the place to Whitfield.

He remembered Thomas Whitfield well, he said, because the former tenant always stopped down to pay his rent in cash and because he moved out so fast, with two and a half months remaining on his lease. "Said the company was transferring him. Didn't put up no squawk about paying his lease to the end, either," Constantine said.

The date Whitfield took off—January twelfth of last year—was what made Reavis and Matson straighten where they sat. January twelfth was the day after the last Boston murder.

Matson, inching closer to the man with a limp: "What did Mr. Whitfield look like?"

"Big. Six-one, six-two, maybe even bigger," the Korean War veteran said. He looked Reavis's way. "But not as tall as Mr. Reavis over there. A hell of a lot more meat on him, though. I'd say he goes about two hundred, maybe a little more. Age? Late thirties, I'd say." Constantine touched his head at the temples. "Touch of gray."

"Mustache, beard, scars, tattoos, anything like that?" Matson said.

"Don't remember nothin' like that. Mr. Whitfield was a real good-looking guy. Not movie star looks, mind you. More rugged good-looking. Never saw him with a woman, though. Didn't talk about them, either. You think the guy's queer?"

Matson managed to say without a growl, "I doubt it. What else can you tell me about him?"

"Had a real good job, a lot of education. Sometimes when he brought me the rent, we'd talk. Mr. Whitfield could use the big words when he wanted." Constantine coughed. *Cigarettes,* Reavis thought, *that's what they do to you.* "I never saw him talk to anyone but me. Kept pretty much to himself."

"Did he fill out a rental application?" Matson said.

"Yeah. Sure." Toby Constantine sat forward. "Want to see it?" When Matson nodded he did, the old man got up and hobbled over to a battered wooden desk. "I'll get it for you."

Constantine brought the form over to Matson. Reavis scooted over on the sofa and they studied it together. Whitfield had lived in Newport Beach, California, before Boston. He worked for a company out there called Atlas Investments. Didn't ring any bells with Reavis.

"Atlas Investments?" Matson said. "Did you call them to check on Whitfield's employment, Mr. Constantine?"

"Sure did, chief," Constantine told Matson. "Always call the employer. Only good business." He paused to scratch himself under the arm. "I spoke with the president. Forget his name right now. He said Mr. Whitfield had been with them for a long time. He in some kind of trouble?"

Matson said, "He might be. We're not sure yet. I'm going to need this application." Nodding at the application he'd been holding, palms against the edges. "Your prints on file anywhere?"

"Army took 'em. Infantry. Korea."

"Would anyone have handled this application other than you and Whitfield?"

"Nope. Just the two of us."

Matson got up, ready to leave. "Thanks, Mr. Constantine. You've been a lot of help."

Reavis liked to watch Matson. Pummeling and squeezing, he commanded answers. Reavis couldn't do that. Didn't have the bulk for it. The badge either. "Wait one minute, please, Mat." Reavis took hold of Matson's arm and, looking at the superintendent: "You say you and Mr. Whitfield talked sometimes?"

"It wasn't nothing special but, yeah, we talked. Man always paid his rent in cash, so when he stopped down with it, sure, we'd usually talk."

"Did he have much of a temper, could you tell?" Reavis didn't want to leave until he'd learned as much about Whitfield as he could. Maybe it was only a coincidence that Whitfield had left town the day after the last Boston murder, was a member of Executive Fitness. Maybe . . . but Reavis had a feeling.

Constantine didn't answer right away, then he took his time. "He *seemed* to be easygoing enough. But you got the feeling . . . there was one thing. Nothing with me . . . something happened with some clerk in a store. He was mad." Constantine looking hard at Reavis now to make his point. "Real mad, had to catch himself when he was telling me about it. All she did was make him wait or something like that. It was more like his pride was hurt."

Constantine shook his head. "No, Mr. Whitfield wouldn't be someone to mess with. Know what I mean? It wasn't nothin' you could see too easy. But it was there."

Constantine looked like he wanted to say more but didn't know whether to go on, so Reavis said, "Go ahead, Mr. Constantine."

"He always wanted to know about my family. How I was with them. I'm divorced and he asked stuff like did I see my kids much when they were growing up, what we did together, did I still get along with their mother, things like that. He was lots more interested, though, about whether my ex was a good mother to the kids, wanted to know if she worked outside the house. He asked a lot of questions about her.

Funny, when I asked him about his family, you know"—the man with the bum leg glanced quickly at Reavis—"just to be friendly, not to pry, mind you; he'd never say nothin'. Acted like I hadn't asked; went and changed the subject on me. Did that two or three times when we talked."

Constantine coughed again, then stood and rifled the pockets of his wrinkled gray pants. He pulled out a crushed cigarette pack, red and white, and frowned at it before he squashed it more. He looked from Matson to Reavis. "Either of you two gentlemen got a smoke?"

Both Reavis and Matson said they didn't smoke, so Toby Constantine turned awkwardly on his bum leg, leaned toward the ashtray beside his recliner, and pushed butts around. Then picked one up and pulled it straight. Reavis could remember doing the same thing when he was out of cigarettes, before he quit.

After lighting the butt, Constantine chuckled (at first Reavis thought he was coughing again) and gestured at the ashtray. "Something else about the guy." Constantine wheezed when he blew out the smoke. "Those days we'd be talking . . . sometimes he would come over and empty my ashtray. Wouldn't be long after that, maybe he'd put the paper I'd been reading together, set it somewhere all squared up. It was almost like he didn't realize he was doing it. He was like one of them housewives who can't stop picking up."

"You say anything about it to him?" Reavis asked.

"What was to say? The man had a thing about being neat, that's all. He was a nice guy. Why bug him?"

"Mr. Constantine, you said he liked to talk about your family. Anything else?"

"When he talked about himself, it was only about his job. You could tell he was real proud of it. Not that he bragged, mind you. Told me he was some kind of vice-president, traveled all over, something about looking for places to open branch offices. Talked about the job a lot. Gave a person the idea what he did was real important. You know what I mean? Never said how much he made or anything, though. Too much class."

Constantine's eyes widened. "Hey, there was something else. Mr. Whitfield's a lawyer. Yeah. I knew there was something I forgot to tell you. Reason I know is when I gave him the lease to sign, he took a long time looking it over. I kidded him about that. Said something like he couldn't understand all them big words, could he? That's when he told me he went to school to learn how to be a lawyer."

Reavis leaned forward. "Did he tell you what school?"

"No sir, he didn't." Constantine gave an elaborate shrug. "I asked him, but that was another one of them times he didn't answer me."

Reavis did his best to hide his frustration. "Anything else? You mentioned he traveled a lot. He ever say where?"

"No. And I asked, too. Just said he'd been back and forth between the coasts a lot."

Reavis had brought his laptop and flash drive with audio output with him and played all five call-in recordings.

"Recognize that voice?" Reavis said.

"That's Mr. Whitfield on each one. I don't get it. How could that be, one man calling to report hearing shots five different times?" Constantine said.

Now they didn't have to contact the last man on their list so they returned to police headquarters. When they were seated in Matson's office, Reavis went first: "Think Whitfield's the one?" When Matson didn't answer right away, Reavis came right out with his thinking. "I do."

"No doubt about it, Clifford."

Matson then picked up the phone and dialed. "Hello . . ." Then he held the phone out from his ear and looked at Reavis. "I called the number Constantine gave us for Atlas Investments. A recording, Clifford. I'm getting a recording." He glanced at his watch. "What time is it out in California?"

Reavis held his Timex out so he could read the time. "It's nearly five here," he answered. "Must be about two out there. There ought to be someone in the office. If it's any size."

Matson set the phone in its cradle. "A recording," he said. "What do you think of that?"

"What was it Constantine said the guy did?" Reavis said. "Wasn't it that he looked for places his company could open new offices? How big could Atlas Investments be if they don't even have someone around to answer the telephone in their main office in the middle of a business day?"

"What was I supposed to do?" Mason said. "Tell some damn recorder that we think the guy they have looking for new properties might be out there killing women?" Giving it some thinking. He snapped his fingers. "I've got an idea."

Matson tugged a black loose-leaf notebook out of his right-hand desk drawer. He paged quickly through the notebook, found what he wanted, picked up the phone, and dialed another eight-digit number. Then tucking the phone between his ear and left shoulder. "Yes," he said, when he got an answer. "This is George Matson of the Boston Police Department. *Superintendent* George Matson. I'd like to talk to the chief." Looking where he had his finger on the notebook page. "Bill Milligan still chief out there?"

"Bill," Matson said when Milligan got on, "George Matson. Boston. Can you have one of your men check out a Thomas Whitfield for me?" Then Matson gave him the address Whitfield gave Toby Constantine.

After that call, Matson called the wage tax collector in Newport Beach, California and, after that, the one in Boston. Thomas Whitfield hadn't paid wage taxes in either place. Finally, the Boston Police superintendent called another number. "Mr. Constantine," he said into the phone, "when you called Atlas Investments about Mr. Whitfield, did you get an answering machine? . . . You did? How soon did they get back to you? . . . I see. Okay, Mr. Constantine . . . No, that's it for now. Thanks."

Matson seemed puzzled when he looked up at Reavis after hanging up. "Constantine got the recording, too. The president of Atlas called him back the next day."

The phone buzzed and Matson picked it up. "Yeah, Bill, thanks for getting back to me so quick," he told the caller. "So no one ever heard of him, huh? Spell that for me, will you?" Matson wrote something down. "Thanks, Bill, I owe you one." And he said so long and hung up.

Matson looked up from what he had written. "Clifford, we're getting somewhere. That address in California . . ."

"Yeah?"

"A phony. A guy"—Matson looked down at his notes—"named Roselli has lived there for the last five years. No Thomas Whitfield has ever lived at that address. I think we might be onto something. Otherwise"—he looked up at Reavis again—"why the phony address? Man gives a phony address, he's got to be hiding something."

Twice more Matson called Atlas's number. Twice more he got a recorded message.

"What's the voice on the recording sound like?" Reavis said.

"No accent." Matson must have seen what Reavis was getting at. "Can't tell if it's the same guy called in the murders or not. Could be, though.

Now that you mention it, it did sound a little muffled. Like someone trying to disguise his voice."

It was almost six now. Reavis called the airport and found out there was nothing out of Boston to Phoenix that night. The killer had been in Phoenix right before Boston. So that's where Reavis would have to go next. From Matson's office he booked a 10:40 p.m. flight to Pittsburgh, then another tomorrow out of Pittsburgh to Phoenix.

"Nothing till ten forty?" Matson said.

"No. You want to get a beer at Joey's?" Joey's was a cops' bar, not too far away.

Matson got a funny look on his face, looked down at his desk and said, no, they'd go somewhere called the Pirate's Den. He explained that when he would stop at Joey's all the cops would get quiet because the boss was in the house. He couldn't go to Joey's. And he sure missed being with all those other cops.

# CHAPTER TWENTY

"Marsha."

Marsha looked up from the case she was working on and out at her secretary Carol, who was leaning over her desk, hand over the telephone. Carol, mid-twenties, four months pregnant and beginning to show, said, "There's a Mel Sadecki holding for you."

Marsha had been thinking a lot about Mel Sadecki in the week since they met. Actually, she'd done a lot more than thinking. Interested, curious, wanting to know where he lived, she had looked up his phone number and address on the Internet.

"Thanks, Carol, I'll take it," she said as she got up to close the door. Carol liked to listen through the door to Marsha's private calls. And though Marsha really liked her, she knew her secretary liked to gossip. Door closed, seated again, she took a deep breath and lifted the phone. "How are you today, Mr. Sadecki? Need an attorney? Not calling from jail, are we?" Marsha was joking, but having a tough time feeling comfortable.

"No, Ms. LeGrange, fortunately not." She heard him chuckle. "I was calling out of concern for your health."

"My health?"

"Yes," he said. "I've been giving your health a lot of thought and I came to the conclusion that you needed to do something a little more stretchy and aerobic than Nautilus workouts."

"Oh . . ."

"Now don't get angry," he said. "I want to emphasize that I am making no remarks that should be taken as disparaging. You look to be in excellent condition." There was a pause on the other end; then she heard what sounded like a nervous laugh. "I'm calling to express my willingness to provide you with a little racquetball competition some lunch hour."

"When?" she said, not at all surprised at her eagerness. Giving no thought to the fact that not many days ago she'd been looking forward, in the same way, to playing racquetball with Lester Wilkins.

They agreed on the following Tuesday and as soon as she got off the phone she checked her Tuesday schedule. The Matvey case was scheduled for a pretrial conference with Judge Gorshak in the afternoon. She called her opponent on Matvey and, after some arm twisting, settled the case within the settlement authority that her insurance carrier client had granted her. No need for the conference. That done, if Mel wanted to have lunch or something after racquetball, she would have her afternoon free.

Tuesday took a long time coming and when it did Mel picked her up at the office and they walked the three blocks from there to the Arena. On the way over, she got out of him that he'd never been married. "Too much traveling, I guess," he said. "How 'bout you?"

She punched him in the shoulder, said, "Same as you, too much work. Only I don't travel much."

At the Arena, she changed quickly, but Mel, in shorts and a gray sweat-shirt with the sleeves cut off, was first on the court. When Marsha ducked through the door wearing the snug shorts that went with her canary-yellow T-shirt, he had just slammed the blue ball against the front wall.

She warmed up hurriedly, first her forehand shots followed by a few backhand shots. Then just one to the ceiling. No stretching. They hit for serve, and he won.

Marsha set herself quickly and he served. She hammered it back at him with no trouble, but she wondered if he was taking it easy on her.

Soon her muscles warmed, tendons and ligaments stretched. After a while, as they began to test each other's limits, the shots got tougher.

Soon she could feel perspiration running down the sides of her face and her T-shirt begin to cling. He won the first game 15–9.

His sweat shirt got darker down the middle of his back and under the arms. He had unusually large wrists and was light on his feet for how big he was. There was no *easy* now. Mel Sadecki was giving it everything he had.

His powerful arms kept rocketing the ball at her and she had to extend herself more and more to get it back to him. She'd nick the side wall and drop it off the front wall so he'd have to run in, then she'd follow with a shot to the ceiling to drive him back. Marsha fought his power with her finesse. The only sounds on the court were the echoes of ball against racquet and ball against wall, heavy breathing, and sometimes a grunt. The second game went 15–11. His way again.

Her competitive burners were turned to high. They went on like this for close to a half hour in the third game and she led him 11–8 before he nailed a shot that flew low and fast, first off the front and then off the side wall. She lunged for it and her momentum carried her into Mel, who couldn't get out of her way fast enough. They came down together. It felt good being tangled up with him, so she took her time working her way loose.

Marsha scooted on her hands and rear end to the back wall. There, Mel joining her now, they both slumped, exhausted. When she got her breath back, she elbowed him, saying, "I could have reached that shot if you hadn't gotten in the way. That's interference, Mr. Sadecki."

He laughed. "You should be thanking me for saving your life." He was breathing easier now, too.

Mel said, "You are wasting your time practicing law. You should be a racquetball pro."

She edged closer to him as she pretended to give turning pro some serious thought. Then, as if deciding, she shook her head. "No, I'm over the hill, Mr. Sadecki. Too old."

"I should be so old." He got up easily to his feet and turned to reach down for her hand. "I'm starved. Let's grab a fish sandwich at the Oyster House. You have the time?"

"What's the matter, scared some girl will whip your butt?"

"I'm conceding." Now just looking at her with a real nice smile.

She took his hand and let him pull her up. "I don't know if I can make it that far," she said, frowning. "It's five or six blocks from here, isn't it?"

He held out an arm. "Here, lean on me. I'll get you as far as the locker room. After that it's up to you." He had a big smile. "After we're done showering, we can hit the Oyster House."

She glanced quickly at him, and then away. *Here, lean on me. How long had it been since she had leaned on anyone?*

Mel showed Marsha to a steel chair in the "square" seating area of Market Square when they got there. (Four streets lined with mostly restaurants bordered an area shaped like a square, which the city had reserved for tables and chairs.) "Why don't you just watch the people and I'll go get lunch? Wait," he said, "until you see the fish sandwich you're getting."

It was one of those early May days. The sky was cloudless, air crisp and not too hot yet. A shirt-sleeves and blouse kind of day. Happy, Marsha sat there, looking around the square. *Funny*, she thought, *I've lived in Pittsburgh for years, first law school and now practicing law, with a clerkship in between, yet I've never been here.* She looked around, trying to spot Mustache Pete's, according to *Pittsburgh Magazine*, Pittsburgh's newest trendy night spot. There it was, the window with nothing but a mustache painted on it. No sign.

Market square seemed, on this sunny day at least, like a secluded green valley nestled among tall, ice-shrouded mountains—the nearly all-glass PPG Place Buildings with their high spires—and brown and red hills, the older two- and three-story buildings; some had dates in the early 1900s embedded in concrete squares on them.

The people she saw were as much of a contrast as the buildings: Shirt-sleeved, white-bloused executives, the men's arms draped casually over the backs of chairs and benches, the women, hands in their laps and leaning back in their chairs, one leg over the other. Most angled their faces at the sun. College kids carrying books, Frisbees, or both (probably headed for Point State Park) walked by. As did four men she guessed were retired.

She saw two sad cases clutching brown bags with bottles poking out, lying prone on the grass, the pigeons walking around them. *What a shame,* she thought. *So young.*

In her peripheral vision she noticed a sudden movement. A man. Did she know him? She leaned forward to get a better look. Yes, the back of his head, all she could see, did look familiar. If he knew her, though, why had he turned away? Because she was sure that that was what he had done. That planted some anxiety in Marsha.

She was still thinking about that man when she heard, "One fish sand-wich and one large Coke." Mel was back. She turned, holding out both hands to grab the huge fish sandwich and forgot about the man across the square.

Mel had not exaggerated about the size of the Oyster House fish sand-wiches. Good. She was starved and made short work of both the sand-wich and the Coke Mel brought her.

He caught her licking the tartar sauce off her fingers and burst out laughing. She reddened. Looked away. Then she shrugged and laughed too. She seemed to laugh a lot with this man.

She got the urge to talk about herself, something she rarely did. Putting her hand on Mel's shoulder—she seemed to find a lot of reasons to touch him—she began, "Mel, I can't remember how long it has been since I've had so much fun. It has been nothing but work for me. For too long."

Mel started to say something but she moved her hand from his shoulder and held it up. "I know; I have no one to blame for this all-work, no-play life but myself. First I had to make some money to help pay for college, a job at night, work all weekend. Then law school: more part-time work." (The kind of part-time work in law school, she did not dare mention.)

"Study," she said. "Classes. Keep those grades up so you get a job clerking for a judge, Marsha." Shaking her head. "Next: Work day and night for Judge Kaufman. He was a wonderful man, Mel. He tried to get me to slow down." More head shaking. "Now it is the law. Office during the day. Lexis-Nexis, WESTLAW, most nights, and more weekends than not. Pride in some accomplishments, sure, but there has not been much laughing."

Mel spoke slowly and all he said at first was, "I know what you mean. Me, too. Too much business."

Finally, he shook his head and broke into a big grin. "Look," he said. "You want to have fun. So do I. Let's you and I do just that. Let's have some fun together. What do you think of that radical idea?"

Her grin matched his. "We owe it to ourselves."

They spent the rest of their time at Market Square talking about the people they saw. Once, she got the uneasy feeling again and had to wonder why. *What is bothering me? On a day like this?*

"Is Lester Wilkins the managing partner at WW&D?" he said.

"Yes. He's a nice man. He's out of town on a big case now. Do you know him?"

He looked like he wanted to ask her more, but he said, "No, I don't actually know him. We talk at the Arena, though. Seems like a decent guy."

"He sure is," she said. But didn't put much on it.

They left a little while later.

On the walk back neither said much, not thinking they had to. Right in front of her building they stopped and he surprised her by taking her chin in his hand, tilting it. At first she thought he was going to kiss her, and maybe he was, but what he did instead was look into her eyes, as though he were trying to read her thoughts. He held her chin and looked at her like that long enough to make her blush.

Then she grinned and so did he, that little-boy, shy grin. She noticed that there was some moistness at the corners of her eyes. Probably from the sun. That's it, she was looking into the sun.

Then it was goodbye, we'll have to do it again, real soon, from both of them.

Inside, after she got to the elevator, she didn't notice Larry Haski until he yelled to her. "Going up, Marsha?" He was holding the elevator door for her.

She hurried to get on and almost bumped into Jeff Guilfoyle, who was on his way to the elevator, too. *Thank goodness,* she thought, *now I don't have to ride up to WW&D all by myself with that woman hater. Was he the one whom she had seen at Market Square?*

Marsha got that anxious feeling again.

# *C*HAPTER TWENTY-ONE

As a hungover Clifford C. Reavis, thirty-five thousand feet above the ground, dozed his way across the country from Pittsburgh, Pennsylvania, to Phoenix, Arizona, Jackie was pounding around the track at the Hampshire High School in the North Hills, near Pittsburgh.

By now Jackie had learned that Lester Wilkins would be gone for quite a while to Atlanta. He was out for Jackie to frame. Last night Marsha LeGrange turned up the strain Jackie was feeling higher yet. He had let himself into her condo once again. And even by her front door, crouching, listening, he could smell the marijuana. He knew where she kept it. It wasn't a new smell to him there. He stood tense, ready to bolt, thinking maybe she had a visitor. Hoping it was a man. Hard as he strained, though, he could hear nothing but her heavy breathing. Sleep breathing. He made for her bedroom.

As usual, the night light was on, but tonight the dim light was ringed with a marijuana haze. The drawer in her nightstand was open. Her right breast poked out above the satin sheet. He clutched at his throat. He could feel his cock start to grow. He wanted to rub it on her.

Jackie bent over her and slowly pulled the satin sheet back. His cock was threatening to blast open his pants zipper as his gaze traveled down her body. Then he caught sight of something—the side of her hand rested on her right thigh near her mound; something was in her hand, dangling loosely. He couldn't tell if the something was white or pink because the light was so dim. He leaned over to get a better look.

The vibrator. The one he had found in her nightstand drawer. That's what the fucking thing was. Shaped like a cock, with pimples on it.

He realized he was gasping. How long had he been doing that? Had he said anything? Made a noise? He studied her. Sleep mask in place. Sound asleep. Jackie started to breath normally.

First he turned the bedroom light on. With her sleep mask on, Marsha didn't even flinch under the bright overhead light. She never flinched. Then he leaned over and gently removed her thumb and two fingers from her phony lover. Next, he gingerly picked it out of her open hand. Her fingers curled and he jumped back. Holding his breath again, he stared at her, watching as her hand took hold of the sheet, and she rolled over on her left side.

He didn't want to have to kill her now, but would if she woke up. He was gonna kill her all right, but he had a certain order he had to do it in. He was big on doing things in the right order. She hugged the pillow to her face. *Mel* was the name he thought he made out as she hugged the pillow to her face.

*Mel!* The rage came on and he went for her. Only holding back at the last minute.

Still enraged today, he ran around the track. Near blind with his feelings, he stepped on a pebble and his ankle started to twist. He was quick enough on his feet to take the weight off before the ankle twisted and hobbled him. Nevertheless, he stumbled a few more paces before he was able to right himself. How long had he been thinking of the way she looked last night? How many laps had he run, thinking of that naked bitch?

He looked around. Still alone. All alone on a gray day. There were puddles in the track from last night's rain. Puddles and dead worms.

Jackie pounded along, trying without success to forget last night. "I'm going to rip you, bitch. You'll lie there and beg. You will grovel."

Faster he went, nearly mindless now.

"Bitch! Lying, fucking bitch! I've been lying to you too. The name you call me isn't my real name. It's my Pittsburgh alias. Every time we talk, it's a lie, because you don't call me by my real name. You call me by that Pittsburgh alias. I'm the big lie in your life." His feet smashed the asphalt. Faster yet he went, still screaming, but now there were no words. He stumbled again. Righted himself again. More screaming. More stumbling. On and on.

Finally, he stumbled for the last time, then crashed, bouncing on the track and rolling off into the grass, still wet from last night's rain. He lay there gasping for air. Then he tasted salt. Tears.

"Don't cry. Don't be weak. You'll get her. Then you won't have to cry anymore." That was the pep talk he kept giving himself.

His muscles were relaxed from all the running now. But soon, he knew, they would be knotting up again. Only getting Marsha LeGrange would cut those knots. Only then could he sleep right, go back to Dutton, South Carolina, where he was born and raised, and see Miss Sarah again. Sarah Lee Simpson was better than a momma to him.

He sat there ripping out clumps of grass. Soon, he vowed, there would be one less woman to make a fool out of some dumb bastard like he was when he was a kid. He thought of how her eyes would look when he spread her legs and climbed on her. Then she would know who the fool really was. He laughed. And then some more. He couldn't stop.

After he was laughed out, he remembered once again that Miss Sarah was always telling him to look on the bright side of things. That's what Jackie would try to do now. Here was that bright side:

1.      Marsha LeGrange and Jackie talked; they knew each other,

2.      Marsha LeGrange did not know his real name,

3.      Marsha LeGrange only knew him by his Pittsburgh alias,

4.      Now he had her vibrator, and

5.      He had never failed before.

# CHAPTER TWENTY-TWO

11:05 a.m. Phoenix time. As Reavis was getting off the plane, flight bag tucked under his left arm, he turned to tell the flight attendant she had really beautiful hair. Her "Watch out!" was too late to keep him from smacking his head on the top of the door opening. Tears came to his eyes. All he ended up saying to the flight attendant was, "Don't worry, I'm okay."

He didn't call Matson until he checked in at the Royale Motel in Scottsdale, where he'd stayed the time he was in Phoenix for the Association convention. He liked their late buffet breakfasts.

"I had some luck here, Clifford." Matson's voice sounding like an explosion in Reavis's ear.

"Softer, Mat," he had to say.

"To much to drink with me last night?" Matson said.

"Yeah." He would leave it at that, not wanting Matson, who would get on him again about how clumsy he was, to know about smacking his head on the plane exit. "What did you come up with?"

"The manager of the bank Whitfield used here turned out to be a pretty nice guy. Seems Whitfield showed him a California driver's license when he opened a business checking account there for Atlas Investments, and the manager still had the number from it. Whitfield had authorization to fully manage the account from his company's president. I called the California Bureau of Motor Vehicles and it is getting me Whitfield's picture by e-mail. I'll send a copy to your cell when it arrives."

"Good. How much did he have?"

"What are you talking about?"

"In the checking account," Reavis said.

"I thought you'd never ask. Withdrew over ten thousand the day after the last murder here. But he left over five million in the account. It's still there. He accesses it online with a password and username. There's been a lot of wire transfers into the account since he opened it. My computer people can't trace him to a current address. He nixed getting either hard-copy or e-mail statements. The address he did give the bank was his place at Toby Constantine's. Atlas Investments must do pretty damn good—and I'm still getting that damn recording when I call them."

"Atlas Investments. California. That's where the answer is. I know it," Reavis said.

"Yeah," Matson said, "but first Phoenix."

Sure, he could have called the Phoenix Health Club, saved a plane trip. But the only way he could be sure he got all the information he could was to be looking at its manager, face to face, seeing what records they had on Whitfield. Reavis was sure the manager would come up with something Reavis wouldn't have thought to ask. Just like what happened with Toby Constantine, when he had to urge the Korean War veteran on and the man had gone into how Whitfield, who worked for Atlas Investments, always had to know how Constantine, and especially his ex-wife, treated their kids.

As he headed the rented Impala towards the Phoenix Health Club, Reavis thought about how stirred up Matson had sounded on the phone. Not bad help, George Matson. The city of Boston was going to have a real tough time strapping its superintendent down from now on. George Matson should never have taken that damn job in the first place. He wasn't meant to be desk-bound. Reavis couldn't understand how anyone could be, for that matter. Without thinking, he shook his head and then felt another slash of pain squirting down his right side from that smack on the head he took walking out of the plane. His headache was getting worse, too.

He was on Camelback Road. Sprinklers were going everywhere there was greenery. Reavis thought it must take a fortune to keep this place green. What a contrast the green around the homes and shopping centers were to the stark, rusty-looking hills where it ended. What would happen if the concrete canals ever dried up? How long would it take the sun to bake everything back to rock, sand, and cactus again?

The health club was only a fifteen-minute drive from the Royale Motel. It sat off by itself in a sprawling shopping center. White, with a dome roof, and palm trees spaced around it; it had four empty wrought iron tables with blue and white umbrellas out front.

A green lizard darted across the walk in front of him as he made for the entrance. The door had a decal on it, a man and a woman showing off huge muscles, holding up the world. Mr. and Mrs. America, Reavis guessed. Did anybody really look like those two?

He found out soon enough. A man who could have been the twin of the man on the decal, white T-shirt that showed off his muscles and white slacks, early thirties, greeted Reavis in the lobby. He stood back and looked Reavis over.

"Something I can do for you, sir?"

Reavis, who made himself take his eyes off the women's aerobic class bouncing around in a workout room to his right, said, "Manager in?"

"I'm Art Manning," the man said as he held his hand out. "This place is mine. How can I help you?" Then he said, "You've come to the right place. We can put some meat on your bones."

Reavis liked the way this Art Manning did not crush his hand when he shook it. He also liked the way he said the place was his, not making any big thing about it, just telling. Far more important, though, Reavis needed Manning to take to him.

Because he was not going to get any help from the Phoenix Police Department. Earlier he had called Jack Mason, the Phoenix Police superintendent, a man Reavis knew from at least a dozen seminars. Mason was out of town, though, and Reavis got his deputy. "Mr. Reavis," the man told him, "we can't walk into a place of business and demand that they show us their records." Reavis thanked the guy and hung up, wondering how Jack Mason ever ended up with an asshole like that for a deputy superintendent.

Reavis handed Art Manning the letter from Matson that said he was a liaison to the Boston Police Department. Manning took his time reading it. Then, looking puzzled, he asked, "How, in Arizona, can I help the Boston, Massachusetts, Police Department?"

For an answer, Reavis handed Art Manning the newspaper clippings about the three Phoenix murders. He snuck another look at the aerobics class as Manning read them. When he thought Manning had enough time to go through all the clippings, he took his eyes off the third woman from the left in the front row, short blonde, a little young, about fifty, and turned back to him. "Know any of them?"

Manning shot a look at him, as if asking where Reavis was going with this. "Sure. They were all members here. I know all my members. Funny," Manning said, shaking his head, "I also knew the three men pretty well. Hell, a lot of the people knew them. Ralph Marcinko was a county commissioner. None of the three seemed like the type, you know, to go around raping and murdering women. But the police . . . the papers . . . TV"—shaking his head again—"they all seemed so sure. And the women. I knew them all, too. They came here a lot." Manning gazed levelly at him. "What about these people, Mr. Reavis?"

"Marcinko and the other two did not kill those women," Reavis said. "I'm certain one man killed all three and I think he was a member of this club. In fact, I'm sure your club is where he selected his victims. He's been doing the same thing at other high-end fitness clubs all over the country."

Manning let out what Reavis would call a sigh of relief. "I was very interested in all of the cases," he said. "I made sure to read and watch everything about each one. But . . . the papers. The TV. Everything. There was so much evidence . . ."

"He's not a member here anymore, or at least not a regular. He was done here after he'd committed the three rapes and murders and framed three men for them. The killer has been raping, killing, and framing some other man for his crimes about once a month. At least that's the way it's been since his first murder here."

Reavis continued. "He has moved on now; I'm sure of that. There have been two murders in Pittsburgh, about a month apart. They were both like your three here. Before Pittsburgh, three in Boston, too, *since* the ones in Phoenix, each of those also a month apart."

Reavis got out his digital recorder with the two Pittsburgh and three Boston call-in recordings now in it.  "Could you listen to these? You'll hear the voice of the man who reported the Pittsburgh and Boston murders. See if you recognize the man's voice."

"Sure, I'll do anything I can to help. I always did wonder about those killings. It bothered me that they were all members here. But I never thought it was anything more than a horrible coincidence . . . there was so much evidence."

Manning motioned to him. "Come with me, I'll listen to them in my office."

At his office, Manning sat Reavis, who started the first call-in recording. By the end of the second recording Manning had straightened in his seat. After the fifth, his mouth was open and his eyes were wide.

While Manning had been listening, Reavis looked around. On the desk were pictures of a striking woman, thirty, he would guess; she was the woman leading the aerobics class Reavis had been watching. The other pictures were of three little girls with blond curly hair. Displayed on the walls were finger paintings, each signed by a different young artist. One of the youngsters made backwards Ks.

Manning interrupted Reavis's inspection of the photographs. "I know that voice," he said.

He rose from his seat and went to a file cabinet and took out a thin file. "The man on those recordings is Donald T. Lamont," he said as he handed Reavis Lamont's file.

When Reavis opened the file and saw what was in it, he nearly choked. On the right side of the file were Lamont's vital statistics, in tiny, precise writing:

| | |
|---|---|
| Age: | 40 |
| Height: | 6-1 |
| Weight: | 200 |
| Color of hair: | Brown |
| Eyes: | Blue |
| Diseases: | None |
| Medications: | None |
| Family Medical History: | Unknown |
| Employer: | Atlas Investments |

What caused Reavis to choke was the employer's name. He had to work hard not to show his excitement. Instead, he asked, pointing at the Family Medical History, "What does this 'unknown' mean?"

"I asked Lamont the same question," Manning said. "He told me he was an orphan. But something about his look when he told me that . . . I didn't buy it. Parents killed in a car crash, he said. No other family."

Reavis handed the file back to the man in the white T-shirt, pointing to the printing on the right side of the file. "Lamont print this?"

Art Manning took a look. "Yes," he said. "My printing is horrible, so I have the clients fill everything out. See how small and neat LaMont's printing is?"

Reavis nodded, and leaned forward. "Tell me about Mr. Lamont," he said.

Manning said, "Lamont was built. Worked out only on the Nautilus equipment. Never touched the free weights." Manning looked hard at Reavis. "Mr. Reavis, Lamont could push those machines around like very few members here *ever* could." Then Manning looked down at his hands, grew silent.

Reavis motioned, wanting him to continue. "Go on, Art, don't worry about whether what you might say is important. Say what you are thinking."

"Well, he was always asking me questions about my family. These pictures on my desk." Indicating the pictures of the blond woman, the three little girls. "My wife and I have three daughters. He saw the pictures when he came into the office to see about joining the club. He seemed disturbed that my wife ran aerobics classes here part time." Manning paused. "He seemed okay with everything when I told him she started back here after the youngest started school. He had this pissed look on his face until I told him that. You had to be there. It was bizarre, that look he got. Then he tells me that it was his opinion that a momma's gotta be with her little ones all the time. 'A momma needs to do the raising of her kids,' he said."

Manning gave his head a puzzled shake. "I almost told him that what my family and I did was our business, but he caught himself and apologized, said it was a big thing with him, women taking care of their kids. He brought up being an orphan again."

"The orphan thing . . . ?"

"Yes. I asked him about that, tried to get him to talk about it. But he changed the subject."

Reavis had no doubt now. There had to be something about his mother. "Lamont" asked Manning questions about his family and they were the same kind of questions "Whitfield" had asked Toby Constantine. No doubt Lamont was the man Reavis called Whitfield—Atlas Investments, their descriptions, those questions about family, and Art Manning recognizing his voice on the call-ins.

Just as important, though, was he was beginning to see a way to get to the man.

What kind of childhood must this man, who went around slaughtering young women, have had? Would knowing help? After all, a thing could happen to one child and it would affect them one way, some other child—same kind of thing—it would affect entirely differently. But it seemed pretty certain that this guy had no mother around when he was little. Or that she came and went as she saw fit. Maybe lied to him. Made him feel like a "nothing." And that it bothered him.

Anxious to hear more, Reavis said, "How about anything else he might have said? His work, what he liked to do with himself in his spare time—sports, hobbies, anything."

Manning rubbed his chin. "He was a real good-looking guy. He looked younger than his age. You can see there," and he pointed at Lamont's file, "he's forty. Dark hair. I don't remember any gray. He was a real neat freak. He would straighten things out on my desk as though I wasn't even in the room. He always arrived in a suit. To talk to him, he sounded smart, you know, like he had a pretty good education. I think he did say he'd been to some kind of graduate school."

"Law school?" Reavis asked. Whitfield had claimed he went to law school.

Manning's eyes widened. "Yes, that's it. That's what he did tell me. But I don't think he was a lawyer." Manning looked at Lamont's folder. "Investments. That's what he did. Land, or something like that. Looking for real estate to invest in so his company could build a new office, I think he said he did."

Same story Whitfield told Constantine, *again*.

"There was something else," Manning said, getting up and going over to the table against the wall, then returning with a heavy black notebook. He flipped through it, then stopped, squinting. Then flipping the pages again, stopping, putting his finger on something, turning the book around so Reavis could see what was under his finger. "Look," Manning pointed out, "Lamont's name, then one of the victims' names. He didn't talk to most of the women here"—nodding his head, now remembering—"but I saw him talking to her a couple times."

Manning turned the book around and began paging slowly through it again. Then he closed it, nodding his head, convincing himself. "This is our sign-in book," he said. "Where all the members sign in for their Nautilus workouts. Every page with a victim's name on it, Lamont's name is on the same page, real near the victims, as if they came in about the same time. Another thing, he only came in the evening; that's when the business crowd came to work out. We had a lot of good-looking career women come in then."

# CHAPTER TWENTY-THREE

Tonight, a Friday, Jackie did not go into the Nautilus room. Instead, he waited until he knew Marsha would be strapping herself into the first Nautilus machine. From outside the room, not letting her see him, he studied her as she lay on her back, breathing deeply, getting ready to start. Then she did, pushing with her legs, first one, then the other, moving the weight as her lips silently counted the repetitions. Her eyes were tightly closed as she concentrated on doing the exercise. He liked to stare at her when she concentrated like that.

She would be the most special one yet.

Unconsciously, he licked his lips. He liked getting close enough to see the tiny hairs on the insides of her smooth thighs, which he could not do right now. Soon he would be that close and more, asking her the two questions. And if she lied, she would have to die.

It was a warm night, so Jackie decided to wait outside for Marsha. She came out of the Arena close to seven thirty and headed down Fifth towards Grant. There, she made a left and passed the UPMC Building. Four blocks later, at Second Avenue, she made another left. After that she walked on, eventually passing the Allegheny County jail. Once she made a right onto the Tenth Street Bridge, Jackie knew she was on her way home. *No hurry,* he thought, *let her get home, settled.*

He doubled back, got his car at the First Avenue parking garage near the Public Safety Building, and headed for her place. All the way over to the South Side his forearm muscles were bunched and his fingers had the steering wheel in a death grip because tonight he had something special planned for Marsha LeGrange.

There was still some daylight when he drove past her place, but he could see a light on behind the curtains in her living room. She was home. When she went out she only left the bedroom light on.

Jackie kept going, turned right at the next block and headed toward East Carson Street, where he parked his car in the eighteen hundred block and headed for a pay phone.

Marsha had been a little down because she hadn't seen Mel at the Arena. Now that Mel had just called, though, saying he just wanted to check in, she was in good spirits. He had been busy with something this weekend, he told her, but he hoped they could get together sometime next week, maybe work out, play some racquetball, and then go out to dinner or something.

She was in the kitchen waiting for the Stouffer's frozen lasagna she had in the microwave and thinking about what she could wear when she and Mel went out to dinner. The phone rang again. She hurried to the living room to get it, answering it before it rang for the fifth time.

In a voice, high-pitched, one with a southern accent, a man said, "I have something of yours, Marsha."

She went along with it. "Oh you do?"

All she could hear was breathing.

"Who is this?" She pressed the phone hard against her ear. "Mel?"

Still no answer.

"Hank? . . . Jeff . . . come on, who is this? I've got lasagna in the microwave and I'm famished."

"Look in your nightstand," the voice with the southern accent whispered. "Last night I borrowed something you keep in it. Though that's not where I found it."

Marsha felt the breath go out of her. All I keep in the nightstand, she thought, is the toy. No one could know about that.

She got herself under control and, hiding her panic, let the caller hear only contempt. "Who is this?" she said. "I don't know you and I don't let little redneck boys in my bedroom." She quietly hung up, too late remembering what she had read about anonymous callers. That they got their kicks from hearing you talk, the fear in your voice, your reactions to them.

Jackie's face got hot. Anger whacked him. *Little redneck boys.*

"The little red necked boy died in Dutton, South Carolina," he said. Enraged, he ripped the pay phone off the box, unaware that Marsha LeGrange had already hung up.

Marsha ran to the bedroom and tore open the nightstand drawer. "Oh my God. It's gone." Then she lost all the strength in her legs and her body sank down to the rug. For a while she had neither thoughts nor feelings. Numb. Then there were no thoughts, only feelings: Shame. Panic. Rage.

Finally there was thought. Questions, mostly. What did she do with it this morning? She couldn't remember. Had her sex toy fallen to the floor when she fell asleep? Sometimes after her special evenings she did find it on the floor. Had some man really been in her bedroom? *No*, she tried to tell herself. *Impossible.*

She began crawling around on the floor, looking for it there and under the bed. It was neither place.

She jumped up and tore the covers back, looking first behind the headboard, then between the mattresses, and finally she looked behind the nightstand. She ran to the dresser and ripped open the lingerie drawer. When it was not there she opened all the other drawers. Not finding it in the bedroom, she ran to the bathroom. Maybe she had carried it in there last night. No, it was not anywhere in the bathroom, either. It wasn't anywhere.

In a full-fledged panic state now, she went back to the bedroom and started tossing everything out of the drawers, pulling all the covers off the bed. It was nowhere . . . gone.

Marsha dropped on the bed for the second time, head in her hands, eyes closed tightly. She had to remain calm. She must think clearly. *Could someone have been in my bedroom?* she wondered, appalled by the thought. If so, why? Who? When could he have been in there? While she slept? After she left for work? How did he get in? She always kept the condo locked, didn't she? . . . or had she forgotten this morning?

The doors. She jumped up and ran to the front door. Then the back. Both were locked. Her shoulders sagged. She looked at her hands. They were trembling. This time when she returned to the bedroom, she sprawled face down on the bed. Her thoughts would not stop whirling.

She lay there needing to call, to be with someone. She didn't want to be alone. Not now. But who could she call? Mel Sadecki? She shook her head. No, she believed that something had started between them but it had not gone on long enough for her to do that. What would she tell him, anyway? That someone took her little plaything?

She got her mind to focus on who the caller might be. Someone who used a phony southern accent. Could it have been Mel? He said he was from the south. After all, she asked herself, how well did she really know him?

Or how about Hank? Jeff? Larry Haski? Even Lester Wilkins. He could have come home for the weekend. Then terror struck her down to the floor again. What if it was a former client. Someone from Cleveland who recognized her here in Pittsburgh. No. It couldn't be. She'd worn an expensive wig when she sold her body.

As she paced from room to room, she realized it could have been any of them, or—more than likely—it wasn't any of them. No, it couldn't be someone she knew, or had sold her body to. She would not let herself believe that; it was just some phone freak.

She would look again. That is what she would do. Then she would find the damn thing. But not until morning. She would probably find it then. Maybe in the bathroom. Probably somewhere she already looked. Yes, that was it. How many times had she found something she had looked for everywhere, always finding it someplace she had already looked? Sure, tomorrow she would be a lot calmer, better able to look for it. She was high last night. That's all. She must have put it somewhere when she was high. It had to be around somewhere. She would find it tomorrow. That is what she told herself.

# *C*HAPTER TWENTY-FOUR

Hard as she searched, Marsha could not find it Saturday morning. Her phone rang a lot that day, all weekend, in fact. But now, hiding from the sound of it in bed, she could not get out to answer it. Because some man knew about her special evenings and that was him, she was sure, who was calling to taunt her with that knowledge.

Would he be back? Every time she heard a noise, she dug her heels into the mattress, pushing herself harder into the headboard. She knew she should call the police, but how could she? What would she tell them? That someone had broken into her home? "Oh," she could picture some stocky police officer asking, "and did he take anything, ma'am?"

What was she going to tell him? "Nothing of value, officer, only a sex toy that has been in the family for years."

*Some man knew.*

What if it was Larry Haski? She imagined coming upon him having coffee with the guys, him looking at her, smirking, then leaning across the table and whispering her private business to the others. In her mind she saw them all look her way, then break out laughing. Even

Jeff Guilfoyle. She twisted the pillowcase. If anyone at the office ever found out, she would have to quit. But quitting her job at Wilkins, Wilkins & Dunn would not be enough; the story about her special evenings would follow her everywhere she went—the *Virgin Marsha* and her vibrator.

In the middle of a Friday afternoon in Arizona, dinnertime in Pittsburgh, Reavis lounged by the motel pool, two Royale Motel towels over his bony white legs, the sun at his back. He finished all he could do in Arizona and there wasn't anything he could think of doing in California over the weekend. So he decided not to leave here until Sunday.

The towels kept slipping off his legs and, as he reached down to pull them up again, he caught a woman on the other side of the pool staring at him. Smiling. He could tell she liked what she saw. She looked to be in her mid-to-late fifties. Really put together. She was about as young as Reavis would go.

She rose, walked over to the pool bar, nothing jiggling, and sat on one of those high stools. At another time, he would have gone over, struck up a conversation, maybe bought her a drink.

But two other women were on Reavis's mind today. Peggy was one. He missed her. He did not have a name for the other woman yet, but he knew a lot about her: She would be good looking; she would have very dark hair; she would be thirty to forty, single, well-educated; and she would be starting to have some success in her profession. And she would be hooked up with a guy who had some bucks.

At five p.m. Arizona time he returned to his room for a nap. When he woke up he phoned Matson. "Have you tried Atlas again?" Reavis asked after filling Matson in.

"Yeah," Matson answered, "Still nothing but a recording."

"If it wasn't the weekend I'd fly to California tonight," he said. "But if no one is at Atlas during the week, they sure as hell are not going to be there over the weekend. Besides," he admitted, "I'm shot, the beer last night, the jet lag and all. Don't worry." *Who was he telling that to, Matson or himself?* "We're getting closer. Now we are certain it is Whitfield and that he belongs to the same health clubs as his victims. So if he has not moved to another city, for sure we will find him on the membership list of the Fitness Arena in Pittsburgh."

"Yeah," Matson said. "We are closer. But he probably is, too, Clifford."

Reavis was all too aware of that.

"Anything on the photo from California DMV?"

"No DMV photo from California yet. I'll have to get on their backs. We should have received it already. But I did get the information on the prints from Whitfield's lease. Constantine's were a match to him. There was another set. No match."

After they hung up, Reavis thought about what he and Matson had learned:

1. Whitfield belonged to the same health clubs as his victims,

2. He was good looking,

3. Big,

4. Very strong,

5. He was about forty,

6. Had dark hair, maybe with a little gray in it,

7. He liked to talk about mothers taking care of their kids, staying home with them,

8. He probably at least attended law school, and

9. He was obsessive about being neat—an order fanatic?

Did talking about his job, mentioning that he went to law school, boost Whitfield's self-esteem?

More and more Reavis believed that after he visited Atlas Investments in California he would have all of his answers and that by the time he got back to Pittsburgh, Matson would have e-mailed him the California DMV photo.

A thought brought him straight up in bed. Suppose he was already too late? Damn, he should have grabbed a *Pittsburgh Post-Gazette* at the airport this morning. No problem. He got the Internet on his cell phone and clicked on to the *Post-Gazette* and *Tribune Review* online versions. Then he checked the Pittsburgh TV Web sites: KDKA, WTAE, and WPXI. No murder in their headlines.

He called Peggy a few minutes before eleven Pittsburgh time and asked her to tune in to KDKA. If anything had happened they'd have a reporter on the scene. It would probably be the lead story.

"Okay, the news is just coming on," she said.

Reavis kept quiet as long as he could. "Anything . . . anything at all, Peg?"

She answered, "A man was arrested for killing his common-law wife's four-year-old boy, and the usual fire and accident stories are all they are promising to bring us."

"They'd have promised a murder if there was one. At least we have one more day. Good. Thanks, Peg. Call me on my cell if you hear anything." He wanted to ask her if she missed him as much as he missed her, but he couldn't work up the courage.

"When will you be home, honey?" she said.

"First part of next week. I hope. I'll get a Sunday flight to California, so I get to Atlas Investments first thing Monday. Peg . . ."

"Yes?"

"I think I'll know who he is by the time I leave there. Should know what he looks like, too, when Matson sends me his California DMV photo."

She didn't say anything.

"Did you hear, Peg?"

"Yes. I'm scared, Clifford. I don't want anything to happen to you."

After trying to ease Peggy's worry, failing and finally saying so long to her, Reavis called Bobby Doall and filled him in, too. Bobby, like Reavis, was late to bed, late to rise. Also like Reavis, he owned rental properties now and freelanced as a consultant for online businesses. Two years earlier he'd even started an online company that he then sold for a couple million, Reavis having to drag the price of that deal out of him. Bobby didn't need to work on Reavis's rentals for money. It was just something the two of them could do together now, two buddies, Reavis a little older. Well, maybe a lot older. Two guys who didn't need to work at all; two guys who just did things that interested them.

Bobby said, "I agree with you, Clifford, there's nothing you can go to the police with; you're right, the guy will just run if he knows they even suspect him. You're going to have to find a way to psych out the guy, get in his head, throw him off his guard. You know, I think what you do, once you find out who he is; you get in his face at the Fitness Arena, get in something about his mother when you do."

"I like the idea, Bobby. Be thinking about what I can hit him with at the Fitness Arena, something that will get him off his game. I agree, we have to come up with something to say about his mother. I can get in his face safely at the Fitness Arena with you there. Hey, can you get me the name of all the female members at the Arena?"

"Sure, but not this weekend. I don't know the weekend people that well. First thing Monday okay with you?"

"I hope, Bobby. I'm worried we're running out of time."

"I'll get them to you ASAP."

Before he left the Royale Motel in Phoenix on Sunday, Reavis called Toby Constantine in Boston. "Naw, nothing like that. It was just how much time the ex spent with the kids, how well she took care of them when they were growing up. Did she ever leave them for long periods of time. Nothing like did we beat them, molesting, anything like that."

Next, Reavis called Art Manning's Phoenix health club. His conversation with Bobby Doall had given him an idea. He got Art Manning on the phone. "When you were talking about how you and your wife raised your family, Art, did LaMont ever say anything about being mistreated, molested, anything like that as a child? Did he ever even give you a hint that anything like that had gone on when he was a kid?"

"Definitely not. He focused on how much time we—mostly my wife—spent raising our kids. Stressing she should always be with the kids. Never abandon them. He actually used the word 'abandon' a couple times."

By mid-evening on Sunday Reavis was settled at another motel, the Ali Baba in Costa Mesa, California.

Reavis called Peggy just before eleven p.m. Pittsburgh time. She told him there was nothing in the papers. They waited. After she got into the evening news, she told him there were no murders at all that Sunday.

Before she got off, Peggy told him she missed him and Reavis was able to get the words out that he missed her, too. He hadn't sounded too slick to himself doing it. Beth Reavis had been the last woman he'd ever said that to.

# CHAPTER TWENTY-FIVE

Bobby Doall got back to Reavis first thing Monday. Bobby, always a man of his word, sent Reavis an e-mail with all the Fitness Arena's female member's names. After Reavis got the names, he called Pat Tazer. "Taze, we're sure the next female victim's going to be a member of the Fitness Arena. I've got all the female members' names. Can you run them in the computer for women who called the Pittsburgh Police to complain about being harassed?"

Tazer said he could, so Reavis forwarded Bobby's e-mail with the female members' names to him.

Then he took off for Atlas Investment's address. It turned out to be a shopping center in Costa Mesa. At the fourth place he stopped, a cheap-wig shop, Reavis got the manager just opening up. He gave her a chance to let some sun in before he said, "Ever hear of Atlas Investments? Supposed to be here in the center somewhere." He showed her the Ali Baba Motel stationary on which he had written Atlas Investments's address. "This is the address I have for them."

The woman, about forty, a redhead with freckles and a big chest, shook her head and turned away to finish opening up. Then she stopped, turned back to him. "Have you tried the mail drop place yet?" she said.

"Mail drop place?"

"Yes," she said. "Two doors down." Pointing where. "A lot of people who only need an address to get mail use it. *Strange looking people.* Wait till you meet the guy in charge. A real sweetheart."

When he got there, he saw how he had missed it before. It had just a metal door, no number on it. There was no name printed on the door to identify the place. He went inside and saw what looked like a wall of post-office boxes. A man gouging his teeth with a toothpick slouched in a slat-back chair at a desk behind the waist-high counter. Reavis moved toward the guy.

Who would not look up.

Reavis began to drum his fingers on the wood counter. Only then did the guy turn, looking as if he was trying to decide whether to get off his ass and come over or just ask Reavis what he wanted from where he sat.

Finally he got up and sauntered over. First body odor, next the smell of stale wine, and, last, the smell of rotten teeth broke on Reavis like one wave after an other. Body Odor leaned on the counter, turned his head only a little, and spat out part of a wooden toothpick. "Do something for you, pal?"

Reavis realized that there was only one way to handle this guy, so he dug five new twenties out of his wallet and spread them on the counter, which was pockmarked with cigarette burns.

The man who stank so much looked at him. "For what?"

"Atlas Investments," Reavis answered.

The man, whose front teeth were half eaten away, nodded for Reavis to go over to a door and be let in. Then the man pointed to the chair he had been sitting in.

"Sit," he said.

Reavis did that while the man got a file out of a scratched gray file cabinet. He tossed it on the desk in front of Reavis and moved away.

ATLAS INVESTMENTS the folder read. Reavis looked to the postal box numbered 612. *Suite 612, an office that measures seven by five by twelve inches.* Atlas Investments was a postal box in a room managed by a man who stank. A mail drop.

The file did not contain much. Instead of a billing address there was a note stapled to the inside flap that said, "Pays six months in advance." The phone number for Atlas Investments was the same one Reavis had. Atlas Investments had rented the box for the last five years. That was it. No names. No addresses.

Reavis kept his face expressionless. "Does Atlas get much mail?"

Body Odor, now chewing a filthy nail, would not look at him. "I don't check customers' mail."

"That won't get you the hundred." Reavis sat back, folded his arms and watched greed struggle with conscience.

Greed slaughtered its helpless opponent. "All right," the guy said. "Okay. When the mail comes in for Atlas, like with a lot of them"— BO nodded toward the mail slots—"I pick up a little extra by calling the number you see in their file, leaving a message there's mail here, where it is from. In a day, maybe two or three, I get called back and told where to send it."

"Who?" Reavis leaned forward. "Who calls you?" He could feel his stomach tighten. "Where do you send it?"

"Different places for Atlas Investments. Pennsylvania last couple months."

"Where in Pennsylvania? Pittsburgh?"

"Yeah." The man looked at Reavis as if he wondered how Reavis would know that. Then he started working on his ass, scratching.

Reavis, exasperated, said, "What about a name and address?"

"Different names for each city."

"Whitfield, Lamont?"

"Could be." He gave an imitation of a man trying to think. "Yeah, probably."

Reavis believed the man was not working hard enough for the hundred. "I don't see anybody's name and address here." He handed the file over.

"It should be."

"Show me where, then," Reavis said.

The man stopped digging at his rear end and reached for the file. He looked in it, shook his head, and then looked at Reavis. "It must have slipped out of the file."

Reavis wanted to grab him. All this way, this close, and this foul-smelling excuse for a human being loses the killer's Pittsburgh name and address.

Something, probably the way he was looking at the guy, must have tipped him to what was on Reavis's mind. "Don't worry, pal, he'll call again. I can get his name and address for you then."

"Nah," Reavis said, trying his best to act like it didn't matter. "The more I think about it, the more I think that this isn't the Atlas Investments outfit I am interested in anyway." He didn't want it to get back to Whitfield that there was someone asking questions about Atlas Investments. "There are a lot of firms with the name 'Atlas' in them. I'll just keep looking."

Outside, after he'd let the stinking clerk keep one twenty, sitting in the rented Chevrolet, waiting for the air conditioner to blow the hot air out, Reavis mentally kicked himself in the ass. If only he hadn't said *Whitfield* and *Lamont*. If that bastard inside had only saved Whitfield's Pittsburgh name. Now what?

*Now what* turned out to be apartment C-110, Lockhart Towers, Newport Beach, California, the address where Whitfield claimed to live before Boston. Reavis checked his notebook to refresh his memory. He remembered now. The Newport Beach police chief had called Matson back, said a guy by the name of Anthony Roselli lived there. Reavis had written the name down.

When he got to Lockhart Towers, Reavis knocked on Roselli's apartment door. No answer. Then he tried the apartment next door. A woman answered. Late twenties, she was tall, blonde and, like everyone else out here, she had a tan.

"I'm trying," he said, "to get in touch with a neighbor of yours. Anthony Roselli. Know him?"

She was chewing a mint but he could smell the light scent of last night's whiskey. "You mean the mystery man?"

"What do you mean 'mystery man?'"

"I've been here for over four years and I have never seen Mr. Roselli. No one has. No one comes in or out of that place."

He thanked her and left, then hit two other people on the same floor, getting the same answers. No one, it seemed, knew Anthony Roselli.

Another dead end.

Reavis straightened to his full height. *Or was it really a dead end?* He got on the Internet on the cell phone Bobby gave him last Christmas, got the number for the Newport Beach tax collector. "My name is Clifford Reavis," he said when he got her, "and I'm working with the Boston police on a case. What I need is some information on an Anthony Roselli, apartment C-110, Lockhart Towers Apartments."

"Hold on a minute," she said. "Was that R-O-S-E-L-L-I?"

"Yes, first name Anthony."

"Hold on, Clifford Reavis who is working with the Boston police on a case," she told him. When she got back on she said, yes, Anthony Roselli paid wage taxes. "What would you like to know about him?"

"Does he work for Atlas Investments?"

"Yes," she said, "Anthony Roselli does work for Atlas Investments. Is that all you need to know?"

He said it was, thanked her, and hung up.

# CHAPTER TWENTY-SIX

Marsha made it to work on Monday, and was glad she did. Because this Monday things at the firm were hectic, which was exactly what she needed. The phone did not stop all morning and right before lunch Jeff stopped in to ask her if she wanted him to pick up any take-out for her when he came back from lunch. She did her best to smile and shook her head no.

Marsha had to leave her office for a short conference with an expert witness on one of her cases. When she got back from the conference there was a message from Carol that Mel had called. He didn't leave a number. She called him at his home but just got his answering system. Next time she talked to him, she'd have to get his cell number.

A little after two, Carol walked in with a FedEx package. *Good*, she thought, *that gear is in on my products liability case*. She would get it out to the metallurgical engineer who the firm had retained as its expert witness so he could inspect it, let her know if it was defective and tell Marsha whether, in his opinion, it caused the mine accident that killed those seven coal miners in West Virginia. She tore at the brown paper.

But there wasn't any gear in the red, white, and blue package. *It was the vibrator.*

Someone *had* been in her bedroom.

Someone who knew where she worked.

Marsha wet herself, though she didn't know it until later.

Now, though, she sat frozen, unaware of the spreading wetness on the back of her skirt.

It took her ten minutes to discover the back of her skirt was wet. Mortified, she got up and backed over to the closet. Squatting, never taking her eyes from the door, she felt around on the closet floor until her hand struck her gym bag. She found a pair of sweats. She dug them out of the bag and with them in hand she inched her way along the wall until she got to her office door. Which she quietly closed and locked.

Nearly losing her balance, she struggled out of her sodden skirt, pantyhose, and panties, then pressed herself into the corner of her office, where she moved her legs into the sweats. Back at her desk, office door now open, there she was, wearing a lovely silk blouse over sweats.

She had always felt safe in Pittsburgh. Home, her condo, had always been a comfort. No longer, though. Now she saw it as a prison.

But there was nowhere else to go. She would have to take the bus, like she had in the morning, because she was too terrified to walk home. After she got on it, she made sure to sit next to a woman, and studied each man who got on. She could sense the stares from the other passengers—a blouse and sweats, the new look? She got off the bus two blocks from her home and got rid of the vibrator, now inside a brown lunch bag, in the first trash can she could find. When she got home and opened her door, she yelled, "Hello."

What was he going to do? Holler back, "I'm in the bedroom, Marsha."

She made herself go in, telling herself that she'd had martial arts instruction. Big deal! First, she turned on the light by the door, then every light in the living room. When she got to the bedroom, she reached around the door, flipped the light switch, jumped back into a martial arts stance, and listened. She reached under her dresser and slid out her journals. They had to go, too. The journals she shredded in her home office. She left the condo with their hard covers and dropped them in the nearest trash can. Then hurried back, looking over her shoulder as she ran.

Should she call the police? Maybe so. But she got only as far as reaching for the phone before pulling her hand back. What would she tell them?

Imagine the police going around to her neighbors, maybe even people at work, asking, "Are you the one who took Ms. LeGrange's little plaything? What does it look like, you ask? Well, Ms. LeGrange tells us it is light pink and has small bumps over the one end. It looks like a penis; it isn't a real one, though, but it was all she had." Marsha buried her face in her hands, overwhelmed.

She had one friend who would never let her down. Carrie Stockhausen. She picked up her phone and dialed Carrie. She got her, first ring, and told her everything.

"Why didn't you call me before, Marsha?" Carrie didn't wait for an answer. She said, "I'll be right over. Don't let anyone in but me. Do you still have the taser that Marilyn supplied us?

"No, I got rid of it. I didn't think I'd ever need it again and it was illegal. Do you still have yours?"

"No, I got rid of mine. Same reason. Illegal."

In part of what she called her "orientation," Marilyn had given both Carrie and Marsha taser guns, which they could keep beside their bedside tables in the bedrooms in Marilyn Moore's eight-room home, where they earned their money.

Marilyn also had a man with a black belt give them a short course in self-defense. Then Marilyn gave Carrie and Marsha a much longer course in how to find out what a man needed to be pleased sexually; and then she told them how to provide it. There were days each spent watching videos; and more days asking and answering Marilyn's questions. After that, each was set up with known "easy" dates for their first month at work.

Marsha heard a knock on the door. It was Carrie, who hadn't lost a bit of her looks. She was, maybe, an inch taller than Marsha. Marsha always thought Carrie was more beautiful than she was. Carrie gave Marsha her vote. Both got the best customers from Marilyn's high-end whorehouse. With the quality of escorts Marilyn provided her male customers, it was a seller's market for her. Marsha showed her a long knife that she found in her kitchen. "Think I should keep this by my bed?" she asked.

"Marsha, how deep you sleep, anyone who gets into your home will see it and he'll have the weapon. I keep a Bic pen near my bed. Why don't you do that? They're sharp, too, and an intruder isn't likely to think of it as a weapon."

"Do you think it was any of the men we spread our legs for at Marilyn's?" Marsha said.

"I can't imagine any of our former customers doing anything like that," Carrie said. "Neither of us ever had any major trouble with them, had to push our panic buttons, let alone use the tasers. "I'm wondering though, Reggie Arthurs, the one you thought you were falling in love with . . . "

"Marilyn shut that down fast, didn't she?" Marsha said. "What she told me made sense. We might have started with love but that love would always have the way we met be there to destroy our relationship. I miss him sometimes. Remember, we became whores in Cleveland so we wouldn't meet any of our customers in Pittsburgh. Reggie was from Cleveland and as far as I know still lives there. No, it couldn't be Reggie."

Carrie said, "Also, you and I always watched on the way back to Pittsburgh to see whether we were being followed. Marilyn even had her bouncers follow behind us to see whether we were being followed. Just to be sure. No, it wouldn't be Reggie Arthurs. Or any of our other clients. They wouldn't have waited this long."

"I guess I agree," Marsha said. "I don't believe the guy that's got me so worked up is one of our old customers." She put her face in her hands. "What am I going to do, Carrie? The man had to be in my home to get the vibrator. How did he get in? I'm always careful to lock the doors."

"Let's get you out of here for a while until we decide. Why not stay at the Madison Hotel until we can see where this is heading. And you must call the police. Just put a matching pair of panties and bra in the FedEx box you received and call the police, tell them what's happened—except for what really was in the box you got at work."

And Marsha did call the police. After that, she told Carrie to take a ride and come back in a half hour. If the police were still there, to just wait outside in her car until they left. After the police left Carrie could help Marsha pack and take her to the Madison, which was only blocks from WW&D's offices. She could either make the short walk to work from the Madison or work her files out of the hotel room.

"Could you send a female officer?" she asked when she called the Pittsburgh Police. The dispatcher, a man, replied, "We'll do our best. If there's one on duty and she's not working something else. Otherwise we have to send whoever's available."

Marsha couldn't make herself look at the short, stocky police officer who did show up, when he pulled her underwear out the FedEx box. After he left to canvass the neighborhood, she spied on him as he went door to door.

Officer Patterson came back to tell her that none of the neighbors saw anything suspicious. "They all say they never see anyone at your house, lady. Most of them say they don't know you, that you keep pretty much to yourself." He shrugged. "I told all your neighbors to be on the lookout for anyone suspicious. Not much more I can do. Call if you hear from the guy again." Then he left.

Jackie had watched a gorgeous young woman enter Marsha's, stay an hour or so, leave Marsha LeGrange's condo, get in a car, and drive off. He saw Officer Patterson, too. He watched him arrive, go inside, come out again, go from door to door, return to Marsha Le-Grange's and, finally, leave. The whole thing had not taken forty-five minutes.

He would love to know what she told the middle-aged cop. It had to be some kind of lie. Women like her didn't have it in them to tell the truth. He wished he could have seen the look on her face when she opened the FedEx box. He wondered if anyone else was around, maybe Carol, her secretary, if they saw the vibrator and what she told them if they did. Jackie laughed. She must have been scared shitless.

He imagined how his momma would look if something like that happened to her. It was natural for him to think of his momma when he thought of Marsha LeGrange. They were two of a kind.

Upset. That is what his momma would have been. His momma was always getting upset. Jackie dug his nails into his thighs. Janice Simpson's momma, Jackie's grandmother, "Miss Sarah" everybody called her, had always been after him not to upset Janice when she came home, saying she was probably home for a long time before she had to fly somewhere again. First when she would come from college, later from one of those fucking jobs of hers. Miss Sarah always dressed him up for his momma's visits. Told him to be on his best behavior. Why did she have to go and tell him that? He was always good. He never got in any trouble. Not when he was little.

Yet he could remember at least three times that he overheard Miss Sarah asking his momma, "Why does Jackie upset you so?" Janice Simpson never did answer. If she would have, he would have heard, listening as hard as he did. All she did was cry. Each time. His momma left earlier than she was supposed to those times, too.

What had he done to make her leave so early? Why did she act like she hated him so many times? What was so important about school, then work? Why did he upset her so? Why didn't she call or write him when she was away? That was the big mystery—what he ever did. He even asked Miss Sarah about it, what he did to make his momma leave him before she was supposed to, act like she hated him. "It wasn't you, John Lee. They called from work. She was angry that she had to leave so soon. She has to travel a lot. She's very important. They need her everywhere," Miss Sarah would tell him. "Mr. Randolph's going to take her to the airport." Then she would always look away. Not wanting to see the brokenhearted look in his eyes.

Mr. Randolph drew his thinking. That one used to be around Miss Sarah's a whole lot when Jackie was real little. Hadn't he called Mr. Randolph "Daddy" then, when he was real little? Didn't he remember Mr. Randolph telling him, "That's okay, Jackie, you can call me 'Daddy' if you want."

Wasn't that evidence Mr. Randolph was his real daddy? Fuck it. What did it matter? Old man Randolph hadn't stood by him any better than his momma had. He hadn't married her, made her stay at home, had he?

Jackie left before Carrie Stockhausen got back, so he didn't see them leave with two of Marsha's rolling suitcases. It wouldn't have mattered. He still needed a man to frame.

# *C*HAPTER TWENTY-SEVEN

Reavis, still in California, almost out of people to question, places to go. Final stop. So far, because the door was open only a crack, Reavis could only say that the manager of Lockhart Towers was young, had dark brown hair and one brown eye. The young man seemed anxious to get rid of Reavis, who could hear a baby crying inside.

Maybe his *CLIFFORD T. REAVIS, CERTIFIED INVESTIGATOR* card would help. He had a couple made, complete with gold seals—and his photo—bought at a business-supply office. It looked official, this card he issued to himself. He slipped it through the narrow opening.

The young man took it, gave it a look, and smiled at Reavis as if to say *Why didn't you tell me*, as he opened the door.

Reavis followed the apartment manager into the living room. There were little kids' toys all over and a thirty-two inch TV in the corner. College textbooks, notebooks, and pencils threatened to smother the card table in the corner of the room. The young man, who said his name was Tim Mincer, motioned for Reavis to sit, then turned and yelled, "It's okay, Sandy. It's for me."

Mincer shook his head. "Baby's been up most of the night and I've been studying for finals at Cal State. The oldest, only three, is at Grandma's until finals are over." Mincer handed Reavis's card back to him. "I'm going into law enforcement when I graduate."

Reavis smiled, nodding his approval, then looking as official as he could, handed the Cal State student Matson's letter. Mincer's lips moved as he read it. Then his eyes opened wide and his lips formed the word "murder." "What can I do to help?"

"I'm looking for an Anthony Roselli," Reavis said. "I show his address as apartment C-110 here in Lockhart Towers, but I can't get an answer when I knock on his door. His neighbors tell me they've never seen the man." Reavis lowered his voice. "By the way, Tim, this is all confidential. I can depend upon you to keep it that way, can't I?" He was letting Mincer, who wanted to go into law enforcement someday, know he was in on something big.

"Oh sure, you can depend on me," Mincer said. "Anything I hear stops with me." Giving himself a tap on his chest with a closed fist.

It was time to let the criminal justice major see how important this case really was. "Boston isn't the only police department interested in Mr. Roselli, Tim. We think he might be involved in as many as two dozen murders." He paused to let that sink in. "Frankly"—earnest look, putting his cards on the table—"I would like to take a look around his apartment."

Mincer drew back a little, started to fold his arms over his chest.

"Now." Reavis paused again, gave the college student a look and nod of the head that said he didn't have to worry. "We both know the police can't get into Roselli's apartment without a search warrant. But we also know his landlord can if he has a good enough reason." Reavis winked at Mincer, getting him ready. "I saw smoke coming out from under Roselli's door when I was there. Think you'd better take a look?"

The future police officer, eyes slowly widening, a smile growing on his face. "I might need some help putting out the fire," he said. "Would you mind helping me out, Mr. Reavis?"

"My civic duty."

After they got to Roselli's apartment and opened the door, their mouths came open in unison. Because inside there was nothing but carpet and curtains and a phone hooked up to an answering machine. That little box, Reavis would bet his last dollar, had to be Atlas Investments.

You could have heard dust settle. That was how quiet it was after Reavis played back the answering machine message recording. The only message made the whole trip worth it: "This is Thomas Wilberforce of the American National Bank in Pittsburgh, Pennsylvania," the message began. "Every six months on accounts over ten million dollars, it's the bank's practice to call and get a verbal renewal from the account holder to make sure that the account holder's written authorizations and requests to allow an employee to possess signature and account management authority over the account continues to exist." Wilberforce finished this tongue-twister by identifying the killer by his Pittsburgh name as the customer in question. The banker left Atlas his private number.

At Los Angeles International Airport, while waiting for a flight to Pittsburgh, Reavis got on his cell phone and called the Fitness Arena. A woman answered.

"I'm from out of town and I was supposed to meet a Pittsburgh customer of mine to play racquetball," he said. "But I lost the paper with the name of the place we were supposed to play. I am almost sure it was the Fitness Arena. Could you see if he's a member for me?" Then Clifford Reavis gave her the name.

She said she could and when she got back on, said, "Yes, he is. Would you like him paged, sir?"

"No need," Reavis said. "He won't be there yet. Tell you what you can do, though; you can give me his office and home numbers so I can call and tell him I'm going to be a little late."

That she could not do. Rules, she said.

At the airport, Reavis got on the Internet with his cell phone again, clicked on "Favorites," clicked again on "White Pages" and there filled in Whitfield's Pittsburgh name and only "Pittsburgh, PA" for the address. Soon he had Whitfield's full Pittsburgh address and phone number. When Reavis dialed the number all he got was an answering machine. The voice on that machine, however, was the same as the one on the call-in recordings. No doubt.

He called Matson and Bobby Doall to give them the guy's Pittsburgh alias, phone number, and address. Bobby Doall thought he knew who the guy was, but had never talked to him.

# CHAPTER TWENTY-EIGHT

Marsha had registered at the Madison Hotel, where she'd be fine with her laptop. If she couldn't face going to the office, she could work in the suite for a couple of days. The office was only three well-lit blocks away, so she could either drop by the office to pick up case files or have a legal assistant from WW&D bring them to her. If she had to, most of what she needed from the firm she could access online with her WW&D online password or her Pacer account.

Carrie was with her. "Second thoughts. Can we be sure there isn't any way the guy who's bothering you could have been one of our sex clients?" she said.

Marsha said, "Marilyn took such good precautions to protect us, Carrie. I can't see how, especially because it's been so long since we did it and when we were whores we were only in Cleveland. The guilt's still there below the surface. Maybe that's part of my reason for no love life. That's the damage. I don't, though, see this problem starting in Ohio."

Carrie said, "I'm staying with you tonight?"

"Please, if you can" Marsha said.

"Of course I can. Marsha, you're my best friend. You'd do it for me, wouldn't you?"

"Anytime," Marsha said.

Reavis's flight landed at the Pittsburgh International Airport about the same time Marsha and Carrie were getting settled into the Madison Hotel. As soon as he got off the plane he was on his cell to Peggy.

"Clifford, are you home?" She sounded happy to hear him.

"Almost," he answered. "I'm at the airport. Hungry?"

"A little. I could eat."

"Good. As soon as I pick up the Monte Carlo out of long-term parking I'll be on my way to see you. I'll pick up some calzones at Vincent's on the way in and bring them over. That is . . . if I'm invited."

"You get over here. Invited? I've missed you, you big hunk."

Reavis stopped at Vincent's Pasta and Pizza, just off the Greentree Exit of the Parkway West (aka I-376 West), where he picked up a steak calzone with extra peppers, extra cheese, and extra onions for himself; for Peggy, he got a regular steak calzone. He'd probably eat half of hers, too.

Peggy lived in Mt. Lebanon, a suburb of Pittsburgh, about a fifteen-minute drive from Vincent's. She was at the door waiting, arms outstretched, then pulling him against her red soft cotton T-shirt. He felt dumb, holding a bag of calzones and getting an erection.

"It feels like you missed me," she said. "Your face is a little flushed. I'll bet you took one of your little blue pills, too. Did you?"

"Guilty," he said. "Devil that I am."

"Well, you'll just have to wait. I want to hear all about your trip." Her eyes shined as she looked up at his. "I'll make the wait up to you."

Her kitchen was compact, mostly lavender, paisley-design wallpaper. She had a vase of red roses on the kitchen table. Then there was the stainless steel, the sink top, her carving knife set, utensils hanging from stainless steel hooks.

She set two plates and two sixteen-ounce cans of Iron City Beer on the table. He took the calzones out of their bag and put each one on the plates Peggy had out for them.

"Clifford, how was California?" Peggy, her face a little flushed, was sitting across the table from him, her calzone only halfway to her mouth, regarding him with a worried look.

*Why the worried look?*

Peggy's eyes narrowed; she continued looking steadily, right into his eyes. The look still a worried look, but now motioning him to answer the question, *How was California?*

He told her all he'd found out, including Whitfield's Pittsburgh alias and address.

"It could be four or five of the men I see at the Arena," she said. "There's a lot of big, good-looking men there. Two or three I know have only been there for a short while. I don't recognize the name."

He looked at her, feeling good about how close he was getting.

Peggy put her calzone down. She hadn't eaten much. She was frowning. "And his next victim?" she asked. "Do you know who she's going to be?"

"I will, if she calls the police. Pat Tazer is looking into that for me. He may already have it. The killer almost always takes something personal from his victims' bedrooms. Then he calls them, says he has whatever it is he took. Next he sends whatever he took back to them. Mail or FedEx. He must like to terrify them before he kills them. But not all of them report it to the police. Stacy Bonato, for example, thought it was another resident at the hospital, some guy playing a joke on her. She never did call the cops."

Peggy leaned forward, brushed quickly at her hair. He was aware of a tightness around her eyes and mouth. She said, "So maybe you find out who his next victim will be." She paused. He saw that her hands were clenched, the fingers white. "Then what?"

*Then what, indeed.* Reavis was silent. Thinking. He remembered how it had been with Paul Petro. There had been no question that time. He would kill Petro. But he had not cared about himself that time. What did he have to lose then? Things were different now. Now he had Peggy, someone, something—a lot—to lose.

The two men, Beth's murderer, this new killer, would not separate down deep in himself where it mattered. Even though he knew it wasn't Petro's intent to do all the killing he did.

What would happen if he did try to kill this guy? Was that what he was going to do? For some crazy reason did he need to kill this man? Like with Petro. If so, how was he going to do it? The guy was young, strong, and killed with a knife. Clifford Reavis was neither young nor strong. Could not fight off a knife.

He was staring at the napkin that he was twisting in his hands. Now he looked at Peggy. Her elbows were on the table, her hands were fists and she was trembling.

"I don't know, Peg. I don't know how I am going to stop him."

"*You* don't know how you are going to stop him? What does stopping him have to do with you?" she said. "That's not your job. Your job is to help Newton Sylvester. What about him?"

He hadn't been giving much thought to Newton Sylvester lately. His thoughts had been on the women, their killer. He nodded, thinking about Sylvester. "That is one good thing. Sylvester will be all right. We'll get copies of all the call-in recordings and I know they will all match up on voiceprint analysis. That, and the fact that the murders all happened in the same way, the same kind of evidence, and how Sylvester did on the lie detector test will work in his favor (even though the polygraph results are inadmissible, they are convincing). And if the voiceprint expert says it's the same guy on all the call-in recordings, then Tim and I are pretty sure the DA's will agree to postpone the pending trials, including Mr. Sylvester's."

"Then that should be it, shouldn't it, Clifford?" She was staring at him. "You are done. Right?" Her eyes were wide, searching his, wanting him to say that was it, that he was through with the case.

He couldn't meet her eyes. "He's not going to stop, you know."

She reached across the table, got his right forearm and tugged at it. "Clifford, look at me."

He did not want to but she waited him out.

"What did you just say?"

"I said he is not going to stop."

Peggy stood, hands on her hips. "That has nothing to do with you. Can't the police stop him?"

"No."

"Why not?"

"If they arrested him, which I can't see them doing with just the evidence of the call-in recordings, some similarities in evidence in the cases, the fact that he was in each town at the time of the murders," he said. "He would be out on bail in hours."

"Bail. No judge would let him out on bail."

"Peg," he said, "one of the things they don't teach you in law school is that when judges look at setting bail they look at how strong the prosecution's case is. How strong do you think the case is here? Some voiceprints? They are not the same as a confession. He's not confessing on those recordings. What's left? Bring Toby Constantine and Art Manning in to testify he was in Boston and Phoenix at the time of the murders there? A judge might not even allow them to testify, deciding that their testimony was far less relevant than it was prejudicial. There are no witnesses who can put him at any crime scene." Reavis shook his head. "No, Peg, there just isn't enough of a case against him to hold him without bail. I can't even see the police arresting him, let alone the

DA getting an indictment on that little evidence."

"But that's not your problem, is it?" Shaking her head. "No. No. No." The look she gave him told him not to make it his problem, that she didn't want that.

His chair made scraping sounds as he pulled it closer to the table. He was slow to go on with what he said next. "It has something to do with Beth, Peggy."

She moved from where she was standing and walked slowly around the table to him, putting both hands on his shoulders. "You've never talked to me about her."

"I know . . . maybe . . . maybe now is the time." He put his head down. "It isn't just she died, I loved her, she was pregnant with our baby . . . " He turned to look at her. "Do you know what happened to her?"

She nodded. "Yes. I called Pat Tazer. He told me a drunk killed her and the baby in a car accident."

"Did he tell you anything else?"

"No. He wouldn't. He said there was more but that you would have to be the one to tell me that."

Reavis didn't know where to start, or even if he should. "There is more." He paused, trying to gauge how she would react. Then he dove right in. "I tried to kill him, the man who killed Beth. Not just once. More than once." He stopped talking, worried what she'd think about him now, not knowing if he could say the rest.

She took his head in her hands and gently lifted it so that they were eye to eye. "You were in a rage, Clifford. He killed the woman you loved. Your unborn child. Anger is one of the feelings you get when someone dear to you dies. That's how I felt about Harry's dying of cancer, making me a young widow with three little girls to raise. I was angry at him for smoking. I was angry at the cigarette companies. I was angry at everything. . ."

"I was more than angry. I was enraged!" His voice cracked.

She still gently held his head in both hands; still looked at him eye to eye. He didn't know if he could say the big part, about waiting too long before trying to push Beth out of the way of Petro's Jaguar. How that meant he was a coward. *What would she think of him if he told her that?*

"Tell me," she whispered. "It will be okay."

"I think I waited too long." He heard himself groan. "I'm pretty sure I froze for a fraction of a second before I jumped at her to push her out of the way. I think I could have saved Beth if I'd been a fraction of a second faster." He couldn't look at Peggy.

He pushed back his chair, rose, stood there, knowing he was losing it. He bolted away from her and into the living room where he threw himself onto the couch and pulled a pillow over his head. He was crying now, the loud, moaning kind. And he was ashamed. Now he could never look at Peggy, not after what he told her and now doing all this crying.

It wasn't long before he felt her sit beside him. He pulled the pillow tighter around his ears. She gently removed it, put her hands on him. Her face brushed against his and he could feel that it was wet, too. Her breath was warm in his ear as she told him over and over how much she loved and respected him, how bad she felt about his hurting and that he was no coward.

Later, he was saying it was goofy, but he knew it had something to do with not saving Beth that made him need to try to save Whitfield's next victim. That it had to be him doing the saving because, if the police were let in on it, Whitfield would probably get on to them and get away. And that wherever he went he would keep on killing.

She was saying how she agreed the killer wouldn't stop, that she was scared for Reavis, that she now understood it had to be him to stop the madman who looked like a businessman. He would think later that this was the first time he could really believe she loved him.

When he was all settled down, she nudged him, saying, "You want to finish what we started when you just got here. Let's check how well that little blue pill is working."

Clifford Reavis just grinned. What a wonderful change of pace. His mood and train of thought did a one-eighty.

"I've got the red lace set on," she said.

"I was hoping."

Reavis took her hand and led her to the bedroom and she took her T-shirt off to show him the pretty red lace. Then she reached back and unsnapped her bra, letting it fall to the floor. And rushed into Reavis's arms. *Perfection.* Clifford Reavis took care of the panties. And—not long after that—the woman who was in them.

Afterwards, Peggy fell asleep. He reached over to brush some still-moist hair off her forehead and she made a little sound. Young people, he thought, much more relaxed now, smiling to himself—*they think they invented it.*

Tonight was the first time he told Peggy he loved her. Oh, he figured she knew, all right; but this was the first time he ever came out and said the words. After he said them the first time, though, he kept saying them.

It killed him to leave her love-filled bedroom. But he had to.

# CHAPTER TWENTY-NINE

Reavis was up early—for him. First thinking he was still at Peggy's. Then realizing, no such luck. There was a message from Pat Tazer on his answering machine. "Hey, Bones, I've called you on your cell and the call wouldn't go through and this is my third call on your land line." Tazer's voice got louder. "I've got something for you. The next victim is a neighbor of yours. Marsha LeGrange is her name. She's safe for now. I'll tell you why when I talk to you."

Reavis called Tazer. "Shoot," he told the big cop when Tazer got on the phone.

Tazer brought him up to date. Told him the next victim was going to be Marsha LeGrange. After he'd finished, Reavis told him he still wanted to come in, read the file and get his thinking on the case. Also, that he might have something else for Tazer to look up.

Next he called Whitfield's number about ten thirty and got the man still at home.

"Is Ruth in?" Reavis said.

"I'm sorry, sir, but you must have the wrong number."

Reavis apologized and hung up. The man who answered the phone was the same man whom he'd heard on all the call-in recordings, but that was no surprise.

A half hour later Reavis pulled his Monte Carlo into the upscale three-building condominium development where Whitfield lived. He was listening to a song on one of his CDs, Johnny and Joe singing "Over the Mountain." He lowered the volume and took in Whitfield's building, the middle one of three.

Each building front was a combination of brick, made to look weathered, and what looked to be stained wood, close to the brick color. There were ten to twelve units in each building. There were no garages, just carports. He drove slowly past each one, speaking the plate numbers into his digital recorder.

After he had them all, he called Tazer and told the man he was heading for the police investigation bureau on the North Side.

He needed to know which car was Whitfield's, his thinking being that as long as he could find the killer's car, then he would always know where the man who drove it was.

Tazer was on the phone and scribbling something when Reavis got to his office. When he saw Reavis, he put his hand over the mouthpiece, waved his hand at a chair, said, "Sit your skinny ass down," and went back to talking and scribbling.

After the big man hung up, Reavis told him about Arizona and California in detail, and told him the killer's Pittsburgh alias and address. He said to Pat Tazer, who had said not a word while getting filled in, "What about this Marsha LeGrange?"

For an answer, Tazer looked down at the paper in front of him. He pushed it at Reavis, who read:

Marsha LeGrange
1812 Sydney Street
Pittsburgh, Pa. 15203

Tazer looked at Reavis, raised his eyebrows. "She's a neighbor of yours, Clifford, thirty-two, a lawyer over at Wilkins, Wilkins & Dunn in the UPMC Building. I got in touch with the investigating officer, who says she's out-of-this-world beautiful and has a body to match."

Pat leaned back in his chair. "She got a call at her home while you were in Arizona. Didn't do anything about it then. But when she got her underwear sent to her at work, that's when she called us. She's scared, because someone had to get into her house to get the underwear. She's staying at the Madison Hotel downtown until she can decide what to do about the intruder."

Tazer pushed himself straight up in the chair again, leaned and stretched his big body, and grabbed two papers stapled together, the "Police Incident Report." Handed it to Reavis.

"How long you think she has before he makes a move on her?" Tazer asked.

Reavis said, "It could be anytime." Knowing the victim's name was changing how he felt. His stomach was beginning to knot; he could feel sweat trickle down his spine. He was not sure if he was scared or excited. Maybe both. He set his recorder on Tazer's desk, nodded at the tablet in front of the big man, getting ready to push the *play* button on the recorder. "Write down these plate numbers, Pat."

Neither said anything as Pat Tazer punched the numbers into the computer behind him. Reavis walked around the desk and watched as information on each plate came up. He didn't recognize any of them.

"We strike out?" Pat Tazer said.

One of the cars was owned by National Car Rental. "Call National," Reavis said, "and ask who rented the Town Car."

After Tazer got off the phone with National, he turned the paper he wrote on so Reavis could see. The name on the paper was Thomas Whitfield. The address: Anthony Roselli's in California. He'd shown National a California driver's license for identification.

"Taze." Reavis took his time. "Tell me what you think. I figure . . . I make this official, you guys stake him out or something, he'll probably spot them and get out of town. Then we probably lose him long enough for him to get two or three more women in some other city. He'll come back and get Marsha LeGrange, though. The man's obsessive. Me. I don't look like a cop. I think I can get close to him."

Tazer, a couple times looking at Reavis, a couple times looking away, didn't say anything right away. Finally, not saying a word about Reavis putting him on the spot with his employer if anyone ever found out what he knew and when: "Yeah, this isn't one for us. But what the fuck are you going to do? Even if he doesn't spot you?"

That was the question. "I've got a gun." He looked at Pat Tazer, waiting for a reaction. Getting none, he said, "I can always shoot the bastard."

All Pat did was look back. Finally, he said, "Clifford?"

"Yeah?"

"Will you use it?"

"I went after Petro, didn't I?"

Pat Tazer continued looking him over, gauging him. "That was different. Petro killed your wife and child."

"I don't know." Reavis removed his glasses and rubbed his eyes. "It should be different, but I just don't know. I'm getting the same kind of feelings I got with Petro."

Tazer was leaning on the desk again. "You just can't wait outside where he lives and pop him."

"That's what I want to do. But that makes me a murderer. First degree. But I could catch him doing something," Reavis said slowly, working it out as he talked. "I could shoot him then. Couldn't I?"

"Catch him *doing* something?" Tazer said. "Doing what? What do you mean?"

"Something like breaking in to where Marsha LeGrange lives. Which he is going to do. If there's anything I am sure about it's that he will attempt to rape and murder Marsha LeGrange in her condominium. That's what he did with all the rest—raped and murdered them in their homes. And it will be a lot closer to sooner than later with Marsha Le-Grange. He's overdue and now—no doubt at all—we're sure he's here."

Slowly, Pat rose and walked around to the side of the desk, stopped, now looking at Reavis, who had moved back to where he was sitting. "Sounds like a plan." Pat Tazer looking like he wanted to shake a finger at him. "If you shoot him, make sure he dies." He was not smiling.

That's what it came down to: catching Whitfield breaking into the young woman's place, Reavis going in right behind him, being able to pull the trigger and not missing. But could he? Would he be in time to save Marsha LeGrange, or would he freeze and be too late? Again.

On the way home he got his cell out and called Bobby Doall to fill him in on what alias Whitfield was using in Pittsburgh and to give him Marsha LeGrange's name and address.

"I know her, Clifford! I know her!"

"Talk to me, Bobby."

"You would pay to watch her work out. She is outstanding. I've talked to her a couple times. In fact I've been putting some slow moves on her. She's good people. She's an attorney and from what I hear, a good one."

"I thought you didn't know the names of many of the people who worked out there, Bobby?"

"For someone who looks like her, I make exceptions."

"How about the killer? Do you know him?"

"Only a little," Bobby said. "The guy's put together. That's about it. We may have talked, probably did at one time or the other, but I don't know. Remember, I couldn't recognize his voice on the call-in tapes."

"Okay, Bobby, be ready for my next call. I'll probably need your help to come up with a plan."

"You've got my number," Bobby said.

Jackie, who had not seen Reavis speaking the Town Car's license number into his recorder, had been imagining how terrified Marsha LeGrange must be. And he was loving it. Getting whatever she wanted. Because she looked good and smelled nice. Marsha LeGrange, who told people what she thought they wanted to hear. People like Lester Wilkins. Just trying to beat some guy out of a promotion. Lying if she had to. Anything it took. Just like his momma and Marie Martieri—say something, anything, as long as it got her what she wanted.

After thinking about Marsha LeGrange and his momma, he thought back to his second year of law school, when he had finally put everything together about women like his momma and Marsha LeGrange. The bitch who finally clued him in was Marie Martieri, who was beautiful in a dark Italian way and owned a superior body. Only about a third of the students in his law school class were women when Jackie went to law school. Now, he had heard, lots of times law classes had more women in them than men.

He had done real well his first year of law school and somehow Marie Martieri had found out, started sucking around him, bugging him to help her in the evidence and tax courses. She asked him over to her place to help her study, fucking his brains out that very first night. Climbed all over him five minutes after he walked into her apartment. Telling him she'd been dying to fuck him since she first saw him the previous year.

Then one day in the law library Jackie Simpson overheard Todd Morrison, a rich kid from old Boston money, and Marie Martieri, talking. "Marie," Jackie remembered Todd Morrison saying, "what is it with you and Jackie Simpson? You lowering your standards? Hitting on some redneck."

He would never forget her laugh, way too loud for the law library. "Him. Nothing," she said to Todd Morrison. "I always tell you everything, honey." She gave a vicious laugh.

Todd Morrison, whom she let everyone know she was going with, said, "That asshole. He's got brains and looks, but you can't educate class." *He*, meaning Jackie, the one without class. They both laughed.

"I'm just using him to help me get through this damn place. You don't think I'm letting him have anything that's all yours, do you?"

*One lie after another.* There she was, admitting she was only using him. Then Jackie watched as she put her arm around Morrison—with other people around, something she never did with Jackie. And they shut the books they had in front of them and left them on the table. Then went off to Todd Morrison's place.

Jackie was already good at getting into people's homes by then and that is what he did later that night—got into Todd Morrison's apartment. Marie Martieri and Todd Morrison were there, Morrison passed out in his bed from screwing and whatever they'd been drinking. The scent of marijuana was also strong. Marie Martieri, who was not in much better shape, but awake, was tugging on her black panties while she sat swaying on a bedroom chair.

Jackie decided to show himself, and Marie, not at all frightened, struggling to stand, her panties half on, laughed at him—her fool. He took three long steps over to her and pounded her in the face. Breaking off some teeth. That changed her attitude and she started begging him not to hurt her, mess her face up. His answer was to crunch her nose with his second punch, throw her over his shoulder, and take her into the bathroom to give her a look at that lying face with the broken nose and front teeth missing. She was saying she would do anything if he wouldn't smash her face again. That set him off even more, just as much as—he was certain—Marsha LeGrange's begging would when he got to her.

He would never forget the look in Marie Martieri's eyes when she saw herself in the mirror. Then it was back to the bedroom with her still over his shoulder. Todd Morrison, stoned, passed-out-drunk, never moving, not even when Jackie raised a leg and kicked him off the bed and onto the floor. So he could rape two-faced—now broken faced—Marie Martieri.

Jackie dumped her on to the bed and did what he wanted to her for a long time, watching the fear in her eyes as he slammed into her, then watching those lying eyes go dead as he kept at her, making her do anything he wanted her to do, the bitch bleeding all over Jackie's cock and Todd Morrison's sheets.

After he'd had enough, he pounded her unconscious, got off her, and went to the kitchen. He was on his own high now. Higher than he ever knew he could get. He got a knife. Who knows how many times he slammed it into her? What he did remember was that Todd Morrison never moved, lying there on the floor, passed out.

Jackie lifted Morrison and dumped him on Marie Martieri's body, moved him around on her bloody dead body, placed the bloody knife in Morrison's right hand, and squeezed Morrison's fingers and hand around the knife handle.

All Todd Morrison did was murmur something about a blow job.

When Jackie got to his apartment, he put all his blood-soaked clothes and shoes into a plastic bag, which he drove across town to throw in a dumpster.

Next he called the campus police on Todd Morrison, saying he heard a woman screaming in Morrison's apartment . . . and Todd Morrison did ten years for voluntary manslaughter. Never got to practice law.

He could remember grinning the whole way home, knowing Marie Martieri would never again tell him, "Come on over this afternoon, Jackie. I'm horny." The afternoon, so she could be with Todd Morrison later. The whole time she was fucking Jackie, she was after Todd Morrison and his money. Todd Morrison? Never again would Todd Morrison get away with calling him white trash, giving him those looks like John Lee Simpson was a nobody.

That first time with Marie and Todd, it was like he was getting his momma and Stuart Randolph back in a way, his momma for abandoning him all the time, looking at him with that hate in her eyes sometimes, conning him into thinking she was back to stay every time she came back home. He laughed to himself. That she loved him. *Fat chance!* And rich Stuart Randolph for taking her away from Jackie.

Even then he knew the real reason why he felt so good about Marie and Todd. That's why he knew he wasn't crazy. It only took that once to show him how good he could feel, and how to get that feeling. He was taking down rich, important people—like Todd Morrison was bound to be, and Mr. Randolph already was—and he was shutting the lying mouths of the women, women like his momma.

Jackie let out a laugh that would have frozen the sun. What he did with his victims, the men as well as the women, made how he felt about things ease up. Made him feel like a big deal. Take care of the hate. Get him loose. It was better than booze and dope. It wasn't any more complex than that.

Knowing what he could do to people like Todd Morrison and Marie Martieri gave him a feeling of power—lifted him up. At first, he didn't actually have to be doing it; just knowing he could was all he needed. By simply looking for types, feeling the hate, raping and killing the ones who lied like his momma, framing some arrogant prick, Jackie Simpson controlled how good he felt.

Over the last couple of years, though, he realized he had become addicted to doing it, no more than three in every city when he traveled, now really hooked, working hard to reach the peak of feeling he got with Marie Martieri and Todd Morrison.

Marsha LeGrange would give him the best feeling ever. Jackie sure needed her to hook up with some guy like Lester Wilkins—*yesterday*! Jackie's needs were strong. He needed this next fix bad and soon.

That's what he was thinking and feeling when he got Clifford Reavis's wrong number call for a woman named Ruth.

# $\mathcal{C}$HAPTER THIRTY

After leaving Pat Tazer, and talking to Bobby Doall, Reavis called Tim Garrity. Newton Sylvester's attorney said his voiceprint expert would have the analyses conducted pretty soon. Even if the call-in recordings matched, Garrity thought it could be tough getting the DA to drop the charges against Sylvester. "Best bet," Tim said, "is to keep postponing his trial. See what more, and better, evidence Reavis could get on Judith Jenkins's real killer. We've had preliminary talks and the DA seems to be willing to postpone."

"Are you going to tell Sylvester?" Reavis asked.

"I told him that your theories and what you've learned are the reason I want to postpone the trial. I don't want to get his hopes up until I'm absolutely sure."

After talking to Tim Garrity, he called Bobby Doall again. "Bobby could you get your buddies who work at the Fitness Arena to check out the days and times both Whitfield and Marsha LeGrange worked out and get back to me?"

Reavis then reached for the phone to call Matson. But then a thought struck him. Why not get a recording of the killer's voice? That would really pin it down. He could call Whitfield, using some pretext, and record the conversation. Which was not legal. A technicality that he would worry about later. All he had to do was figure out a good enough reason to keep him on the phone long enough to get a good sample of his voice. What he finally decided to do was pretend he was taking a survey on television viewing habits.

"Six-eight-seven, three-three-seven-seven," was the way the man Reavis had tracked from coast to coast answered his phone for the second time.

"Mr. Crawshaw?" Reavis asked.

"No, I'm sorry, you must have the wrong number," Whitfield said.

"Well, sir . . . actually . . . anyone can help me. My name's Clifton Weston. I'm retired, pick up extra money doing television audience surveys. Make five dollars a completed survey. I just have a few questions if . . ."

"I'll be glad to help you make your five dollars," the killer said. "Fire away."

Reavis had his digital recorder hooked up to the phone before he made the call. An idea began to form. A way he could learn more about the man. "Okay, these will just be general type questions, sir. I won't even need your name." *That should put him at ease,* Reavis thought. He looked at his hand, the one holding the phone. The fingers were white. He was worried the man on the other end of the phone would hang up. He wanted to have more than a sample of Whitfield's voice now. Now, he wanted to find out as much as he could about him.

Reavis was telling himself to take it easy, keep the tightness he felt out of his voice. "Let me get my question sheet here. Bear with me, please. I had it in front of me a minute ago. One minute, please. Don't ever get old like me. Oh, here."

Reavis started asking his questions, general ones, about the killer's age, how long he'd lived at his current address, the number of people in his family. Was there a change in the killer's voice when he asked about family size? Reavis couldn't be sure.

"The next question," Reavis said, "is about income. I'll give you the ranges. And he did.

"Over $250,000," Whitfield answered.

"Wow." Reavis tried to make the wow sound spontaneous. "Single, young and making that kind of money." Then as though he were catching himself: "Gee, I'm sorry, sir; I just got carried away. It's not often I get to interview anyone making *that* kind of money." Making himself sound worried: "We're not supposed to say things like that, you know. It just slipped out." *Come on, you bastard, take the bait. Start talking about yourself.*

"No problem," Whitfield said. "I've been lucky, I guess. I work for a California investment company. Caught on with them right after law school."

There was the law school again, like in Boston and Phoenix.

Whitfield was warming up. "I guess you could say that I grew up with the company. I was lucky enough to recommend some situations that turned out well."

This killer, this man who was supposed to be making over a quarter million a year from a company that was just an answering machine, but who Reavis knew had over ten million in one bank account in Pittsburgh and five million in another in Boston, was telling him about "recommending situations," how big a man he was.

"The company," the killer went on, "showed its appreciation by giving me regular promotions. Now I'm something they call the vice-president of acquisitions."

"Vice-president?" Reavis put as much awe into his voice as he could.

"Yes," Whitfield said. "It's the kind of job that has me doing a lot of things. Right now, for instance, I'm here in Pittsburgh looking into real estate opportunities, distress situations, now that commercial real estate is taking such a hit. Not as much here in Pittsburgh, though, but more than usual for here. I've located some interesting opportunities.

It is usually left to me to make the final decision about moving forward on those kind of situations."

Again, the same kind of story he used in Boston and Arizona. Didn't he change anything? A vice-president, that's how he had to see himself, as some big-deal officer in a company. "Vice-president of acquisitions," Reavis said. "That sounds like a lot of responsibility. You must be under a lot of pressure. How do you handle it all?"

"What was that?" The man sounded guarded now.

So Reavis backed off. "I was just saying that you must be awfully busy."

"You're right," Whitfield said. "It does keep me pretty busy." Sounding like he was more at ease now that they were back to questions about work only, how busy he was, not about how he could take pressure.

"I'm jealous," Reavis said.

"I've just been lucky."

*Yeah, you bastard,* Reavis caught himself thinking. *But soon your luck is going to run out.* Once again, his emotions were working on him: Anger. Rage. Not to mention hate. He couldn't let them show. Not while he had a chance to probe Whitfield's motivations, maybe find a weakness in this man who, so far, had raped, murdered and framed so many human beings with impunity. "I would like to know what kind of television programs a man like you watches."

*That's it, the kind of programs he watches, get some ideas from knowing that.* "That's what this next batch of questions is about, too, about the television programs you watch, how many hours a week you watch TV, things like that."

Reavis had a thought: somewhere he could go with this. "Let's see. I lost my place again. Oh, here it is. How many hours a week do you watch television? The answers can be: less than five, five to ten, ten to twenty, twenty to thirty, or more than thirty hours a week."

"With my schedule, less than five."

"You really must be busy. I guess you have to be pretty selective about what you watch then. That's what this next question's about. What is your favorite kind of program. Let's see, the categories are: *news, reality shows, sitcoms, cop/detective*, and *other.*"

Where he was heading: After Whitfield's answer, Reavis would ask him which shows he liked, what it was he liked about them—questions whose answers might reveal something about this madman.

"Other," the killer answered.

"Other?"

"Yes, I like shows about animals—National Geographic specials, programs like that."

"Frankly, I'm surprised," Reavis said. "That's kind of an unexpected answer from a man like you." He was gently prodding the man to tell him why he liked those shows.

"Not really so odd," Whitfield responded. "The way animals act, live together, I think, is similar in many ways to how we act toward one another. How many times have you heard people use the expression 'survival of the fittest'? Take a look around you. What happens to the young? The old? The poor? I'll tell you what; they get swallowed up, stepped on, eaten alive. And by whom?" he said. "The rich. The powerful."

It came all the way through the phone, about the rich and powerful; the hate, it was in his voice. And then it hit Reavis. *That's why he frames men like Newton Sylvester? Hate. But why the hate?*

" . . . Some animals hunt in packs," Whitfield was saying, "others, alone. Let me ask you this? What's the corporation takeover specialist other than a lone hunter? How is he any different from a jungle cat? Quietly stalking what he wants?"

There it was in the interviewee's voice. As though he were saying, "See, that's what I respect. That's who I am." Reavis sat back. *Or am I,* Reavis asked himself, *getting carried away by this survey?*

With a change in tone to one laden with scorn, the killer went on. "Other animals hunt in packs. Take politicians, for example. And I'm not only talking about men who run for office. I am talking about political bosses, the money men, too. Have you ever been around them when they were all sitting there deciding how to split the money pot—who would get what?" Reavis thought he could hear just a trace of a southern accent now. "You know, political contributions, payoffs, whatever?"

Now he was positive the killer framed rich, powerful men because he hated all of them. What else would Whitfield tell him? Keep flattering him, Reavis told himself, keep him talking and don't let him realize that he's talking about himself.

"You've really opened my eyes," Reavis said next. "I never looked at things that way before." Then, laying it on: "But I guess that's why I'm on pension, downsized from a mid-level management job, and you're a vice-president of some big company. Say, what is your favorite kind of animal show?"

"I like the ones about the big cats."

*Just like you, the panthers and the leopards*, Reavis wanted to say. *Sure. All you're doing is living the law of the jungle. Kill or be killed. Hunt or be hunted.* Crazy? Sure. But the man he was talking to was out of whack. A madman posing as a corporate executive.

The tangled way he felt about Beth Reavis's murderer and how he felt about this guy, once again, was getting to Reavis. He could feel the rage building and he made himself hold the phone more loosely, slow his breathing, as a way of keeping it in.

And he took a deep breath before he asked the next question. What about Whitfield's family? According to Toby Constantine and Art Manning, the killer had shown an abnormal interest in the way their wives were with their kids. Reavis believed that how Whitfield felt about his mother might hold the key to why he killed.

"Are you still there?" Reavis asked. The man said he was. "Sorry, I've been thinking about all that you've said. But how can you compare the family life of animals to ours." *Go, you son of a bitch*, he willed Whitfield, *tell me what was so different about your family, the way you grew up, that made you kill. Or were you, like your jungle cats, simply born to kill?*

Reavis could hear the man's breathing getting faster. *Go on, answer me, you piece of shit.*

"What do you mean—compare animal families to human families?" There was a hesitation about Whitfield's speech.

"Well, you know what I mean," Reavis said. "Sometimes the male animals don't even hang around long enough for the female to have her babies; and the females of some species kick the kids out as soon as they can." Reavis realized that he was leaning forward in his chair.

"Not most animal mothers. They stay with their young until the cubs can go out on their own." Reavis could detect a whiny quality entering Whitfield's voice that hadn't been there before.

Reavis was having a tough time controlling his breathing, was breathing faster than normal again. Leaning more, too. In combat. "Well, I'm no expert." He was no longer trying to be the inoffensive survey taker. "But it was my impression that animals force their young to fend for themselves, many times too early. Just abandon them. You know. Leave them all by themselves. Like you said. Survival of the fittest. When you look at it that way it doesn't sound so cruel, does it?"

"*No.*" A shout. "*Not* most mothers. Most mothers stay by their young till they're big. They never leave them. They take care of their young. They love them!"

Reavis was standing now. "Aw c'mon, sir," he said. Making sure the man heard the doubt in his voice. "No. That's where people and animals are different. How many humans throw their kids out, abandon them. With human mothers it's a matter of unconditional love?"

He didn't wait for an answer. "Hell, it's human nature." *Concentrate on mothers*, he had to tell himself; it's women he kills. "Especially for mothers, to protect their children, even long after they've grown up. Human mothers love their kids, want to be with them."

"Not mine!" Whitfield wailing now.

"Oh?" Reavis said softly.

But there would be no more. Whitfield had hung up.

Clifford Reavis sat for a long time, playing and replaying the recording he made. Jungle. Big cats. Rich, powerful men. Law school. Vice-president. His mother abandoned him. Reavis heard the hate. That whine Reavis heard in the psychopath's voice when he screamed, "Not mine!"

He no sooner got off the phone with Whitfield than Bobby Doall called back.

"Clifford, the guy works out only on Mondays, Wednesdays, and Fridays. Marsha LeGrange varies her schedule, but they've been working out a fair amount on the same day and at the same time. Except when he was out of town for the Boston and Phoenix murders."

Reavis told Bobby about the conversation he just had with Whitfield. Bobby said, "I think Whitfield's mother abandoned him. That he had to think she didn't love him. Even hated him. Maybe she abandoned him for some rich guy."

After getting off the phone with Bobby, weighing what Whitfield had to say, Bobby's thoughts about the man, he caught himself smiling. He was learning a lot about Whitfield.

But would he be able to use it?

# CHAPTER THIRTY-ONE

Reavis was still playing the recording of Whitfield when Matson called. He told Matson about the hate Whitfield showed for rich men and his belief that Whitfield felt abandoned, maybe even hated, by his mother. And they talked about how they might use what he had learned.

Matson agreed with Bobby and Reavis, saying that they should be able to use Whitfield's feelings about his mother to throw him off, give Reavis an edge. Matson continued pressing the idea on Reavis about trying to catch the killer breaking into Marsha LeGrange's and shooting him. Getting an edge on the man by using what Reavis knew about him and how he felt about his mother to weaken the man.

Matson then said, "One thing before I forget: I got his picture in from California DMV. It's pretty grainy. I showed it to the bank manager up here and he said, yeah, he was pretty sure that's the Whitfield he knew. Toby Constantine, the apartment manager, said the same thing."

Matson laughed. "What's it matter? Pretty soon, you're going to know what he looks like, anyway. I'll e-mail it to you now. Oh, one other thing. Seattle's call-in recordings have come in. I listened to them. It's the same guy. Big surprise. I'll get them to you for Tim Garrity's man.

I'll send the rest to you as soon as they get here."

Reavis said that he would be looking for the DMV picture. "Bobby checked out their records and learned Whitfield and the LeGrange woman work out the same days."

Reavis went on, "Just like everything else he does, always the same. Even to who, how, and when he kills. You look at every case. Not a thing different. I'll bet he's the kind of guy who, if he brushes his teeth before shaving every day, wouldn't feel right all day if that day he shaved first. Tomorrow is Wednesday. I guarantee he will be at the Fitness Arena tomorrow night for a workout. I'll be there to meet him and try out a few of our ideas."

Next he got Bobby Doall on his cell again and they agreed on a time to meet before heading for the Fitness Arena.

An hour earlier, Jackie had slammed the phone down on that survey taker. Yet he still could not shake the bad feeling that call left with him. Not good. He was the kind of person who needed to keep things under control.

He rose, went to the bathroom. There were some spots on the mirror that he had somehow missed, which were more evidence that he had not been operating right. He could not put up with things like spots on the mirror. He got the Windex and a clean T-shirt, went back and wiped them off. He looked in the medicine cabinet; moved some bottles around, so they would be in the right place. Everything seemed out of place. The closer he looked, the more he saw—hairs on the toilet bowl, in the bathtub, soap not centered in the soap tray.

Next he went to the bedroom and kitchen and straightened everything out there.

*Was he really that out of control?*

Learning that Lester Wilkins would be in Atlanta for probably months had almost put him over the edge. The night after he found out, he went to Marsha LeGrange's. And almost dragged her out of her bed. He went for her three times. Who knew what held him back? After that night, he had to force himself to stay out of her house for the next two days. That's what he made himself do. To test his will. Otherwise, he wasn't sure he could keep from raping and murdering her with no one to frame.

Even Nadine had come in for a week. Nadine was as perfect a woman as he could find. But some nights, even when Nadine was in town, he still visited Marsha LeGrange's condo late at night.

Exercising usually helped him when he got uptight, but it was Tuesday. He had just worked out yesterday. Working out two days in a row didn't give your muscles time to recover, build back up. He took a long, deep breath, letting it out in a sigh, knowing he would be drawn to Marsha LeGrange's condo. That gave him some relief, thinking how terrified she must still be from what he'd already done to her, with the call and the FedEx package, but it kept him pressing for the fix, too, needing to smack her around, get her under him, do anything he ordered her to do. It worked both ways.

Looking around his home, he thought: *Dirty dishes, everything out of place. Marsha LeGrange is the reason things are getting out of order.* Finally, smiling now, he thought, *but I am getting to her, too.*

Jackie let himself into Marsha's and padded all through the apartment. He could smell her scent everywhere, strongest in the bedroom. It had a flowery kind of smell, like blossoms.

He went through her dresser drawer and all her closets, poking into her secret places. Her journal was gone now. She must have gotten rid of it. Like his momma, all she cared about was work, getting ahead. That's all she ever used to write about in that journal. Other than Lester Wilkins and Mel Sadecki. He liked where she wrote about being called the *Virgin Marsha*. She really hated that nickname, the *Virgin Marsha*. Wouldn't everyone at the office love to know about her little sex toy? He couldn't find the vibrator now, so he decided that she must have gotten rid of it, too. He sat in the little chair in the corner of her bedroom and thought about telling everybody. How could he do that? Let everyone know about Marsha and her pulsing boyfriend?

Reavis, after getting off the phone with Matson and Bobby Doall, called Garrity. "Tim, I called Whitfield and pretended I was a survey taker." He went on to tell Garrity about what Whitfield  had to say, how he had more than simple mother issues, and discussed with Tim some of the ways he was planning on using those issues to throw off the rapist, murderer and framer of innocent men. He didn't mention anything to Tim about the illegal recording of the interview. Tim didn't need to hear that.

B efore doing that he called WW&D and learned that Marsha LeGrange wouldn't be in that day. Tazer had said she was registered at the Madison, so he called there and asked to be put through to her room, hanging up when she answered. So, she was still there. Now, a block before her home, a condominium, he nearly missed Whitfield's National Car Rental Town Car.

It was parked on the opposite side of the street from the young Le-Grange woman's condominium. Her condo fronted on the street. The bastard, he was sure, had to be inside her home. That didn't worry Reavis, because Whitfield's next victim was still at the Madison. He would wait for the psychopath to leave and then follow him, see where he went. He was anxious to get his first look at the man he would always call *Whitfield.*

Reavis got an itch beside his nose and, without thinking, scratched it, then smelled gun oil. He looked at the gun beside him. He must have grabbed it when he saw the killer's car, got gun oil on his hand.

Before leaving Marsha LeGrange's condo, Jackie went to the front window, straightened a blind just enough, and looked out. He didn't notice Reavis in his pickup. Who he did notice, though, was his momma. Jackie let the blind snap closed. She must have followed him. How did she always find him so easily? His momma was headed for Marsha LeGrange's front door. Was she here to tell on him? That he was someone Marsha LeGrange knew? That Marsha LeGrange talked to that *someone*. That her John Lee Simpson was getting things right so he could kill her? Did his momma know all that?

Quietly, he ran to the kitchen, letting himself out the door that opened onto a sidewalk that surrounded the condominiums. He hurried out to the front corner of Marsha's building. When he got there, he peered around the corner, then quickly had to pull his head back. Janice Simpson, his momma, was knocking on Marsha LeGrange's front door. What was she here for? It had to be to tell Marsha he was after her. He put his hands to his face like a little kid who thinks that will hide him, and pressed himself against the brick wall of the building. At least ten minutes passed.

He heard footsteps. Her walking away? She must have been standing at Marsha LeGrange's front door all this time, quiet, sneaky, not wanting to miss a chance to tell on him. Making believe she left.

*How could she always find him?*

"Set it down a minute. I'm losing my grip," Jackie heard a man's voice say. Taking a chance, he looked out. There was a delivery truck double-parked beside a car. Legally parked behind the delivery truck was a black pickup. A guy wearing glasses was in the pickup, but he couldn't get too good a look at him. There were two delivery men, too, trying to lug a refrigerator up the street. That was who he heard. And now a lady came out of the condo next door to Marsha's and started getting on the delivery guys about not dropping her new refrigerator. Now was as good a time as any to get away, so he headed for his rental car.

On the drive home he gave a lot of thought to how his momma could find him all the time. What he decided was that it must be the cars—the names he used when he rented them. He'd used the name Whitfield in Boston to rent cars there, too. And she had seen him there.

With his momma knowing where he was, now more than ever he had to get Marsha LeGrange and get out of here, go somewhere safe, away from Janice Simpson. And he had to do it soon. For his own mental health. He would go to his grandma's, Miss Sarah. She was always glad to see Jackie.

There was one thing, though, that he never considered: leaving Pittsburgh before he finished with Marsha LeGrange and Lester Wilkins, or a Lester Wilkins substitute. No, of all the women who acted exactly like his momma, Marsha LeGrange did, and actually looked like she could be her sister. She had gotten to Jackie the most. He had waited a long time for her—way too long!—and he wasn't the kind to quit. Lester Wilkins, or someone like him, would be his usual icing on the cake.

Reavis saw no one around other than the older woman who walked to Marsha LeGrange's front door. She had some kind of black attaché case in her hand, probably selling something. He watched the delivery truck double-park in front of him. After that he saw the two delivery guys and the woman next door to the LeGrange woman's condominium, too. He didn't know it yet, but he totally blew catching Whitfield leaving Marsha LeGrange's. He looked at the Timex on his wrist. It was getting on to five now; parking places on Sydney were starting to fill.

A man reached in the pickup's window and put a grimy hand on Reavis's shoulder. He was a skinny guy with a red face. "Hey, buddy," the guy said. "You're in my spot." The little bastard turned and pointed to the house Reavis was parked in front of. "I live here."

Reavis was getting ready to leave anyway and didn't want to draw undue attention to himself. Because he expected to be spending a lot of time in front of Marsha LeGrange's. So all he did was lean his head out the window and say, "Take it easy, pal. I was leaving anyway."

Reavis hadn't seen Whitfield leave, but the Town Car was gone when he went down a block to turn around and came back to where it had been parked. He must focus better—he missed the guy getting out of the LeGrange woman's condo.

But Reavis would be face to face with Whitfield tomorrow, anyway.

# CHAPTER THIRTY-TWO

Marsha went to work Tuesday. She didn't check out of the Madison, though, because she wasn't ready to go home yet. Now, Wednesday, she spent all morning brooding and pushing files around on her desk.

She heard something, looked up, and there was Larry Haski.

The look on her face betrayed her. "What's the matter?" he said. "Looks like you've been having a bad day."

She studied him for a second, wondering again if he could have been the man who stole her vibrator. "Headache, Larry . . . I guess I am feeling a little under the weather." She held his gaze, trying to decide whether he was laughing at her behind that innocent look on his face.

"I've got some aspirin," he said. "Want me to get you some?"

*Why all the solicitousness?*

Haski had a tough time looking her in the eye. "Marsha, I've got an apology to make. I guess I've made it a little rough on you around here. Jeff Guilfoyle and I were talking the other day at the Arena, and he agrees with me. In fact, he brought it to my attention. It's just that it's getting close to the time they should be considering me for partner here. Maybe even past the time." His shoulders sagged and he sighed.

He turned and looked at her now. "Anyway, I'm sorry." And the look on his face told her that he really was.

Marsha broke down and started crying. She would not have done it if she hadn't gotten the freak's phone call and her vibrator hadn't been stolen and then FedEx'd to her. His kindness was just what she needed. It released her from her terror, if only for the moment. The next thing she did shocked her. She heard the words as if someone else had spoken them. "Larry, some man broke into my condo, was in my room, took some of my underwear, and sent it to me here."

She found herself just pouring it all out, Larry listening, being so understanding, telling her he would be scared, too, if someone broke into his apartment. He was saying all the right things. He came around her desk and put his hands on her shoulders, working them into her tense muscles (in a nice way) on both sides, until they finally let loose, softened. Something else she needed.

They both started feeling awkward after a while, and he moved from behind her and walked over to one of her client chairs and sat. With perfect timing he switched the conversation to talking about the cases they were working on. He even mentioned that he had to make another trip to Arizona and how much he hated the heat there. After a while, he got up, gave her arm a tender, easy squeeze, and left, smiling a goodbye to her.

Still Tuesday. Reavis had been getting edgy ever since Whitfield disappeared from Marsha LeGrange's. He wanted to make sure Whitfield was home, hadn't left town. So early that night he took off for the man's condo, now in the Monte Carlo, in case Whitfield had seen him in his truck outside Marsha LeGrange's.

Reavis got to where the killer lived, a short drive from the South Side, hit 279 North, kept on it until he reached Exit 10, Hampshire Township, made a right and drove two blocks. The Town Car was there. So he pulled right up to it, got out of the Monte Carlo, and felt the hood of the killer's rental car. Cold. Whitfield had been home for a pretty good while.

He backed up and parked and trained his gaze on Whitfield's apartment. He was still worried Whitfield would leave Pittsburgh, start killing somewhere else. That was why he made Peggy promise she wouldn't tell Marsha LeGrange that Whitfield was after her. Because if she knew for sure who was harassing her, Marsha would tell the police. It would save her life, but after the police questioned the killer, he would simply take off. One, two years later, having a much better idea about Whitfield's needs now, Reavis believed Whitfield would return to Pittsburgh for Marsha LeGrange. Her life would be saved. Temporarily. That's what he had to keep telling himself. But what about the other lives? The women in other cities before Whitfield came back for the LeGrange woman? Knowing he might save other women would not help much, though. Not if the killer got Marsha LeGrange before he started up somewhere else.

No. Reavis was all but sure Whitfield would not leave Pittsburgh before he made a try for Marsha LeGrange. He would not leave, because killing women, Reavis was certain, was what he had a strong need to do. And three was his number. No more. No less. He was an addict, Reavis was sure of that. Whitfield had his get-high ritual: the way he frightened women by stealing their underwear, calling them, sending it to them, then raping and murdering them, then framing innocent men. And a big part of this ritual was three murders in each city. Recently, one after the other until he got his quota of three in the same city.

How badly did Whitfield need his fix? Was he getting desperate? That was what Reavis, Matson, and Bobby Doall had decided to work on: getting Whitfield desperate enough to make a wrong move. Give them an edge they sorely needed.

# *C*HAPTER THIRTY-THREE

Reavis was not outside Whitfield's place five minutes when the man—who looked like anyone else you might run into in Hampshire Township—appeared. Whitfield's gaze wandered around the parking lot. He acted casual enough, but Reavis could swear that the killer stiffened when he saw the Monte Carlo.

Then Whitfield took off, running. Headed for his rental Town Car. But right before Whitfield got to his car, he pivoted, slowed to a fast walk and headed for the street. Reavis had a quick decision to make: get out and follow him or stay in the car and wait for Whitfield to come back. At the speed the other man was walking, though, it didn't look like he would be coming back.

Reavis pushed at the door, got it open, got out and hustled after the younger man. He tripped and nearly fell, righting himself in time to see the killer round the corner of the last building. Hobbling now, Reavis took out after him, worried that he was going to lose Whitfield.

He need not have worried, however, because what happened next was that he nearly ran into him.

Jackie had flopped into his chair after the second call to California. He was sweating, panicked. In California, his informant told him, a man had been asking questions about Atlas Investments. Skinny. Tall. Somewhere in his sixties. Wore glasses. A man who asked about Pennsylvania. Pittsburgh. "I wrote down his name, It's Clifford Reavis," the California man said. "Oh, he mentioned the names 'Whitfield' and 'LaMont,' too."

The second call he made got to him even worse. That time a young-kid building manager held out on him, Jackie could tell, when he asked if anybody was around asking about Roselli. All the kid said was, "No. Why? May I help you?" Jackie slammed down the phone, just knowing that the kid on the other end was looking for more information about Jackie. To tell someone.

He couldn't move from the phone for a while after the second call. Jackie sat, his gaze wandering unfocused around the room. Was it some kind of credit check? That's what it had to be. Maybe from the bank. Wilberforce's bank. The signed authorization, all those wire transfers dropping into the account wasn't enough?

It couldn't be the rapes, executions, and frames. That would be impossible. Nevertheless, he went back over each one. Weren't all those rich bastards in prison or on the way? Weren't cops and DAs alike satisfied with their convictions? Sure they were. He had followed each case online. So why then was anyone looking into Atlas Investments? Who was Clifford Reavis, the tall, skinny guy who wore glasses?

He made himself get calm, think clearly. Didn't he pride himself on his nerves? He never panicked, did he? That real calm feeling always came over him when things got tight. Hell, the danger, the excitement, that was part of it. Wasn't it? *Sit back, breathe right, get calm,* he told himself.

He had a way of making himself calm. Taking a deep breath. Letting it out real slow. Then another. Let that one out. In. Out. Getting the rhythm. Heart slowing down now. Thoughts no longer racing. There you go. Getting there, to that calm place within. Very, very calm.

Now he could put his mind to it. Again, he went over each of his crimes, looking for weaknesses in the planning, in how he went about each one, thinking maybe he left some clue behind. He shook his head. No, he couldn't find a flaw.

What about Marsha LeGrange? Could she have hired someone to investigate him? No. That bitch had no idea who he really was, what he was up to. No one at Wilkins, Wilkins & Dunn did.

Did she have any idea that she'd talked to Jackie, whom she didn't know by that name? She wouldn't even talk to him if she thought she was talking to someone named John Lee Simpson, a poor southern boy, the bastard son of Janice Simpson and Stuart Randolph. *Did she have any idea how long he'd spent checking her out, selecting her and deciding that she would be next? How very long he had waited for his chance?*

He had to watch becoming too sure of himself, even though nothing ever gave him any reason not to be. He got up, an idea taking shape, and went over to the window. Looking out, he saw a silver car he'd never noticed before. He couldn't tell if anyone was in it—the setting sun was reflecting off its windows. Something about that car made him wonder. Instinct, maybe? Jackie trusted instinct.

He got into sweats, checking his look at the mirror near the front door. Then he took a couple of steps outside. He pretended to be just seeing what kind of evening it was, looking all around, just letting his gaze touch quickly on the silver car. It looked like some kind of Chevrolet. He wasn't good on car types. He still couldn't tell if anyone was in it.

Jackie decided to make like he was going for his car, then, at the last minute, head for the street. Maybe the suddenness of his move to the street would flush someone out of the silver car.

That's what he did. He took off towards the Town Car, but veered away from it. Somewhere behind him he heard a car door open and slam shut. Not looking back, he slowed to a fast walk. When he got to the corner of the last building in his complex, he stopped, pressing himself against the wall, listening hard. He heard footsteps. Someone was coming. Fast. He straightened. Tensed. The footsteps getting closer. Whoever it was made a lot of noise. From the sound, he judged that they couldn't be more than ten yards away. That's when he moved out again, heading back the way he'd come.

A tall, skinny guy with glasses. Older. Maybe. This guy had to be Clifford Reavis. He made sure that he kept his face friendly, showing no shock, so the man he thought was Reavis wouldn't notice how wired he was. He kept walking, but stopped in front of the tall old guy with glasses, who *had* to be following him.

"Hi, Jackie said. "I know you from somewhere, don't I?" And then held out his hand for Reavis to shake. The old guy took it. "Aren't you Clifford Reavis? Didn't we meet somewhere before?"

The guy's eyes opened wide behind those glasses. "I sure am Clifford Reavis, but I'm not sure about meeting. You do look familiar." Then Reavis said Jackie's Pittsburgh alias, asked if that wasn't who Jackie was. Reavis said, "I think your mother's showed me your picture, so we haven't met but I know a lot about you. She tells me you work out at the Fitness Arena. I'm going to be down there tomorrow night. We can talk some more. I've got some news for you about your mother. But I just got a call on my cell—minor emergency—so I've got to head back to my car right now. Great meeting you," he said.

There wasn't any doubt now. Reavis had to be the one who was out in California asking questions. Yeah. Tall, skinny, glasses. The name clinched it. But who was Clifford Reavis and what was he up to? Jackie had a thought: Clifford Reavis was probably working for his momma.

Jackie kept it together until he got back to his condo. He didn't remember how long he had been back inside. The only thing on his mind, the thing he kept turning over and over, was should he stay in Pittsburgh, or should he run?

What would remain in Reavis's mind the longest was the look in Whitfield's eyes when he rounded the corner and saw him. It was like he knew. The eyes that looked out from under Whitfield's long lashes had the look in them. Reavis didn't have to ask himself if Whitfield was on to him. He knew he was. He didn't know how he came up with the idea to bring Whitfield's mother up to him, but was happy that he had.

The man turned pure white when he mentioned his mother.

After he got back to his car, he checked his notebook, and he made a call.

"Yeah?" the voice answered, after six rings.

"Yes," Reavis said, doing the best he could to imitate Whitfield's voice. "This is Atlas Investments again. Can you remember anything else?"

"Listen, pal, I only talked to you, what, a little while ago. I told you everything: The guy was older, real tall and skinny. He wore glasses and was homely-looking, too. Gave me the name 'Clifford Reavis.' I wrote it down after he left. He wouldn't tell me why he was nosing around, other than to end up saying your company probably wasn't the Atlas Investments he was looking for. But why would he ask me about LaMont and Whitfield? Listen, I have your number; I'll call you if I remember anything else. Don't forget that check."

Reavis hung up on the son of a bitch and headed for home. Now he was sure it was that body-odorbastard from the mail drop place who told Whitfield he'd come around asking about Atlas Investments. And smelling like he did, holes in his teeth and all, where did he get off calling anyone homely?

After he got home he called Matson, and they talked a long time, both wondering what next, talking about a man who was insane—a psychopath?—the way he thought and how he looked at things. How could they use what they already knew, both to keep him in Pittsburgh and get him screwed up was what they covered.

Matson thought Reavis telling Whitfield that he knew his mother was a great move. Then they talked more about their plan, based on the theory that Whitfield's mother abandoned him, maybe worse, when he was a kid. After Matson, he called Bobby. Bobby and Reavis put some ideas together, too, and came up with a plan, thought it would work. They would find out tomorrow.

Jackie grabbed the phone as soon as he got back inside his condo. He didn't see Reavis leaving. He needed to talk to his grandmother so bad. See what she might know.

"Hello," Miss Sarah said, and when he didn't answer immediately. "Who is this?"

"John Lee." Jackie didn't like the way he sounded. Already he regretted calling.

"John Lee. What's wrong? You been drinking again?"

"No, Miss Sarah, no drinking. Something might be wrong, though." He had to come up with an idea. "Some strange things are happening."

"Strange things? Where are you, John Lee?"

"You know I can't tell you. My government job is secret. You know that. I met some man today who said my momma showed him a picture of me. When was she doing something like that? Do you know?"

"Your momma didn't mention nothin' like that to me. Boy, your mother couldn't do that on you. It's about time we cleared some things up about your momma and Mr. Randolph. I haven't told you the whole truth. Thought it best for you at the time, you being so little. Your momma . . . Mr. Randolph . . . they both agreed. . . ." She was crying now.

Jackie did not hear Sarah Lee Simpson crying, nor did he hear a word she was saying.

". . . John Lee." She choked, saying his name. "Your momma . . . she . . . you there, boy? John Lee. You there?"

Jackie was all screwed up. His momma showing some guy his picture. What was that all about? So he didn't hear what Miss Sarah had just said. "Yeah. Okay. Sorry to bother you, ma'am. Well I'd best be going." Jackie looked over at the bar and thought about pouring some gin into a glass. "Bye, Miss Sarah. I love you."

He waited before hanging up, though, needing to hear it: "John Lee, you're the love of my life. Have been since the first second I saw you in your momma's arms. Goodbye, boy."

Jackie didn't know how long he had been sitting in his condominium, but the room was dark when he heard a knock at the door, then another knock. He walked to the door, taking his time, and looked out the peephole. His momma was outside.

He didn't make a sound. Couldn't. Just shallow-breathed until he saw her leave. Then he walked to the chair and slumped into it. Jackie was drained, but now he could smile. Because he had his answer. It was his momma. She had hired Reavis to find him. That's how she'd done it in Phoenix and Boston. Same thing here. That explained everything.

He made his hands into fists, thinking he would just have to put up with his momma knowing where he lived. He simply wouldn't answer the door when she knocked, wouldn't let her in. She wasn't going to make him leave this city. He wasn't about to leave this city. Not until he got Marsha LeGrange, he wouldn't. He would never have any peace if he didn't get her. Maybe, though, he shouldn't wait any longer to go after her.

# *C*HAPTER THIRTY-FOUR

Late Wednesday afternoon, Bobby was parked in front of Reavis's home at 5:00. When Reavis got in Bobby's new car, a 1956 cherry-red T-bird, the kind of car Reavis wouldn't let himself buy, he and Bobby went over their plan again. Then they took off for the Fitness Arena, making small changes in how they would handle Whitfield as they drove.

On that same Wednesday, Jackie got to the Fitness Arena before his usual time. After getting inside, something made him glance at the health bar. And he froze. There, grinning at him like some fool, was Clifford Reavis and the big, strong mountain-man-lookalike in his thirties that people at the Arena called "Shoes" for his weird red tennis shoes. Jackie remembering Shoes from seeing him before at the Arena in the free weights room, sometimes in the Nautilus room. Talking to him once. Not a bad guy.

A lot of the younger women who worked out at night made moves on Shoes. The man was strong, but didn't dress for style: not wearing gym clothes that showed off his build. Shoes, going for strength rather than looks. *The guy shaved that beard,* Jackie thought, *he wouldn't be able to keep the women away.*

Seeing Reavis there, smirking like he knew something about Jackie, got to him. What his momma must have told Reavis about him was probably all lies. It couldn't have been good. *Not after I saw the smirk on Reavis's face when he saw me,* Jackie thought. Instead of letting on, though, he acted like it was nothing and headed for the locker room to change clothes for his workout.

After changing, Jackie was now fifteen minutes into his workout, the skinny investigator still on his mind. Jackie wondered what possible reason could make someone like Shoes hang out with the likes of Clifford Reavis. He heard laughing. He looked up and there he was, Clifford Reavis, standing ten feet away, staring at him, arms folded against his chest.

Shoes—maybe the investigator's son but probably too young for that—was with him, not laughing or even looking at Jackie, now starting to move away from where Reavis was standing, to work out somewhere behind Jackie. Out of the corner of his eye, he could see one of the regulars high-five Shoes and hear a couple of other Arena regulars saying things like, "Hey Shoes, what's up?"

Jackie, though, wasn't interested in Shoes; he was keeping his eyes on Clifford Reavis, who hadn't been moving, but was now heading Jackie's way. Which got him tensing up, working on getting into his breathing. Clifford Reavis had a look full of hate in his eyes and Jackie could feel a tic start under his right eye.

*Fuck you.*

Reavis and Bobby Doall, who people at the Arena called Shoes, had plotted on the way over to the Fitness Arena for Bobby to veer off when Reavis stopped and then head for people he knew, before Reavis made his way to Whitfield. He would be the warm-up guy with the gym regulars, getting them ready to start laughing at Whitfield when Reavis went to work on him. It was their plan for Bobby to tell the Arena regulars that Reavis was going to jerk Whitfield around and— Bobby's idea—to tell them to watch the old skinny guy do a job on Whitfield.

Reavis stopped three feet away from Whitfield and stood there with his arms folded on his chest, sneering at him. Bobby and Reavis had talked about the look he would give Whitfield, too, but Reavis didn't have to act like he hated Whitfield: with hate in his own eyes, he locked eyes with the man.

Slowly, he took his eyes off Whitfield's and as he was turning around, looking toward Bobby and the other regulars, said as loud as he could without making it a shout, "So you're the guy they call a 'stud' here, huh? Does that mean you're a real *ladies' man?*"

Reavis knew the word "stud" at a workout place meant a strong guy. Bobby Doall had told him that, but he was headed somewhere else with the "stud" business. "Is that what they mean when they call you 'Stud?'" To the people in the Nautilus room, other than Bobby Doall, it would have sounded like sarcasm. Reavis could hear some chuckles.

Jackie asked himself, *Where is he headed with that stud business?* He didn't mean to, but he looked away. He could feel a slight trembling inside, so he had to compose himself before he could look back at Reavis again and try to stare him down. He turned back to him. Ready now. "What do you mean?" He was trying to keep it cool, was not happy that his voice was cracking. He backed away, no more than a step.

Reavis, hearing Whitfield's voice crack, seeing him step back, moved in on the man. Close enough to hear Whitfield's harsh breathing. "Well . . ." He looked around to see who was listening and was pleased when he saw that everyone in the room was. He gave them all the kind of smile and nod that would let them get ready, knowing that he was going to start jerking this guy around now.

Then he turned back to Whitfield. "What I mean is that you must really be something with the ladies. A real lady *killer.*" He held Whitfield's gaze.

Jackie narrowed his eyes, trying to get a read on the man he was now certain was his momma's investigator. Off to the side, he could see people watching him and smirking. Just like the other kids did in Dutton, South Carolina, years ago when someone at school would call him a bastard. After he'd broken a couple of noses, that had stopped.

Refusing to take another step back, Jackie lied, "I'm married." He kept it vague. He wasn't going to say any more than necessary. What did Clifford Reavis want from him? What did he know?

What Reavis wanted was to keep enough pressure on the killer so that he would screw up somewhere, and this was the way he, Bobby, and Matson had come up with to do it. He pushed his face not three inches from Whitfield's, looking down, spraying out his wet steak-and-onion hoagie breath on the man's face. "I'll bet you do okay with the women, *Killer*." Loud for everyone to hear, then almost a whisper, "I'll bet they scream when you get them under you. I bet they do everything you tell them to do."

Jackie flinched. He could see more eyes turn their way, hear the laughing. He didn't like anyone breathing onion breath in his face, and having to wipe it off. But his only thought was how to get away from this asshole. *Could he know everything?*

Reavis moved closer to Whitfield and stepped on his foot, ground it some. "Come off it with the humble act, boy. *I bet you do your lady killer act all over the country—Boston, Phoenix, Houston, Seattle, all over—don't you, boy?* What's this so-called wife of yours have to say about that?" Clifford Reavis was playing to the audience Bobby Doall had set up. "I won't tell anyone. Maybe you can teach me your moves with the ladies?" Reavis stepped back, looking Whitfield over. "Yeah, when you knock them *dead* with your looks and charm."

Jackie, who wanted to push Reavis away but did not, realized he was glaring, knew he had to put a clamp on his temper. He heard more laughter, too, and that didn't help at all. He reached back, grabbing the handles of the nearest Nautilus machine to keep his hands from shaking. Why was he letting this homely son of a bitch get to him?

Reavis, whispering a chant now: "Lady Killer, Lady Killer, Lady Killer."

Jackie couldn't take much more. He strained at the straps of the Nautilus machine. He was furious, now yelling at Reavis, "What business is it of yours how I do with the women?"

That was when Reavis gave him a look that told Jackie he knew everything.

Seeing Whitfield's red face, white knuckles, the muscles in his chest standing out like bands of steel, the fury in his eyes, was exactly what Reavis, Matson, and Bobby had hoped for and planned. Get the killer mad enough to want to kill Reavis, make him a target, to keep him from leaving Pittsburgh. If he got the man enraged enough, then when he came for Reavis he would kill Whitfield and it would be self-defense.

*Yeah*, Reavis thought, *he wants me.* He grabbed the handles of Whitfield's machine, leaned over by his ear and, in a voice he had no trouble making thick with contempt, whispered, "You and I both know what kind of *lady killer* you are."

He turned his back on the killer, laughing. "Don't mind me, kid. I was just having a little fun." And he walked away. Playing to his Fitness Arena audience.

Jackie couldn't take his eyes off Reavis after that. Every once in a while he saw the skinny son of a bitch whisper something to someone in the room. Who would then look at Jackie, with Reavis, and laugh.

Jackie was seething, feeling exactly like he always felt when them Farr brothers back home used to taunt him about his momma. Back when he was little. They would always be asking him where was his momma. Was she even coming back to see him at Christmas?

He had to get out of here. He cut short his workout and was leaving the Nautilus room, trying to pass Reavis without looking at him, when he got an elbow in his stomach. Before he could regain his balance, Reavis pulled him close to him and whispered, "You no good piece of shit. No wonder your mother's ashamed of you. But you already know that, don't you? Your mother can't stand being around you."

That stood Jackie straight up. *What had his momma told this Clifford Reavis?* Not thinking, blinded by rage, he reached for his tormentor, and sunk his fingers into the man's thin arm.

"Hey. Easy, asshole," Jackie heard him say.

Someone else shouted at Jackie. "Hey! None of that in here."

Jackie looked over and saw Shoes glaring at him. And for a second his mind went blank. The next thing he knew, his arms were being ripped away from Reavis by Shoes, and the man was saying, "He was joking. Okay? That man was just kidding you. Let go of him. You'll kill him."

Jackie managed a sheepish grin and let go. "Sorry," he said. "Had a bad night last night." Then, aware that everyone's eyes were on him, completely undone now, he bolted.

It wasn't until he was standing outside on Fifth Avenue that he realized he wasn't in the locker room, that he was standing on a busy street—in shorts and his T-shirt. Then he started running. Eyes on the sidewalk. Running down Fifth Avenue. Screaming.

Two hours later, after he'd snuck back into the Fitness Arena to get his things, including the keys to the Town Car, Jackie drove around Pittsburgh for an hour before he finally made his way home. He hadn't been there five minutes, however, when the phone rang. He was pressing it against his ear before he realized what he was doing. Then he heard the hated voice again:

"You and your jungle stories, Lady Killer. Your mother can't stand being around you. She's hated your guts ever since you were little."

*Clifford Reavis was the man taking surveys, too.* Jackie didn't know if he screamed this time. He thought he might have. Clifford Reavis was the bastard who got to him about his momma on the phone, pretending to be taking a survey. The man was going to pay for that.

". . . You worthless bastard," Clifford Reavis was in the middle of telling Jackie, "who are you trying to shit?" Then he brought up Janice Simpson again; he wouldn't let up. "Your momma hates your guts. Always has. She's ashamed of you. You worthless piece of shit."

Those words about his momma . . . what were she and Clifford Reavis up to? Why did she have Reavis plaguing him like he was?

Jackie heard Reavis laugh. Next, he heard shrieking. "Stop it! Stop it! Stop it!" someone screamed. Then it came to him who was making all that noise. It was him.

Clifford Reavis kept laughing. When he finally stopped, he said, "You're beneath contempt. No wonder your mother's the way she is with you."

Jackie cringed, unable to respond.

Then, this time, taunting laughter.

*"Don't you laugh at me!"*

Reavis only laughed louder. And hung up.

Jackie was paralyzed. He sat, staring at the phone, waiting for it to ring again so he could pick it up and tell that four-eyed motherfucker what he would do to him.

He had to do something to get himself back under control. So he made himself think about Marsha LeGrange, his momma's twin. He thought about what he would do to her. And the more he pictured it, the better he started feeling. After he thought about her long enough to calm down, he switched back to thinking about Clifford Reavis. Only this time he made himself think the same kind of thoughts about Reavis that he was thinking about Marsha LeGrange. What he pictured himself doing was standing over a dying Clifford Reavis and kicking him like a dog.

It was Bobby Doall's idea to call Whitfield a "lady killer." Reavis thought, too, about how Whitfield reacted to what he'd said about his mother. He could thank Matson for that move; he'd suggested it, thought it might get to the guy, and it sure did.

What surprised Reavis most, though, was the venom he heard in his own voice when he called Whitfield a piece of shit, told him that not even a mother could stand being around him.

But if he was getting to Whitfield—and there was no doubt that he was—then so was the killer getting to him. Reavis couldn't stuff the rage down. He told himself not to do anything crazy, made himself remember that there was something to lose now. Better put: *someone* to lose. Peggy. But didn't he know that logic always lost when it battled emotion? *Would* he try something crazy with *this* killer?

He'd better call Matson.

"How did it go?" Matson sounded worried.

Reavis realized again how much Matson wished he were here. "Pretty much according to plan," he said. "When I finished with him at the Fitness Arena, everyone was with me, laughing at him. When I called him a worthless piece of shit, told him that not even a mother could stand the likes of him, he grabbed me . . ."

"I thought that would work," Matson said.

"Yeah. He would have killed me if we were alone. For a second I thought he would anyway. I had Bobby with me. He pulled the bastard off me." Reavis caught his breath. "He ran out of the Arena . . . . He was so screwed up that he ended up on the street instead of in the locker room . . . with his workout outfit on . . . ran off so fast there was no way I could ever catch him."

"How about you, Clifford. You holding up okay?"

"That's the second reason I called. If you mean, does the guy scare me, no . . . but I do scare the hell out of myself. I didn't realize how much of a piece of me he had. After a while, I wasn't acting. I wanted to wipe the place up with him. Not that I could. And, Mat," Reavis paused . . . "the more I put him down, the better I felt. I really hate that bastard."

"Listen, Clifford. Don't go near him alone without the .38."

Reavis laughed, but it sounded more like a cough. "Don't worry," he said. "I've come to my senses." Serious, Reavis went on. "I made him hate me today, Mat."

"Think he will hang around Pittsburgh long enough to make a try for you?" Matson said.

Reavis didn't even have to think. "Bet on it."

"You mail the letter yet?"

"This morning, before I even saw him," Reavis said. "I put something about his mother in the letter, too, as an afterthought. Now I'm glad I did."

Thursday morning a loud knock woke Jackie up. Disoriented, he looked around and saw that he was still by the phone.

Another knock. He was on guard now. He got up, went over, looked out the peephole. And saw a uniform. The police? He froze. What the hell were the police doing here? He made himself look again, better this time, and let out a sigh. He saw a uniform alright—on the mailman.

He opened the door, thinking he must look like a bum, unshaven, standing in the clothes he'd slept in. "Yes?"

"Certified letter." The mailman held a letter out for him to sign.

Jackie could only stare.

"Did I wake you, sir?"

"No," Jackie said. "No. That's okay. What time . . . day . . . is it?"

The man took a step back. "Are you feeling okay, sir?"

"No. I mean, yes. I'm fine." Jackie tried out a laugh. "It's just that I get absent-minded. Sometimes I forget what day it is." *Why the fuck am I explaining myself to a mailman?*

The man held out the letter again, this time with a black government-issue pen. Jackie searched the man's face, thinking, *Does he think I'm nuts?*

"Would you mind signing for the letter, sir?"

The mailman was gone now; the door was closed and bolted; and Jackie was leaning against it. He ripped at the envelope and a sheet of lined, legal-size, yellow paper fell out. He opened it and read a list of names: Mary A. Jenks, Teresa Arcase, Amelia Banucci, R. A. Lands, Elizabeth A. Hast, Kim J. Weston, Kathy Murray, Mary S. Montgomery, Maxine O. Stein, Patsy Jaczewski, Theodora B. Thomas, Eve W. Rankin, M. B. Thompkins, Eileen Broskey, Charleen T. Cray, Ann C. Wells, Beverly A. Wiley, Chris A. Flowers, Susan Orndoff, Janet Cratsworth, Stacy Bonato, and Judith Jenkins.

There was also a message:

"I'll let you know what it will cost to forget these names." It had a warning, too: "You can leave town if you want, but I'll find you again and then it will cost you even more."

There was a P.S. too: "I know all about you and your mother."

It was signed "Clifford Reavis."

Jackie lurched to the liquor cabinet, grabbing a bottle, vodka or gin, he couldn't be sure which. He broke the seal, pushed it in his mouth and gulped. Gin. He took another swallow.

That same morning, while Jackie was drinking himself unconscious, Marsha awakened with a start. The dream was fading now, but she remembered some of it. In the dream, Mel was yelling at her. She was home now and there were new locks on the door, with deadbolts to go with them.

She'd missed Mel's calls yesterday. He did call twice, though. She wanted more. Was she driving him away? Is that what she did to men?

# CHAPTER THIRTY-FIVE

Jackie was consumed with rage. All he could think about were the different ways he was going to torture and kill Clifford Reavis. He had to stop thinking like that, but when he made himself stop, his terror took over. He imagined Clifford Reavis telling other people what he knew. Maybe even the police. There was only one way to stop the rage and terror—without trying to rape and kill Marsha LeGrange. Because Reavis knew all about him, he could get caught. Instead of framing some rich guy for his crimes, he might finally be the one who had to pay. If he moved before the time was right.

He simply couldn't let the rage and terror beat him.

To begin to ease his terror and rage, he called for a cab and when it got to his condominium he walked out towards it, heading for the driver's door. He told the man what he wanted and when he wanted it. Then handed the cabbie two hundred-dollar bills. The cabbie was back in twenty minutes and delivered Jackie four fifths of gin and four fifths of vodka. He handed the man another two hundred dollars, got the man's cell number, and told him if he needed more, he would call him. And—oh—keep the change.

After the cab driver left, he read Clifford Reavis's blackmail letter for the fifth time and then took his first swallow of gin for the day. For days, and he would never know how many or whether he called the cab driver again, Jackie alternated between blur and blackout. Now it was early blur. He looked at the bottle he held by the neck. Two, three more swigs, he promised himself, and he would be unconscious again. No more rage. No more terror. No more feelings of helplessness.

Someone knocked on his front door before he got the bottle to his mouth. He lowered it. "Go away. I'm busy." *That's it,* he thought laughing, *go away. I'm a busy man.* He laughed again. Laughing did him good. Why should he worry? If anybody should be doing the worrying it should be Clifford Reavis and Marsha LeGrange.

There was another knock.

*Fuck it,* he thought, *I might as well go see who it is.* Jackie got up, steadied himself, and struggled over to the door. Once there, he threw it wide open.

A real cop this time. Reavis must have talked. Jackie made an effort not to sway, telling himself that there was no law against getting smashed in your own home. Was there? "What do you want?" he said.

"Sorry to bother you," the cop said. "I'm just checking on a report of a prowler. Did you hear or see anything strange lately?"

The cop was looking over Jackie's shoulder into his living room. So Jackie moved sideways, not wanting him to see all the empty bottles. "No. No prowler. Go next door. Ask them."

Jackie could see the man's face and neck getting red, the man getting ready to be pissed off, Jackie trying to tell him where to go, and he had the good sense not to want that. "Here, buddy," he said as he handed the young police officer the bottle, "take somma this." He held on to the doorknob so he wouldn't sway, pleased how the cop wasn't scaring him any.

The cop raised his right hand, palm up, and gave Jackie a smile. "No thank you, sir. Not on duty."

"I feel safe knowing that," Jackie said. "You want something else?"

"No . . . that's it . . . I . . ."

Jackie slammed the door. "Fucker doesn't make fifty a year," he said to no one. "Comes around fucking with John Lee Simpson." Unsteadily, he moved to the window, curious, in a foggy way, to see where the man in the uniform would go next.

What he saw when he looked out was the cop talking to Clifford Reavis out by that silver car of his. Jackie stared at them as they huddled, seeing them look his way as they talked. They seemed to be laughing. Reavis handed the young cop something. Then it dawned on him.

Reavis was paying off the cop. For spying on him. For fucking with him.

That was what set Jackie off, thinking those two out there were fucking with him. *That does it,* he decided. *Today has to be the day.* Much as he hated changes, there would have to be one or two, but today *had* to be the day.

Or did there have to be any changes? Who knew? Maybe Reavis had some bucks; maybe he could pin Marsha LeGrange's murder on that son of a bitch. No matter, they both had to die.

Jackie's clouded mind did manage to separate it all: Reavis was a new and different problem. An emergency. But the four-eyed bastard had not called the cops on him. Therefore, most important to Reavis had to be that he wanted the money. He would solve the Reavis emergency by killing him. In his—John Lee Simpson's—own good time. Marsha LeGrange was a need. He could no longer wait to satisfy that need.

This is how Jimmy Groves, the Hampshire police officer, had come to knock on the killer's front door: It was Tuesday and Reavis had been parked outside Whitfield's every day, Marsha's every night. He couldn't keep it up much longer, even with Bobby Doall and Pat Tazer filling in for him a couple hours every day so he could get some sleep. He had to make something happen. When he saw Jimmy Groves, one of Hampshire Township's day-shift police officers cruise by, he waved him over.

"Jimmy," Reavis said, when the cop pulled up beside him, the two cars driver's side to driver's side, "you know the guy I've been watching?"

"The guy whose wife thinks he's got a honey stashed away in there?" Jimmy nodded in the direction of Whitfield's condominium. (That's the message Reavis had given the Hampshire Township Police Department so they wouldn't keep stopping at his car and asking if they could help him.) Jimmy went on, "You got some problem with him?"

Reavis put on a pained look, shrugged. "I'm running up my client's tab and I'm not even sure anyone's in there." He pointed at Whitfield's. "No one comes in or out." He looked at Jimmy Groves hopefully. "Think you could check? You know, make something up, maybe you're looking for a prowler, you're just checking all the people in his building—asking if they've seen anyone strange? Just see if anyone's in there."

Jimmy said, sure, he would look in on Whitfield.

When he got back, Reavis said, "He there?" And Jimmy said, yeah. Reavis showed Jimmy the California license photo of Whitfield. "That him?"

Jimmy shook his head as if he couldn't be sure. "On a good day, maybe," he said. Jimmy nodded back to where the killer lived. "You should smell him, Clifford. Booze. And when he opened his mouth to talk," Jimmy paused, shook his head again, "it got worse. And shaky?" Jimmy arched his reddish-blond eyebrows. "His hands wouldn't stop shaking. He could hardly stand. Looks like he's been at it for days. He all but told me to get the hell out of there." Then Jimmy grinned. "I was in that kind of shape, I'd be the same way."

Reavis was telling Jimmy that he owed him one when his cell rang. Reavis answered it, shrugging his shoulders at Jimmy so he would know Reavis had to take the call. Jimmy took off. The call was from Tim Garrity. "Clifford, all the call-in recordings are the same guy, according to our voiceprint expert."

"That's no shock. Let's hold off calling the DA. I'm sure this guy is close to breaking. I'm outside his condo now and I had a cop knock on his door to see what was up. He came back saying that Whitfield was plastered and that his condo was littered with empty fifths. I saw him looking out his front window at me while I was talking to the cop. That should really fire him up. He's already over the edge, almost too far."

Reavis went on. "I think he's ready to move on Marsha LeGrange, Tim. Maybe even tonight. Because he saw me talking to the cop. Could you hold off calling the DA's office?"

Reavis had told Tim about Bobby's, Matson's, and his plan. Catch Whitfield breaking into Marsha LeGrange's condo, then shoot the man.

"Okay. Good luck, Clifford. Shoot first."

As soon as Reavis got off the phone with Tim, he called Bobby's cell.

"Yeah," Bobby said when he answered the call.

"Bobby, he's going to make his move tonight. I'm sure of it."

"I'll be your backup. Where you gonna be parked?"

"No more than a half block down the street, parked facing the Le-Grange woman's condominium. I'll be in the truck. If I can't find a space, I'll be there on foot. Out of sight if I'm not in the pickup."

"As soon as you move in," Bobby said, "I'm out of my wheels and on my way towards her front door."

Jackie's watch said 10:33, but it wasn't the kind to give you the date. He turned on the Weather Channel, which not only gave him the date, but also the day of the week. Tuesday. He was way behind schedule with Marsha LeGrange. His thinking was blurred, but, he tried to tell himself, it was still early and he had all day to sober up and get ready. He would be sharp tonight. Tonight he would get Marsha LeGrange and, somehow, Clifford Reavis, too.

He got sick, sick again, and then one more time, shaved, showered and put on fresh clothes. Next, he took the seven empty fifths that he found around his living room out to the kitchen.

He sat. He would take time to work everything out. He was still half drunk. He needed a good workout. That was what he would do, have a good workout. He knew he didn't work out on Tuesdays, but he hadn't worked out in days, so he made himself believe that working out on Tuesdays was okay. Just this once. And after the workout, it didn't matter what day it was, he would lose Reavis by parking the rental car in Pittsburgh, pick up his SUV there, and double back here in it. He looked at the attaché case. Maybe wear a disguise, in case Reavis returned to wait for him.

After it got dark enough, he would go get Marsha LeGrange. He still couldn't figure out how he was going to get Reavis. Maybe simply wait for him to show out front again. Reavis would be back tomorrow; Jackie was sure of that. Jackie would sneak out the back door and come up behind Reavis. Reavis would never know what hit him. He rose, thinking he could work out the details later. When he was thinking better.

But what about his momma? How much did she know? Maybe Reavis had told her about them all, all those women he killed. He shook his head. No. She couldn't know. If she did, she wouldn't keep coming around.

Jackie looked around one more time. And nodded his approval. Yeah. Everything was cleaned up and he had everything he needed for tonight in the backpack. He grabbed it and his gym bag and left.

Jackie quickly caught Reavis in his rearview mirror, following him to

Pittsburgh and, after he parked, again behind him on foot as he made his way to the Fitness Arena.

At the Arena Jackie poured himself into his workout, sweating a lot of the booze out. After he was finished, he sat in the sauna and got even more out. Then he relaxed under a cold shower, feeling almost right again.

He stopped at the health bar after dressing and put down two sixteen ounce glasses of orange juice. Reavis sat two tables away, grinning at him, Jackie pretending to pay him no mind. He wondered briefly how the investigator had gotten on to him . . . then let it go. He smirked. He would know soon enough. When he got some time alone with Clifford Reavis.

After he left the arena, Jackie headed towards the Cherry Street parking garage on foot. Once there, he looked over his shoulder, seeing Reavis a half block behind him on Forbes. Then he grabbed the backpack and took off.

Forty-five minutes later, now in his SUV, he parked two blocks away from his place and walked home, making sure Reavis wasn't around before he let himself in the back door.

He felt sharper now. His mood had lifted. The exercise had cleaned him out. He looked at his watch. 4:11 p.m. In four, five hours at the most, he would be at Marsha LeGrange's. He couldn't wait to see the look in her eyes when she saw who he was, began to experience what he had in mind for her.

Reavis hung back, was standing on the corner of Forbes and Cherry Way. Where he found out Whitfield wasn't driving the Town Car now. By pure luck he caught Whitfield in a SUV, waiting to merge from the parking garage into the line of cars stopped at a red light at the intersection of Cherry Way and Fourth Avenue. It had worked, he was sure. He had spooked Whitfield into making his move for Marsha LeGrange tonight. His proof: Whitfield never worked out on Tuesdays and the man had even changed vehicles.

Reavis headed for his own place.

"It's going to be tonight, I'm sure of it," he told Matson on the phone. Then he brought him up to date about everything, included the voice-print expert saying all the call-in recordings were the same guy. He finished by telling Matson about how Whitfield had changed cars at the Cherry Street parking garage.

"Where are you now?" Matson asked.

"Home. I'm going to take a shower, lie down for an hour or so, then go wait for Whitfield outside Marsha LeGrange's. Bobby Doall's backing me up."

"Think he'll be looking for you?"

"I don't see why he would be; he doesn't have any reason to suspect that I know she'll be his next victim. But just in case, I'll take the pickup. He's never seen me in it. With all the drinking he's been doing, I'm hoping that he won't be quite as sharp, that he won't even be looking."

"Yeah," Matson said. "Good idea about Bobby. I think we've got all the edge we're going to get. He's not going to be as sharp as he could be . . . we know it's going to be tonight . . . and he's not going to be looking for you, especially in the truck."

Reavis took a deep breath. "Wish me luck, Mat."

"Luck is in that .38, Clifford. Clifford . . ."

"Yeah?"

"Don't miss."

# *C*HAPTER THIRTY-SIX

Reavis congratulated himself on taking the pickup. In addition to the fact that Whitfield had never seen it, the pickup blended in with the cars parked around it.

Reavis sat up straight when he saw a young woman who fit Bobby Do-all's description of Marsha LeGrange stopping at her condominium and getting out her keys. Bobby was right. She was truly beautiful. She was an inch or two taller than Beth, three or four inches taller than Peggy. Her hands were shaky trying to get the key in the door and she was frowning. She looked scared. He'd feel like that, too, if Whitfield was jerking him around like the man had done with Marsha LeGrange. Reavis was banking on the fact that he, Bobby, and Matson had done an even bigger job on Whitfield than Whitfield had done on Marsha LeGrange.

Bobby was sitting in his car, a block away. Reavis's backup.

She was in now and he could see all the lights in her place go on, first one room, then another.

Marsha let herself in and immediately went around turning

all the lights on. She wasn't jumping at every sound now, but that didn't mean she wasn't still having nightmares about the man who had been in her home.

Instead of getting into something real comfortable, she got into her workout clothes, including the tennis shoes. She wished she'd be able to wear harder shoes, but didn't have any and couldn't think of any to buy. The gym outfit, shoes? She wore them in case she had to use the martial arts defenses Marilyn's martial arts instructor had taught her. The instructor had also told her to use any available weapon.

She would feel a lot better if she could be talking to Mel. She'd called him today and they'd had a real nice talk and made plans to play racquetball real soon. Marsha felt guilty that she hadn't told him about the man who broke into her condo and took her vibrator. She would have liked to talk to him longer, but she'd had to pick up two of Larry Haski's hot cases. He was out-of-town. She was glad that she and Larry had their talk. He could be nice. She liked him now.

But she more than liked Mel Sadecki. She picked up the phone in her bedroom and dialed his cell again, counting off the rings. No answer this time. Where is that man?

She hung up. Marsha wanted some wine; she'd have a glass, then try him again.

She had never called a man in her life. So the first time she called Mel she wondered what she would say. But that no longer worried her. Now she only wanted to hear his voice. She missed him. Was there any chance for them?

Jackie wouldn't have poured himself a drink when he got back home from working out and sweating out the booze in the sauna if something hadn't been bothering him about Marsha LeGrange. Now, four hours later, he was still trying to piece together his thoughts about her. At times, he thought he liked her. For some reason, probably because she was more like his momma than any of them, he had made a point to get to know her. He had gotten sucked in, started having feelings about her, and that was a first.

He brought his glass to his lips; he was only sipping the vodka; look, the ice had all melted, even. He was actually beginning to think that Marsha LeGrange might be a nice person. She seemed to like him.

Jackie jumped straight up, spilling some of the vodka on the rug.

Wasn't that exactly what they all did? Act nice to people, get them believing their lies. Those ones, the ones like his momma, Marie Martieri—and, yeah, Marsha LeGrange, too—were the ones who were best at it. They got you wanting to believe they thought something of you. That was their big trick.

Jackie looked at his watch on the way to the liquor cabinet. Five past eight. He held the glass out. It was about a quarter full. He would pour in some fresh vodka, only enough to half fill it. Then, when he finished the vodka in his glass, it would be time to go. He always tried to kill them at nine. If Marsha LeGrange really was different from all the rest, he would know that when he put the two questions to her. If she answered them right, he would let her live.

Someone knocked. Jackie stiffened, but did not move.

"Jackie. I know you're in there."

It was his lying momma. "Why do you keep showing up?" he shouted through the door.

"I'm your momma, Jackie. You're my little boy. I want to be with you. We should be together. I've always said we would be someday. I've come to be with you . . . like I promised. I want to make things up to you. Now I can."

"You're too late." This is what it always came down to, her saying she wanted to be with him. Now he knew why. Clifford Reavis must have found out about all his money, too, must have told her. Jackie had struck it rich by splitting Nadine Harris's husband's money and estate with her. Not to mention when he found that some of the upstanding citizens he would frame had been hiding money offshore. And how to direct that money to the "Atlas Investments" account. Now that money was Jackie's. But his best way to make money was his special internet business. He named it Atlas Investments for moving his money around. Jackie was Atlas Investments and he was worth tens of millions of dollars.

"Go away," he called through the door. "We'll talk later." He laughed softly so she wouldn't hear. *After I kill Reavis,* he thought, *you will never find me again.* He held up a hand she couldn't see. "Wait, Momma . . ."

Because he just had to know, Jackie opened the door and let her in. She was still beautiful after all these years. But he backed off so she couldn't touch him.

"I have a question, Momma."

"Yes, darling?"

"Do you know about them, Momma?" He had to know if she knew about the women he raped and killed and the men he framed for those crimes.

"Know about what? Who, sweetheart?"

"Didn't Clifford Reavis tell you?"

"Who?" Making it seem like she didn't know any Clifford Reavis.

"Clifford Reavis. Your investigator, that's who." Jackie couldn't keep his voice down. "Do you always have to lie? Can't you see I'm not little anymore?" It took all he had, but he kept himself under control.

She couldn't stop lying. There she was, pretending she didn't know Clifford Reavis, her own investigator. He looked at the watch again: eight fifteen. It was time to go, but first one more drink. He could hold it. His momma upset him and he needed to be under control.

He went for the vodka bottle, which was only half full. Funny, he thought he'd opened a fresh fifth today. Jackie sloshed vodka into his glass and took it all down in two swallows. Then he crept over to the door.

"I have to go now, Momma. You can stay here if you want, but you will have to wait until I get back." No answer. "Momma?" She had that look on her face, the one that always meant she was leaving him. Yet he had opened his front door and let her in.

He took a long last look at Janice Simpson and then he was out the door. This time it was Jackie leaving *her*. She probably wouldn't be there when he returned. He could always sense things about her, like how he always knew exactly when she was going to leave him, back when she used to live with him sometimes at Miss Sarah's.

He called Marsha LeGrange from the SUV.

She answered on the third ring.

"Brad there?" Jackie used a Boston accent.

"I'm sorry," Marsha said. "There is no Brad at this number. You must have dialed incorrectly."

That's all he wanted to know. If she was home. "Sorry," he said. And hung up.

All the way over to her place he gripped the wheel with both hands, thinking what he would do to her. Tonight she would beg; first not to be raped, then not to be hurt, and, last—if she lied to him—not to die. More than once he had to ease up on the gas. The more he thought about her, the tighter he gripped the steering wheel, staring straight ahead, eyes glazed.

He almost missed Reavis. But once again his sharp instincts saved him. He remembered seeing the truck one other time. This time, though, he could see the man in the truck. It was Clifford Reavis. He saw him before the man was able to stuff his long, skinny body down in the front seat.

*What is Clifford Reavis doing parked half a block from Marsha Le-Grange's? Slumped down in the front seat?*

Jackie kept on going until he got to Seventeenth Street, sure that Reavis had not seen him. Reavis had never seen Jackie in the SUV. Jackie parked and got out of it. He was out of sight of Reavis's truck. He bent at the waist, shaking his muscles out, getting loose. He was breathing faster now, getting that high feeling.

That is when it came to him. Let Reavis see him. Maybe he could get the investigator to follow him inside when he let himself into her house. Damn. Why didn't he bring the claw? That's how he got the DNA to frame all those rich bastards. It didn't matter; if he could get Reavis to come in after him, he could set it up to look like Reavis murdered that bitch. Leave them both there dead. Yeah, making it look like Reavis fell, hit something. Todd Morrison all over again. He laughed. Make it look like he slipped in all the blood. There was no time now to set up Lester Wilkins. He would do it with Clifford Reavis instead. Who could he hate more than Clifford Reavis? Everything was falling into place.

What he ended up doing was getting back in his car and driving right past Reavis. He parked right across the street from Marsha LeGrange's. He got out of the SUV, right under a street light, and stretched, then grabbed his heavy backpack out of the SUV, slowly working his way into it, looking around, trying to look wary. So Reavis couldn't miss him.

Then he crossed the street, standing at an angle so that he would be able to see Reavis and that Reavis would be sure to see him as he tried to open the outside door. He didn't have the key to her new lock, but used the picks he'd bought over the Internet years ago for just such a case. He'd used them before; learned how with the instructions they'd come with. He didn't care how long it took to unlock the door. That would make it even more certain that Reavis saw him.

He was in. Quietly. And Reavis—Jackie saw—was on his way. Her condo was all on one level and her bedroom was down the hall, past the room that she used as her office, an open door at the end of the hall.

"Who is that?" Marsha yelled.

Jackie could hear the terror in her voice.

Marsha LeGrange was way overdue. And so was Clifford Reavis.

Reavis wondered what was in that backpack. What did it matter? He said a quick prayer. Got going, shot towards Marsha LeGrange's house, .38 in hand. There was no way he was taking on Whitfield without it. He was holding it so hard, his hands sweating so much, that he dropped the gun. He had to stop and go back for it, get it right in his hand. Was dropping the gun going to make him late again, like with Beth? He got moving faster than he thought he could run.

Clifford Reavis didn't see Whitfield after he whipped the outer door open. He did hear a woman's voice yelling, "I said who is it?" Then all he saw was a black-purple light bursting behind his eyes, as his knees let go on him.

# $\mathcal{C}$HAPTER THIRTY-SEVEN

Jackie, wild to get at Marsha LeGrange, kicked Reavis's leg out of his way. Blood began spilling out the side of the man's mouth. His skull had to be crushed. He would lug him into Marsha LeGrange's bedroom after he got her. Later for that. It was time for Marsha LeGrange. Jackie raced to her bedroom.

Again, Marsha yelled, "Who is it?"

When he entered her bedroom she was standing between her bed and dresser, bent over slightly, arms and hands extended, as though she had been waiting for him.

"Oh, God. Not you!" she screamed. Why is he wearing a backpack?

"Yes Marsha. It *is* me!"

Jackie ran at her, arms out to grab any piece of her he could and smash her against the dresser.

She surprised him and moved towards him, her tennis and martial arts practice paying off instantly as she easily sidestepped him. A fraction of a second later her martial arts instruction at Marilyn Moore's paid even bigger dividends. As he was moving to grab her where she had been, she lifted her leg and slammed the toe of her right tennis shoe at his groin with a snap-kick that she put her entire lower body into. Her foot bounced off his thigh, but pounded into his stomach. Not losing much force at all. As he started to double over she moved at him and dug the point of the Bic pen hidden in her right hand into his right eye.

And took off for the hall and her front door. *Safety!*

He must have had incredible reflexes because he leaped over the corner of her bed to cut her off. He got just a piece of her leg and tripped her. She rolled away from him and was up and getting ready to blaze toward the door again before he could get on top of her. But he was moving with beyond-human speed while bringing his right arm down, the fist on the end of it slamming into the right rear of her skull.

The blow stunned Marsha and she slumped to her knees. He grabbed her hair with both hands and dragged her to her feet. When she was up and standing he removed his left hand from her hair. And lassoed her neck with his left arm.

She tried to slam the heel of her shoe onto the top of his foot. By now he was expecting something like that from her, so he dragged her to the floor, using his own weight and arm strength, her hair still wrapped around his right hand, left arm still around her neck and now squeezing.

Somehow she managed to grab his left hand in hers and give it a ferocious bite. Which loosened that arm's hold. The pain made him let go of her hair but he was fast enough to blast her somewhere on her head, again, with the side of his right fist. After that blow, Marsha lost control of her muscles and went limp.

He was on his knees and moving cautiously toward her, alert for any more of her tricks. He wasn't getting good vision out of his right eye, blood was trickling out of it. Even with only one good eye, though, he could make out that she seemed groggy but still conscious.

She could barely move; there would be no quick kicks, no more sticking him in the eye. Again, he was able to snatch her hair. Which he did with both hands again this time. And he rose and dragged her across the floor, holding the rest of her body away from him so she couldn't kick, roll, or use an elbow or fist on him. He dumped her on her back, moving his hands to her chest to hold her down.

He let go of her, but before she could move he kept bashing the back of her head on the rug until she stopped struggling. Unfocused eyes looked up at him. He looked deep into those eyes, seeing beneath the clouds in them. Very little focus. But yes. There was the terror.

"You bastard. How could you?" All she could do was whisper it.

"Shut up." He rolled her onto her stomach and grabbed her hair with his left hand. Then pulled her head back. He had to be careful, because if he pulled harder, he would break her neck. It was too soon for that. With his right hand he reached into his back pocket for his knife.

Which he let her see.

Marsha's vision was blurred but improving. She barely saw the knife. Her lips were moving but she couldn't make a sound come out. She thought she might pass out. All this from a man whom she had thought liked her.

Jackie could feel her trembling. He took the knife and slit her yellow T-shirt down the back. No bra. That left only the Spandex shorts and what she had on underneath.

He cut those shorts, and the panties underneath them, from the waist, down both sides, top to bottom. After that he pulled her to her feet, hands under her arms. When she was on her feet, but very, very wobbly, Jackie ripped off the T-shirt, slit shorts, and panties. Now she was naked, except for tennis shoes, facing him and his knife. Barely able to stand. Half out of it.

"Well?" he said.

She tried to focus.

"Well?" Again. He made it more intense this time.

Her vision was clearing. She looked at him. "Wh-wh-what?"

"You know," he said.

"No . . . please . . . I don't." She wiped blood from around her mouth.

"Do you love me?"

She was seeing better. She could see that blood was dripping out of the eye of the bastard she got with the pen. *Do you love me?* Had she been out? Was she hearing things right? He sounded like a little boy. So much so, in fact, that her first instinct was to do her best to look around the room *for* a little boy.

"Oh, yes, yes, yes, I do honey," she said without thinking, as though he were a five-year-old.

"Will you come back for me?"

Still the little boy voice, now *screaming with rage!*

"Oh, yes," she said. Trying to sound soothing. Calm him down.

"You're lying! You always do!" Jackie Simpson couldn't stop screaming. "But I'm too big to believe you now!"

His screaming brought her closer yet to full consciousness. Her answer had been wrong.

Her only chance was to get away. She moved at him, but with nothing like the speed and strength she'd had the first time. She did manage to rake her nails down his chest but he pounded her to her knees, her upper body bowing toward him, hands reaching out to stop her fall to the floor. She could tell her nose was broken; she didn't know what else. There was blood everywhere from her nose. Marsha LeGrange, now on her hands and knees. In front of a deadly animal.

He moved closer. Her time had come.

Reavis, dazed, heard a little boy screaming. His gun was on the floor. Five feet away. He could barely make it out. Could not find his glasses. He crawled to the gun, got hold. Then he rose—dizzy. Where was he? His right knee was throbbing. How did that happen? The kid screaming again. Reavis moved toward the sound, dragging his right leg.

What he could barely make out when he got to the bedroom door was a woman, on her hands and knees, who seemed to be naked and bleeding, and a man, who had to be Whitfield—he just couldn't tell without his glasses—standing over her and moving ever closer to her. There was no little boy, though. Reavis knew that. *Whitfield was the little boy.* Whitfield hadn't seen him enter the bedroom yet, the man was focused on Marsha LeGrange as he closed on her. Reavis, bracing himself on the doorjamb with his left hand, leveled the .38 at Whitfield's body with the right.

He aimed high enough to be sure not to shoot Marsha LeGrange, who was on her hands and knees. The killer moving toward her.

Reavis pulled the trigger.

Marsha heard a shot.

The bastard who had hurt her no longer had his eyes on her. He had his eyes on the bedroom door and was moving toward it with inhuman speed.

Soon she could tell there was a struggle going on near where she lay. Unaware of any pain now, adrenaline pumping, she got up, edging naked in tennis shoes toward two bodies locked together on the floor. There was a man beneath the man who had just stripped her. He wasn't moving. Her attacker was on his knees over the other man and he had the knife. He was raising it above his head.

That was when she heard another gunshot. Maybe the police. *Someone,* she thought, *had called the police.* But soon it seemed like two more bodies were rolling around on the floor again and the one on top was the bastard she hated. The first man—she could make out that he was skinny and older—was laid out on the floor. Not moving at all. Dead.

Her eyes were giving her some trouble. Her vision wasn't perfect. She heard noises. Saw different colors. She smelled gunpowder. But she would not give up. Especially now that she knew who had been tormenting her.

Marsha rubbed her eyes. Then she could make out that son of a bitch on top of the second man, who was younger than the first man and who seemed pretty big.

She jumped on the back of the devil to do everything she could do to bring him down. She knew she had to kill or completely disable him to stay alive. On his back the backpack made it feel like Marsha was on a log floating in that place where waves break—constantly moving. Up. Down. Mindless now, she pounded and clawed at him. Keeping her head up, hanging onto the backpack, tasting salt, spitting. Not wanting to sink.

"You son of a bitch. You had no right!" It sounded like her screams were coming from somewhere else—not her mouth—out beyond the waves. "I thought you cared about me!"

The churning lessened. She was being swept away. She fought hard, adrenaline had come to her rescue. She continued to pound, slash, and claw, reaching deep for all the consciousness and life she had. Not wanting to be swept away. Her frenzy took her out of herself; someone else must be doing the screaming now. In some dark place, though, she knew it was her, but her screaming sounded much farther away.

She was being swept by the waves . . . away . . . up . . . out of the water . . . in the air, crashing . . .

Jackie had blacked out again. A shot—*Was it the second one?*—had gotten him somewhere near the right shoulder, making him drop the knife. Now, on his hands and knees, he looked for it. He crawled over the three of them. None of them moving. Blood everywhere. All dead. He felt good. Where the fuck was that knife? He soon found it over by the far wall. He stood, wobbly, and took in the room. The blood that was flowing out of his right eye wasn't making it easy. The eye didn't seem to be working right. Still, no one was moving. Which wasn't good enough for him.

Then he heard someone yelling outside, maybe a siren, too, he couldn't tell. Time was running out. He had to get out of here.

Jackie Simpson got back down on his hands and knees; he wanted to get right up next to Marsha LeGrange; and he crawled over to where she lay on her stomach. She was covered with blood. He raised up over her, could hear his own laughter, like an echo in a cave. Then he brought the knife down on her for the last time, feeling it sink deep. Overkill.

He didn't leave it in her, though.

A siren. For sure this time. Getting closer. The neighbors must have called. *Gotta move! Out of time?*

Jackie Simpson crawled over to Reavis. And he put the knife in his hand and closed the four-eyed bastard's fingers over it. Then lifted him and dropped her on Marsha LeGrange. Reavis would get the blame. Jackie could go.

Even though his right eye wasn't working good, he could see the three or four people outside Marsha LeGrange's condominium when he ran out. He could hear an ambulance getting close. Still no cops. And he still had his wits about him.

He kept running. Now away from them. Looking back: "A madman was in there," he had the brilliance to shout. "I think he killed them . . . . I tried to stop him. The bastard shot me." He held near his right shoulder where he'd been shot. "Got to get to the hospital. I can drive. Tell the paramedics there's three people, all dead or hurt real bad in there. The killer got away. Out the back door."

Jackie staggered across the street, fumbled with the door to his SUV and got in. It took him longer than usual to start it, but he got it going. He had to use his left arm to drive; his right wasn't working right because of his shoulder. Awkward, but he could do it. He was strong. He turned the wheel, angling it out slowly from behind the car parked in front of him. He might have nicked its fender as he swung out on Sydney—still not seeing his best out of the one eye—but he wasn't going to stop and find out if he nicked someone's car.

Jackie felt dizzy. The bullet wound. He felt near his shoulder. Wet. An indentation near the shoulder. Must be where the bullet went in. He couldn't tell if it went all the way through him or stayed in him. More blood than damage. He would be okay if he could stop the bleeding. All that booze didn't help, either; nor did what Marsha LeGrange did to his eye.

Jackie, who had no intention of going to South Side Hospital, was moving fast, soon west down East Carson Street. He made a right turn and headed to the Tenth Street Bridge.

Soon he was on I-279 on his way home.

He was tired. *No*, he realized, *"drained" was a better word. He had waited too long to get Marsha LeGrange. The stress of waiting had taken too much out of him.*

He parked out front when he got to his condo. The first thing he did when he got inside was head for his kitchen, where he grabbed a dish towel. He wet the dish towel and got to work on the bleeding. He couldn't seem to stop it. He'd have to check the shoulder out in the bathroom mirror.

He heard a sound behind him.

He turned to see his momma walking fast toward him with another towel. She hadn't left him this time.

"God, Momma, you're beautiful." The hate was all gone now. She was still here. She had come back for good.

He could see the love in Janice Simpson's eyes.

*Hadn't she left this time?*

He straightened, steadying himself against the sink. Not against pain. The dizziness. There wasn't any pain.

"I'll be good, Momma," he said. "I have plenty of money. You don't have to work anymore. You won't have to leave me."

"Forget about money. Let your momma take care of you," Janice Simpson said. And she started to work on the bleeding. Jackie watched her work. Very gentle she was, first cleaning the wound, next slowing the bleeding down and then stopping it completely.

"There," she said. "You've lost some blood. But I've got that stopped. All you need now is your rest. Put your arm around me and I'll get you to your sofa. I'll be here when you wake up. Right beside you."

Then she walked him slowly to the sofa, humming songs he remembered from when he was real little as she helped him ease himself down. She left the living room but soon returned with a soft cotton cover and tucked him in.

"You're going to be fine, John Lee," he heard her whisper.

# *C*HAPTER THIRTY-EIGHT

The throbbing on the inside of his head and on the right side of his jaw was keeping time with his heart. He had a screaming headache but he couldn't scream. He wouldn't open his eyes. His right eye flickered, let in some light, and he made it close. He felt like finding out where he was would be worse than not knowing, so he kept on counting . . . 78 . . . 79 . . . 80. Someone was moving around in the room. He didn't seem to be able to open his mouth. He wanted to ask where he was, but he was too afraid he would find out.

Her room. He must still be in Marsha LeGrange's bedroom. It was coming back now. He was too late. Again.

"It's about time you woke up."

The voice sounded like Bobby Doall's

"He broke both your upper and lower jaws. You have a concussion, Clifford."

Reavis opened his eyes. It was Bobby.

"Don't try to talk," Bobby said. "Your jaws are wired shut."

He was in a hospital room? He felt dizzy, believed he was passing out.

"Take it easy, Clifford. I'll explain."

Reavis believed he could sit up, but couldn't make it. Instead, Bobby cranked up Reavis's bed, so he was at about a forty-five degree angle. Reavis tried to sit up even more.

Bobby put his hands on Reavis's chest and gently pushed him back down. "Easy, I said. Your jaw's broken in three places. Two on the upper right and one on the lower right. You've been mostly out for a couple of days and you have a concussion—serious."

Reavis began to lose consciousness.

The next thing Reavis remembered was looking up and seeing Bobby Doall another time. Bobby had a bandage on his right ear that Reavis hadn't noticed the first time. He pointed at it. Bobby put his hand to the bandage. "Whitfield nearly bit it off. I don't know how many stitches it took," he said.

*What does he mean, 'Whitfield nearly bit it off'?*

"Like we planned, I was a block down the street and took off when you did. When I got to Marsha LeGrange's front door, there were people outside saying they'd heard a shot and a little kid cry out. The front door wasn't locked so I went in. I could hear struggling in the bedroom and that turned out to be you and Whitfield on the floor. You weren't winning."

Bobby said, "I had my gun out."

Reavis made a hurry-up-and-get-to-it motion with his hands.

Bobby raised his right hand, letting Reavis know he would fill him in, to be patient while he did. "You were out cold and Whitfield was sitting on top of you, had a knife in his hand and was ready to sink it into you. I got off a shot. I must have hit him somewhere because he dropped the knife." Bobby shook his head again. "I've never seen anyone move so fast, Clifford. He was on me before I could pull the trigger again. We rolled around, him getting on top. The last thing I remember was him squeezing my neck. Getting dizzy. I must have passed out. I've never had anyone do a number on me like that. Whitfield got away . . . ."

Reavis wanted to say, *What happened to the young lawyer? How did Whitfield get away?* But he couldn't move his jaw and he was drifting off again.

Reavis must have fallen asleep because the next thing he remembered Bobby was gone and Peggy was sitting beside his bed, humming softly and holding his hand. The sight of her set him off. Tears ran down his cheeks. What good had he done? It was like with Paul Petro—Whitfield was still on the loose. He lifted his arm. It lowered, slowly, like a helicopter landing. He was fading again.

Then it was Bobby Doall on another day. Reavis had most of his senses, was able to sit up and know what was going on that visit. But the headache was still bad. Not to mention the dizziness and nausea. Bobby came over to Reavis, reached in his old frayed-shorts front pocket and came out with a set of two keys, which he handed to Reavis.

Reavis looked questioningly at Bobby. *The T-bird?*

Bobby, nodding his head yes, had tears starting up in his eyes. "The T-bird was never my car. I was going to buy you one for your birthday, but that was too many months away. It's yours and it's parked in one of your garages in the alley behind your house."

Now it was Reavis with the tears. Wanting to say thank you, but unable because of the wired jaws.

"No," Bobby said, then raising his voice while looking right into Reavis's wet eyes. "Thank you. Thank you so much for taking care of me all those years. Thank you for being such a great friend before and after I could take care of myself."

The nurses had Marsha propped up at a forty-five-degree angle. They told her it took one hundred twenty-six stitches to close the wound in her back. She also needed two pints of blood. Without the paramedics' quick work she would be dead.

She remembered a lot of her colleagues at work had stopped in to see her for a few minutes. Even Larry Haski. Especially Larry Haski. He was turning out to be so nice to her.

There were flowers from people, mostly from work, everywhere in the room.

A young woman, who told Marsha that her name was Sharon LeVon and that she was a professor at Carnegie Mellon University with a PhD in computer science, paid her a visit. The tall, attractive woman mentioned that she was frequently given leaves of absence by the university to work on projects for the federal government. Marsha couldn't imagine why she was visiting her. What did she have to do with any federal project?

"You must have found that fiend's knife on the floor," she told Marsha. "A good friend of mine, who is also a doctoral candidate I'm mentoring, Bobby Doall, shot him near the shoulder and the man that did all this to you must have dropped his knife. You must have picked up the knife and started stabbing him; we think you started the stabbing while that monster was fighting Bobby. Don't worry," she said, "there won't be any charges against you. It was clearly self-defense. You must have stabbed him at least six times. Two of them fairly deep. You scratched him up real good too. Plus there were bite marks on one of his hands."

Marsha remembered climbing on her attacker's back, pounding and clawing him, but she couldn't remember picking up the knife and doing it.

Sharon LeVon went on. "They found him dead, inside his condominium, lying on his sofa with a soft cover over himself. All tucked in. A woman had called to report seeing a man covered in blood going into the condo. She was crying. She hung up on the nine-one-one operator when he asked her name. The coroner's office counted one through-and-through bullet wound near his right shoulder. Neither the bullet wound nor the six stab wounds in his back would have killed him, each by themselves, but he bled out. There was blood all over his sofa."

Marsha still couldn't remember grabbing the knife. But she was glad she had.

Sharon LeVon said that the police found a large backpack, covered in blood, near the front door of Marsha's attacker's apartment. In it were disguises and two knives. But what seemed really odd was that there was also video equipment in the backpack. At first, the police couldn't understand why there was a devil's mask, video cameras, and folded tripods in the backpack.

Sharon said, "They found over three dozen DVDs and a high-end laptop in an attaché case at his condominium. And they couldn't get the DVDs to play. They were encrypted. That's when I was called in.

"Marsha, you were not his first victim. He had made DVDs of all of his horrible rapes and murders. And not only did he make the DVDs, but he also narrated them, bragging about his photographic memory, reciting chapter and verse about how he stalked the women and how he sent them their underwear and other personal things. He even sent three of the women their vibrators. He bragged about how he framed other men for each of his crimes. And he named the women he raped and murdered and the men he framed."

Good Lord! Marsha's eyes widened. *What about her? What did Sharon LeVon find out about her? Her career as a whore? Her vibrator?*

Sharon LeVon, smiling now while she lightly touched Marsha's shoulder. "He couldn't get you on a DVD. You stabbed him before he could even get his mask on. There's no information about you on any of the DVDs. His photographic memory of you died with him."

Marsha wanted to cheer! *No one but Carrie knew her dark secret.*

Marsha could tell that Sharon LeVon was as proud of her as—now—Marsha was of herself.

Sharon LeVon said, "Bobby Doall and I put our heads together, and we finally broke through all the locks and encryptions that evil man who attacked you had put in place to block the public's access to his website. It was, of course, members only. These special members made him rich buying copies of his snuff DVDs. He ended each DVD by turning to face his cameras, in his devil's mask, saying, 'See you next time.' What was weird was that he had this tattoo on his left upper back. It was a small red heart with the words BAD MOTHER. He was the one who was one *bad mother* himself.

"We've been able to identify a lot of his customers and we'll discover even more. One is a United States senator who plays the Christian card. Soon, all the cards he'll be playing will be solitaire in a United States penitentiary. He's already singing about who paid him bribes to help get legislation passed. He's hoping to get a lighter sentence.

"We've been able to identify a lot of his other customers, too, from all over the world. Now they'll need their money to keep them out of jail. He was charging $100,000 a DVD and he had over seventy-five regular customers. We know one bank where he has ten million dollars on deposit and another with five million. There's got to be a lot more."

Sharon LeVon straightened some and patted Marsha lightly on the shoulder.

"Congratulations, Marsha, those DVDs got a lot of innocent men out of jail or a penitentiary." She continued: "A man named Clifford Reavis, with my friend Bobby Doall helping out, had been investigating your attacker and he concluded that you were going to be his next victim. Bobby Doall and Mr. Reavis are very close to each other. Almost like father and son. I've met Mr. Reavis several times."

Marsha could feel her anger building. She was thinking: *Two men knew she was going to be attacked by someone who planned to rape and murder her and didn't at least go to the police about it?*

"What's wrong with your friend and that Mr. Reavis? I could have been killed! Why didn't they call the police?" Marsha asked.

"Marsha, Mr. Reavis and Bobby believed that that would scare him off if they went to the police, but they also believed that he would return some day and do to you what he did to the women on his DVDs. They believed that the only way to stop him from harming you was the way they did: Keep an eye on him and on you and move against him when he began his move against you. And that's what they did. Except it was each of you who saved all of you."

Marsha now understood their thinking, which changed her feelings from anger to gratitude; she now felt grateful to Clifford Reavis and Bobby Doall. She'd have been raped and dead if Bobby hadn't shot the son of a bitch in the shoulder. And Bobby wouldn't have been there if Clifford Reavis hadn't learned about her being the next victim.

After Sharon LeVon left, Marsha thought back, went over everything she knew about this man. He must have been stalking her forever.

She couldn't really see where Jeff Guilfoyle was any different from any normal man. She thought he was her best friend at the firm. When

Les Wilkins stopped in to see her here at the hospital, he told Marsha that the man she knew as Jeff even pushed the other partners to hire her. Nothing weird about him stood out at all. Not until he did what he did. She had even believed he was married, thought she had met his wife, liked his two sons. He had pictures of him, his wife, and those two kids all over his office. Why would that woman—whoever she was—come with him to the Christmas party, the firm's summer family picnic, posing as his wife?

Sharon LeVon had explained that, too. The CMU professor told her that there was no Jeff Guilfoyle. There had been one who went to Orchland Law School. He'd been the Jeff Guilfoyle who had been on law review at Orchland, whose graduation certificate hung on the man who used his name's office wall. But the real Jeff Guilfoyle was not the man who had made partner so fast at Wilkins, Wilkins & Dunn. Your attacker made partner because of the so-called rain of new client fees he brought to the firm. All those new clients were one single person: the phony Jeff Guilfoyle, and him alone. He was a true Internet start-up company. Which sold snuff DVDs. And he paid a part of what he made selling the DVDs as fees to WW&D to get and keep his position as a senior partner at her law firm.

No one knows, Sharon LeVon had told Marsha, where the real Jeff Guilfoyle is. Living or dead. No one knows who the man she knew as Jeff Guilfoyle is. What they do know is that the man Marsha killed didn't leave a widow or any children behind.

She had believed he was her very good friend. And he had almost raped and killed her. She'd be okay about that, she believed, because he never could and she had made him pay. He was *her* victim.

Sharon LeVon had told her the police still didn't know his real name. Who was the man she knew as her friend and colleague, Jeff? *Who was that man?* Then she thought, *What does it matter? He was nobody, he was dead and . . . he'd asked for it.*

# *E*PILOGUE

A week after John Lee Simpson's last breath, Sarah Lee Simpson was carrying a load of wash from out back over to the clothesline her John Lee had put in. *There's not much wash anymore,* she thought sadly, *with John Lee and Janice, Jackie's momma, all grown and gone now.*

John Lee was on her mind today, more than usual, because of the call she got this morning from a lawyer from Ohio named Nadine Harris. She said she went to law school with her grandson and had some news for her about him. The woman lawyer also wanted to give her some money. Another gift from John Lee. The woman told her that John Lee was a really good investor and that he hadn't had to work for years.

That not-working part didn't make sense. She knew that John Lee worked for the government. Some secret job that even kept him from calling her sometimes. She told the lawyer that, but Nadine Harris still said it was important for them to meet, that she would fly to South Carolina, rent a car and come see her.

Sarah didn't care about money. It was her John Lee she cared about. She would put the money in savings for him. She couldn't wait to see him again. Then she would tell him once and for all to forget about that money business, that all she wanted was for him to feel good.

Another thing she had made up her mind to tell John Lee was the truth about his momma. She had tried to tell him the last time he called. It had been a few weeks since she'd heard from him, but that wasn't unusual, what with his secret government job. As she hung the wash out to dry, she went over in her mind just what she would say when she saw her grandson.

It would go something like this: "John Lee, there's something you must know about your momma." That's how she would start; she'd worked that much out already.

She pictured him looking at her crossly, the way he always did when she brought up his momma. But she would go on. "You're all grown now, son," she would tell him. "It's more than time you knew. I tried to tell you the last time you called."

He might look at her then.

"Your momma couldn't keep all those promises about coming back for us, boy." She'd make him look at her when she told him that. "It wasn't her fault, John Lee."

He might ask, "What's that supposed to mean?" Or he might just give her a look. But he'd want her to go on. She nodded her head. Yes, she was sure of that.

"Me, your momma—when she was right—and Mr. Randolph . . ." She would take her time, get the words just right, really liked the idea of practicing them out loud. "We all decided to paint it different . . . how it was with your momma."

The next part she would have trouble with. She would have to go over that in her mind a lot more. "Your momma was attacked." Maybe she would just come out with it and say *raped*. "By a crazy man, John Lee." With John Lee's temper, she'd have to watch him close before she said, "That's the way you came to be. Your real daddy shot hisself before the sheriff got him. Your real daddy wasn't right, boy. He escaped from a place for crazy people."

That's what she couldn't picture her John Lee taking, a crazy daddy, and not one killed in an accident, like she'd always told him.

Telling him the rest would be easier. "Mr. Randolph was always sweet on your momma, John Lee, so he was the first person I thought to call when . . . I found her all hurt." Sarah would go on, "I couldn't get your momma to say nothin'; she was just rockin' back and forth on the bed, holding herself . . . ." Sarah Lee Simpson simply couldn't bring herself to think of that crazy man as John Lee's real daddy.

Sarah couldn't stop now. "Mr. Randolph came over right away, but your momma wouldn't let him touch her. It was Mr. Randolph got her to the place she is now. Paid for everything. He set up something legal so the place—it's called a mental institution—will always get its money."

She would look at John Lee, let him know. "She don't get out of there no more. Hasn't been out for years. I talk to her on the phone, visit her using your money to get me back and forth. But she don't get out. They look after her real good though, boy. You were born at that place." She wondered how he would take that, being born in a place like her Jannie was in. But that's what Janice Simpson had wanted. She'd wanted to have that boy so much.

"What that man did to my insides," Janice Simpson had always explained when she was right, "I'll never have another. It's not John Lee's fault."

Sarah pictured herself reaching out to her grandson then, his running over to her, letting her hold him. She would run her hands through his hair like she always did when he was little, those days the other children got to teasing him so bad.

She would say, "We all thought you was too young to know. Then the time never seemed right." Sarah reached up and pinned the work dress she was holding to the clothesline. "John Lee, we made up a story about your momma being in college, then later about her work. She always did want to finish college. That's why she wouldn't marry Mr. Randolph in the first place. She was home from there on Easter break when it happened. It just made good sense to tell everyone, you too, when you got old enough to ask, that's where she was. No one around here knew. Only Mr. Randolph. It was our secret."

She would hold John Lee tight then. "And now you know, too."

Sarah Lee Simpson hung her last work dress on the line and nodded, pleased with her plan. She decided she just about had it all worked out perfect how she would tell her John Lee.

# $\mathscr{A}$BOUT THE AUTHOR

D A V E   R E E S graduated from the University of Pittsburgh and earned his Juris Doctorate Degree at Duquesne University (thanks to the GI Bill). He has been both an investigator and a litigator for many years. Long ago, he learned that the most important thing about a witness, party to a lawsuit, or a person accused of a crime was whether a jury would like and believe them. Thus, he not only had to ask people questions—he had to study them. He draws freely from the events he has investigated and the characters he has had to study to set the scenes and draw the characters in his novels.

WA